80P

PATRICK BUTLER
FOR THE DEFENCE

JOHN DICKSON CARR has brought off another top-notch mystery, featuring the same engaging hero, Patrick Butler, who performed so brilliantly in *Below Suspicion*.

The story opens on a foggy November afternoon in the offices of a staid old-established firm of solicitors in Lincoln's Inn Fields; it was only a small firm, for all its importance, and on this particular afternoon the only people in the office were Jim Vaughan and Hugh Prentice, the senior partner's nephew—and Helen, Hugh's fiancée, a serious young lady whom he had asked in to tea, when he should have been taking a brief round to Patrick Butler in the Temple.

While they were having tea, a client called: a small dark-skinned man in a green fez who said he was Abu of Ispahan, and that his brother was a magician who had been swindled. 'Unless justice is done,' said the visitor, 'there will be murder.' And within minutes, during which Helen left and Hugh and Jim Vaughan discussed the new client in the next-door office, it was done—not justice, but murder. The Persian was found dying on the hearth-rug, stabbed in the back with a knife from Hugh's desk. The murder had taken place practically under the young man's eyes.

It was then that Hugh resolved to get Patrick Butler to help and, if necessary, to his defence. The story begins to race, with a plot full of action and the chase, but all the clues are there. John Dickson Carr says to his reader, 'If you can deduce the solution to this one, you are the sort of connoisseur for whom the author likes to write.'

John Dickson Carr

PATRICK BUTLER FOR THE DEFENCE

HAMISH HAMILTON

LONDON

First published in Great Britain 1956
by Hamish Hamilton Ltd.
90 Great Russell Street, London, W.C.1

305657

PRINTED IN GREAT BRITAIN BY
WESTERN PRINTING SERVICES LTD, BRISTOL

Chapter 1

FOG.

It was not the pea-soup fog of Victorian fame, tinged brown with mud and chimney-soot. It was the soft, clammy, ghost-white strangler of today.

Thickly it materialized in Lincoln's Inn Fields, about half-past four of an afternoon late in November, when the sky was already nearly dark. It muffled the lights in lower windows; it strangled the street-lamps; it smoked upwards to veil other windows above the square.

If you had stumbled up four flights of stairs, you would have seen on the landing closed, heavy double doors bearing the legend PRENTICE, PRENTICE, & VAUGHAN, a sedate firm of solicitors founded in the eighteenth century by an ancestor of Mr. Charles Grandison Prentice, the present senior partner.

And, if you had pushed open these doors, you might have been a little surprised.

Ahead, down a long and broad passage with frayed carpet, the offices on either side were all dark and empty. The only faint light came from two offices, set side by side and door beside door, at the other end of the passage.

The door on the left was closed, though a dim glow showed under the sill. In this office young Mr. James Vaughan, one of the two junior partners, wrestled with somebody's last will and testament, and cursed the day he was born. In the other office Mr. Hugh Prentice, the other junior partner, had left the door partly—even self-consciously—open.

'More tea, Hugh darling?' asked a girl's voice.

'Er—no, thanks,' replied the dignified voice of a young man. 'No!' he added sternly, rather as though he were waving away a knighthood.

'Well, darling, you needn't be so stuffy about it!'

5

'*Me?* Stuffy?'

In Hugh Prentice's office a bright coal fire burned in a grate under a black marble mantelpiece against the wall opposite the door. Up to the fire had been drawn an ancient black leather sofa.

At one end of the sofa, self-consciously, sat Helen Dean. At the other end of the sofa, just as self-consciously, sat her *fiancé*. They drank tea with a kind of precision. It was clear that both would have liked to sit much closer, but both were overcome by the dry, dusty frigidity of Prentice, Prentice, and Vaughan.

Hugh Prentice, thirty-five years old and somewhat severe-looking in a dark-haired, dark-browed way, remained straight-backed in his formal black coat and striped trousers. Over the mantelpiece a broad mirror, slightly tilted, reflected both their faces as Helen turned her head.

Helen herself was anything but severe-looking.

Her bright brown hair, her darker brown eyes fringed with black lashes and set off by a clear, glowing complexion, sometimes made her look eighteen instead of twenty-eight. But the lines and outlines of her green frock showed a maturity far on the other side of innocence.

'Oh, I don't care what you are!' she said. 'But, honestly, I sometimes wonder whether you're going to turn into a dry stick like your Uncle Charles—'

'Here! Steady on!'

'—or whether you're something else altogether. Hugh, When you were at Cambridge, why did they call you Whizzer?'

'They didn't.'

'They did!' said Helen, banging down cup and saucer on the little table which held the tea-tray between them. 'Your own sister told me so. But, if you're going to turn into a robed Lord Chief Justice merely because we're in this horrible office, maybe I'd better go.'

Enough is enough.

With a walloping clank Hugh set down his own cup and saucer. He stalked round the table. He sat down beside her, and seized her.

6

No thunderbolt descended upon them. Only faint wisps of fog curled through the dingy office, pressing blind and blank and white against its windows. The fire shifted and crackled. Then, after a long interval, Helen spoke drowsily.

'Darling!' she murmured. 'Oughtn't you to be working, really?'

Hugh sat up abruptly, as though stabbed with a pin, and looked at her.

'I wish,' he said, 'I wish you would kindly make up your mind about my character—Work!'

'Hugh, don't be cross! I didn't mean that. I was only trying to find out if you loved me.'

'Work?' yelled Mr. Prentice, unheeding.

He rose to his feet. He did not actually fold his arms, but the impression was the same.

'With everybody in this firm down with 'flu, every single soul from my uncle to the office-boy, it might interest you to know that Jim Vaughan and I have been working like billy-o. We . . .'

Here he paused in concern, because a spasm of anguish crossed Helen's face. But it was not mental anguish, as he thought. Helen glanced over her shoulder at the thin leather cushion propped up behind her back. Reaching down between the cushion and the back of the sofa, she drew out a book which had been thrust away there.

'Something,' she explained, 'has been half killing me in the middle of my back. I thought it was you, so I didn't mind. But it wasn't.'

And she held out the bright-jacketed book. Its title was *The Corpse in the Copse*.

'Give me that!' said Hugh, with indecent haste.

Snatching the book from her, he stalked across to a steel filing cabinet between the two windows in the south wall. He dragged open the lowest of the big drawers, which was nearly filled with castaway novels of the same kind. Into this he hurled *The Corpse in the Copse*, and closed the door with a rolling bang.

7

'Can't let 'em lie about,' he said earnestly. 'Makes clients think you're not serious.'

And Helen whooped.

She couldn't help it; she laughed in his face. There are times when even the most devoted girl cannot restrain herself from this, but it always infuriates the man in question.

'And what is so funny, may I ask?'

'I'm sorry, dear. It's you.'

'It is, eh?'

'Hugh, you're a fraud. You'd dearly love to walk straight into some roaring adventure like the ones in those stories, and pit your wits against the crafty villain. Now wouldn't you?'

'Certainly not.'

'Up out of the fog,' continued Helen, becoming dramatic in her turn, 'would slip a mysterious dark-skinned stranger with a foreign accent. "I am Omar of Ispahan," he'd say. And he'd tell you about a corpse in a sealed room; and you'd put on your hat and follow him like a shot.' Helen's face clouded. 'Oh, dear. So would I, really. If I had the nerve.'

'Listen!' Hugh said in some desperation.

'Yes?'

'I have not read a detective story,' he announced, with the voice of one disclaiming drink or drugs, 'in practically a fortnight. How could I? Jim and I even have to do our own errands. Look there!'

At first she thought he was indicating his own broad, flat-topped, neatly arranged desk, which was pushed against the back of the sofa. On the desk burned a lamp with a green shade, throwing an even colder glow on bilious-green walls, but kindling in Helen's brown eyes and heightening the colour of the flushed, lovely face as she knelt with her arms folded across the sofa-top.

Facing the desk was an old swivel chair, with a battered attaché case standing open on the seat. Across the back of the chair lay Hugh's dark overcoat, his grey gloves, and his neat bowler hat. Helen, who loathed bowler hats (on him,

8

anyway) as yet lacked the courage to smash it or spirit it away.

Hugh strode across to the chair. He sent his hand diving into the attaché case, and produced a large, shiny folder of buff-coloured cardboard tied in pink tape.

'This,' he said, 'is a brief. A barrister's brief.'

'Darling, I know that!'

'All right! But it was the devil and all to prepare. And I've promised to deliver it, five o'clock sharp, at Patrick Butler's chambers in the Temple.'

'Patrick Butler?' echoed Helen. '*That* horrible man?'

Hugh smiled. It was a smile of charm and devilment, lightening his face and giving a glimpse of his real character, as he dropped the brief back into its leather case.

'Patrick Butler, my dear, is the foremost advocate at the Bar; in criminal law, at least. They call him "the Great Defender".'

'Don't they also call him "that damned Irishman?"'

'The envious ones do, I agree. That's because he always wins.' Deep admiration rang in Hugh's voice. 'Do you realize, Helen, that he's never accepted a brief from the Treasury? That he's never appeared for the Crown? That, always and for ever, it's "Patrick Butler for the Defence?"'

'Yes!' Helen burst out. 'Yes! Because then he can twist the facts, and go all smarmy with the jury, and get a murderer acquitted on fake evidence—!'

She stopped abruptly. Hugh's smile had altered a little.

'Easy, my pet.' He spoke gently. 'Mustn't say that about anyone, you know, in our profession.'

At the beginning Helen had felt no very real animus against the famous barrister. She had met him once, and several times heard his rich, rolling voice in court, without more than a sense of mild dislike. Now, since so clearly he was Hugh's professional idol, she was beginning to feel she disliked Mr. Butler very much indeed.

'I'm sorry!' she said. 'But I simply can't endure his insufferable arrogance . . .'

'It isn't arrogance at all, actually.'

A*   9

'. . . or his lordly manner of saying "I am never wrong."
Really, now! One of these days, Hugh, that man is going to
come such a cropper that he'll land in a ditch and never get
up again.'

'He hasn't come a cropper yet, has he?' smiled Hugh.

'*Eee!*' said Helen.

'And we mustn't be childish, either.'

Helen gasped. The light of the lamp, flat and bright across
the desk, glittered on her engagement ring as she twisted it.

But Hugh was paying no attention.

'Let us admit,' he continued, pacing up and down with a
pontifical air, 'that Butler's methods aren't exactly orthodox.
He regards the law as an intellectual game to beat the other
fellow. Between ourselves, he prefers his clients to be guilty.
"Where's the sport or the credit, in defending somebody
who's innocent?" That's what Butler says.'

'And *you* believe it too?' cried Helen.

'Oh, it's very deplorable. No doubt. Tut, tut. All the same!
You were accusing me, a while ago, of wanting to live in a
detective story—'

'Yes, and so you do! And you're imitating your precious
Mr. Butler, and even talking like him, at this very minute!'

Hugh stopped short.

'By George, I believe I am!'

Helen did not say anything. Hugh waved it aside.

'The point is that Butler, in a very real sense, does live
amid such events. Ever since that witchcraft affair, six or
seven years ago, he's had a whole batch of cases which could
be turned into proper detective stories: the evidence fully
displayed, the conclusions logical. On the other hand, your
Omar of Ispahan—'

'*Whose* Omar of Ispahan, if you please?'

Again Hugh stopped short.

'How the hell should I know? *You* mentioned the blighter.
You said he might walk in here . . .'

'He's not my Omar of Ispahan, thank you,' Helen said with
dignity. 'He isn't anybody. I just invented him for the sake
of illustration.'

10

'Helen! Is anything wrong?'

'No, no, of course not. Do go on, darling. Please.'

'Very well,' argued Hugh, 'let's use him as an illustration. A character named Omar of Ispahan, for instance, couldn't possibly appear in a proper detective story. He could appear only in a thriller. Not that I've got any objection to thrillers, mind! I love 'em. But they bear no more relation to real life than the Arab dagger I use as a paper-knife. Old Omar, if he walked in through that door now, wouldn't bring me news of a sealed room. He could only gabble about some international dope or white-slave ring, which wouldn't be interesting even if there could be any such thing. Omar of Ispahan, even as a myth, doesn't exist. He couldn't exist. Now do I make myself clear?'

This was the point at which a deep-toned church-clock distantly across Lincoln's Inn Fields began to toll five. Its notes, fog-muffled, quivered against the windows. At the same moment there was a soft but insistent rapping on the outside of the partly open door.

Helen has afterwards said that her heart was 'in her throat'. This is erroneous. There is nothing very sinister about the striking of a clock as someone knocks at the door. But both Helen and Hugh believed this because of what happened immediately afterwards.

A sharp push flung the door to the passage inwards and wide open, so that it almost banged against the inside wall. In the aperture stood as curious a goblin as they had ever seen.

The man could not have been much more than five feet tall. Though he was thin and bony, he seemed bulkier by reason of a long, dark, rather shabby overcoat with an astrakhan collar, such as has been seen seldom in the past fifty years.

His black liquid eyes, in a thin dark-skinned face with a long nose, rolled from left to right either in fear or in excitement. A prominent Adam's apple jerked up and down in his thin neck, above a clean white collar but a rather grubby white four-in-hand tie. On his head, a little sideways, he wore the green fez, with tassel, which marks a devout Moslem's pilgrimage to Mecca.

So he stood there, sweating and rolling his eyes, with fog-wisps curling round him.

'Good . . . aftair-noon!' he said suddenly. His voice, though unexpectedly deep, was not loud.

'Er—yes,' said Hugh. 'Good afternoon.'

The little man cast a quick apprehensive glance to his left; next, more slowly, to the right. Then he ran into the room with four quick little steps.

'You are Meestair Pren-tees?' he asked, after a struggle with the English language. 'You are *the* Meestair Prentees?'

'My name is Prentice, yes. But—'

'I am Abu of Ispahan,' said the newcomer. 'Is it possible, pliz, that I should 'ave wit' you a word in private? Yes?'

Chapter 2

THE last stroke of five trembled away.

Hugh, in consternation, looked at his wrist-watch. He looked across at the brief-case containing the brief he had promised to deliver to Patrick Butler at five o'clock sharp. He looked at Helen, who was still kneeling wide-eyed beyond the desk-lamp, her arms along the top of the sofa.

By no coincidence, he knew, could she have invented out of thin air a name so close to their visitor's. Somewhere, perhaps recently, she had heard or read 'Omar of Ispahan'. Helen knew it too, though she only made a gesture of bewilderment.

Meanwhile, Abu of Ispahan was having a fit.

'I 'ave come—' he began; and then found inspiration. '*Monsieur! Un moment! Vous parlez français, peut-être?*'

'*Un—petit—peu. Oui.*'

'*Alors, écoutez!*' cried Abu of Ispahan, seizing the lapels of Hugh's coat. '*Mon frère, qui est magicien, a été escroqué.*'

'Your brother, who is a magician, has been deceived?'

Hugh, rattled, was not at all sure that '*escroqué*' meant 'deceived'. In a vague way he felt it had some more precise and particular meaning. But he hadn't time to argue; and, anyway, the man in the green fez seemed to accept it.

'*Si, si, si! Et si vous ne m'aidez pas, il arrivera un meurtre.*'

'And, if I don't help you, there will be a murder?'

'Yes.'

With lithe grace Helen slipped off the sofa and sprang to her feet.

'Hugh, I think I'd better go.'

'Yes. I must be off myself, in a minute.'

'No!' said Abu of Ispahan.

Helen wore very little make-up; her hair, shoulder length and curling outwards, was not much disarranged. Without even troubling to examine this in the mirror over the fire-

13

place, she picked up her fur coat from a near-by chair. Hugh, dragging loose from his client's clutch, went to help her into the coat. Helen did not speak to him. On her way out she nodded to Abu of Ispahan and gave him a nervous smile, which he returned with a deep if equally shivering bow.

In the doorway she hesitated.

'Hugh. Are you still taking me out to dinner tonight?'

'Yes, of course. Why not?'

'Well. I just wondered.'

'Now, look here, Helen—!'

'Yes?'

Hugh swallowed hard and restrained himself. 'I'll pick you up at your flat. Seven o'clock. Right?'

'Oh, if you like,' Helen said coolly, and left them with great dignity.

Hugh, that outwardly stolid young man, stifled an impulse to tear his hair. Instead, towering above Abu of Ispahan, he looked down at his client with gloomy Byronic eyes.

'Mr. Abu,' he said, 'come here.'

'Pardon?'

'Come here, please. Take off your overcoat and your ... no. I don't imagine you remove the fez indoors, do you?'

'Non! Jamais de la vie!'

'All right; you needn't get so excited!'

Hugh dragged the astrakhan-collared coat back over the man's bony shoulders, revealing Abu of Ispahan in a tight-fitting dark suit of French cut, with broad pin-stripes. The overcoat he threw across the top of the filing-cabinet, beside a discarded midday edition of the *Evening News*. He dashed towards the fireplace, and whirled away the small table holding the tea-tray. A cup flew wide and smashed on the hearth-tiles. Abu of Ispahan jumped as though shot.

'*Doucement!*' urged Hugh. '*Il faut que* ... oh, hang the French! Come here, sir, and sit down.'

Abu of Ispahan sat down on the sofa.

His host picked up a pair of tongs and dropped three lumps of coal on the dying fire, which gushed out black smoke.

'First, Mr. Abu, let me say that I'd give ten years of my life to hear your story at this minute.'

'Ah!'

'Unfortunately, I can't. I have an appointment, and I'm late already.'

Abu of Ispahan, whose eyes were fixed on him like those of an expectant dog, bounced up from the sofa. Hugh, somewhat unprofessionally, pushed him back again.

'However!' he insisted. 'It shouldn't take me longer than half an hour, three-quarters of an hour at least, to get back here. In the meantime, my partner,' and Hugh nodded towards the office on his right, 'will take down any facts you care to give. When I return . . .'

'No!' said Abu of Ispahan. 'Not partner! *You!* Nobody but Meester Pren-tees! *Trois quarts d'heure, hein?*'

'No more than that, I swear!'

'Good. I wait.'

'Would you wait, sir?' demanded Hugh, accustomed to impatient and domineering clients. 'Have you got the time?'

'Time?' repeated his visitor in French. 'What is time?' An expression of cynicism crossed his dark face; he sat back and folded his arms. 'In my country, in Persia, it is only a gift which allows us to sleep a little longer. Time!'

'In that case,' said Hugh, 'you might care to glance over the newspaper.' Hastily he got the copy of the *Evening News* from the top of the filing cabinet, and gave it to his guest. 'There are cigarettes, Turkish and Virginia, in the box on the mantelpiece. If you want anything else, just sing out.'

'Good. I tank you.'

Hugh donned his overcoat, his grey suède gloves, and his bowler hat. Not until then did he realize that he, like Abu of Ispahan, had been sweating. And, as he closed the brief-case and snapped shut its catch, his flaming curiosity could not be restrained.

'You have said,' he added, diving straight into the bumpy waters of the French language, 'that there will be a murder.'

Danger-signal: look out!

Abu's head twisted round, horribly as though his neck

15

were dislocated. He was so small that over the back of the sofa you could see only his eyes, his wrinkled-up forehead, the green fez with the dancing tassel.

'Who,' asked Hugh, 'is going to be murdered?'

'My—my brother.'

'Why?'

'Money!' said Abu of Ispahan, with extraordinary anguish. 'Money, money, money, money!'

The little man was a master of pantomime. His hands, vivid and fluent, conjured up images of coins piled high, of stacked banknotes, of securities in heaps: even of another batch of banknotes, through which his left thumb greedily riffled.

'But who is going to murder your brother?'

Abu seemed deliberately to ignore this. His gaze wandered away, seeking corners of the office. Back it flashed to Hugh Prentice's hands.

'Your gloves,' the visitor said abruptly.

'My . . . *what*?'

'All my troubles,' cried Abu of Ispahan, 'have been caused by your gloves.'

Hugh's first impressions, either that he had misunderstood the words or that he was dealing with a lunatic, were dispelled by the sharp intelligence, the craft and even slyness, in the eyes burning at him over the back of the sofa.

'Come, you lose time!' screeched Abu, flourishing the newspaper. 'Go!'

Hugh went.

Mechanically he glanced at his desk, to make sure all was in order. Vaguely it seemed to him that there was something missing which should have been there. And, when he thought of the newspaper, another idea flashed through his head. But the little Persian gave him no space to think.

On his way out, beginning to close the door behind him, he hesitated. His state of mind, admittedly, was not that of the normal, ultra-correct Mr. Hugh Prentice. In his fever it seemed to him that this mysterious client might fly away from him, might disappear into the fog, before he could hear the full story.

And so, leaving the door about two feet open, he tiptoed sideways to the closed door of the office beside his own. They were separated only by the two doorposts and the narrow width of the wall between.

Hugh knocked very softly at the other door. There was no reply. He knocked a little louder, still without response.

'Jim!' he whispered—and opened the door.

The other office was empty.

Hugh took two steps into the room, and stared round. Jim's office was much like his own, though it had not the comfortable feature of a sofa before the fire. Jim's flat-topped desk was as littered as Hugh's was tidy; Jim's own battered brief-case stood open on the desk.

'Jim!'

'Yes, old boy?' said a voice, so close behind him that Hugh started.

He whirled round. Jim Vaughan, large and untidy and red-haired, was at his elbow.

'Sh-h!' Hugh hissed. He pushed past his companion, craning round the two door frames, and took another look into his own office.

Abu of Ispahan, who had not yet disappeared, was angrily straightening out the pages of the newspaper, slapping at half-squashed sheets to flatten them. His comments, presumably in Persian or Arabic, did not sound encouraging.

Hugh, without leaving his vantage-point, drew back his head and peered round at his companion.

'Sh-h-h!' Hugh repeated.

'What the hell's the matter with you?'

'Sh-h-h! Where have you been?'

'Me? Down to the gents' at the end of the passage: where do you think? But I repeat—'

'For the last time, will you keep your voice down?'

Jim, fists on hips and sandy eyebrows down over bright blue eyes, stood back and studied him. These two had grown up together; they had served in the same Commando unit;

17

and Jim was engaged to Hugh's sister Monica. Yet, despite their close friendship, they were utterly unlike.

For Jim had grown bulkier while Hugh grew more lean. Jim was lazy but practical, Hugh hard-working but over-imaginative. Though in business hours Jim usually wore the formal black coat and striped trousers, he had now discarded the coat and rolled up his sleeves over speckled forearms. His grey tie was pulled down skew-wiff from the hard collar; his waistcoat had been unbuttoned over the beginnings of a corporation. It was a deadly insult to say he was putting on weight there.

Obediently, all the same, he lowered his voice to a whisper.

'All right, all right! What's the mystery? And where's Helen?'

'Helen left long ago. It seems I've offended her again, though I can't think why.'

'So you can't think why, eh?' inquired Jim, closing his eyes. 'Oh, cripes!'

'Sh-h-h!'

'If that girl didn't think you were God's gift to women, for a reason which completely escapes me, you'd have lost her already. Has it ever occurred to you to pay her compliments? Send her flowers? Make a fuss over her occasionally?'

'I've done that!' retorted Hugh, who sincerely if mistakenly believed he had. 'But I can't overdo it, or she'd think I was soft in the head. Helen's not like that!'

'All women are like that. Anyway, aren't you supposed to be seeing Pat Butler?'

'I was! I am! But that's just the point: I need your help!'

'Oh? How?'

'I've got a client in there. I want you to amuse him, entertain him, keep him occupied so that he doesn't get restless and leave. You speak very good French, don't you?'

'Well, I've been told I do. Why? Is he French?'

'No. He's a Persian named Abu of Ispahan, in a green fez. Unless I help, his brother is going to be murdered. And all his trouble, whatever this means, has been caused by my gloves. He—'

There was a pause.

Hugh, suddenly conscious of what he was saying and of the expression on his companion's face, stopped dead.

'Well, well,' Jim observed. There was another pause. 'By the way,' Jim added, 'did he mention the veiled houri, the nine of diamonds, or the north tower at midnight? Otherwise, by crikey, old Abu hasn't missed a trick!'

'God damn it, Jim, this is serious! Do you think I'm having you on?'

'No. Not at all. But I'll give you ten to one,' replied Jim, pointing a finger within two inches of the other's nose, 'that somebody's been having *you* on. I've often thought, old boy, you'd be the perfect gull for a hoax straight out of a thriller. And now you've had it. So help me, you've had it!'

The minutes were ticking on. Hugh had grown desperate. Restraining an impulse to shout, he did a little dance instead.

'I tell you, this is serious! Look at the fellow! Stick your head round the edge of this door and just look at him!'

'No, thank you. I wouldn't buy this one,' Jim said, 'if he'd swallowed an emetic to give the effect of poison. Hugh, why don't you grow up?'

And then, in Hugh's office, somebody screamed.

Even at this point, perhaps, Jim Vaughan might have made some sarcastic remark. But the screams went on. They soared up, splitting through the silent offices in the cold. They touched to life every dark night-fear of the brain; they cowed listeners by their sheer animal-like pain.

The two partners did not look at each other. Their quick, whispered conversation, in a fog-misted passage with the light of two doors streaming out, was cut off as a string is snapped.

Hugh, still gripping the door-frame, twitched his head round and looked sideways into the office. He ran inside, one knee weakening, but stopped by the swivel-chair at his desk.

Abu of Ispahan was now standing up, after a fashion, between the sofa and the low brass fender. Abu's face, which

19

Hugh didn't want to see, was reflected in the tilted mirror. Part of his body would have been reflected, too, if he had not still held out—shakily and with both hands—the crumpled newspaper.

The newspaper sheets fluttered down. Abu's thin chest arched. His foot banged against the fender; he would have pitched into the fire if a half-blind gesture had not sent him reeling half-way round. His image was wiped from the mirror as he fell.

'Easy!' snapped Jim at Hugh's side.

Hugh ran round the side of the desk, and round the side of the sofa.

'*Easy, I tell you!*'

Abu of Ispahan lay face upwards between fender and sofa. His fez had fallen off, revealing a shrunken bald head. His mouth, open, was childish with pain. He had been stabbed, downwards through his bony chest, with a long and heavy knife—an unskilful blow, because the ivory handle of the knife, without hilt, thrust up close to his body like a badly driven nail.

His back was still arched. His hands clawed and clutched at the knife, while blood soaked down heavily over his coat and waistcoat, and a blood-bubble formed where the hilt of the knife should have been. His eyes were wide open as he struggled.

Hugh Prentice dropped his brief-case on the sofa. Stripping off his gloves, he thrust them into the pocket of his overcoat. Then he lunged across the sofa for the telephone, which slipped and jingled on the desk.

'Jim! Maybe a doctor could . . . ?'

'You know he couldn't.'

Hugh went down on his knees by the struggling figure, and tried to prop him up. Abu fought him, weakly screaming, and Hugh lowered him gently. Most of the newspaper sheets had fallen into the hearth; but one rested with its edge on the bar of the grate.

Suddenly it caught fire. It reared up in flame, a bursting-yellow dazzle as though shaking itself, and fiercely illumined

Hugh's face. And Abu of Ispahan, with slowly rolling eye-balls, recognized the man kneeling beside him. His blood-soaked left hand crept up and fastened round Hugh's right hand, before Abu's fingers slipped off again.

'*Your gloves*,' he said distinctly—and died.

Chapter 3

SECONDS and seconds ticked past, audibly by Hugh Prentice's wrist-watch. The fire, gnawing at its three fresh lumps of coal, snapped in brightness. Hugh rose to his feet.

'Poor devil,' he muttered. 'Poor devil.'

'Yes.'

'Funny thing, too.'

'What's so funny?'

'What I was thinking.' Hugh pressed his fingers over his eyes. 'In the Army, Jim, we were taught to kill instantly and without noise. Oh, I know. That's part of an unreal life; it's gone now; we've forgotten it. But what made me sick, when I first saw this, was that somebody's botched the job and left the poor bloke in agony. Can you understand that?'

'Yes, I understand.' Then Jim's head jerked up. 'But old Abu did it himself, didn't he?'

'No.'

'What?'

'I said no.'

Already Jim, the practical man, had flopped down into a chair. He was running his hand inside his open waistcoat, over a stoutening waistline; and hitherto-unseen freckles had started out against a pale face. Now he half rose.

'But that knife!' he said, pointing as he flopped down again. 'It's yours. It's the Moorish dagger that old Mr. What's-his-name sent you as a present from Morocco; I'd know it anywhere. Look! There's the sheath on your desk now.'

The sheath was made of roughish dark-blue cloth, backed by heavy cardboard inside; its mouth broad and over an inch wide, tapering seven inches to its point to hold the heavy, six-inch dagger with the smoky-brown ivory handle. Hugh nodded, but did not look round.

22

'I know that, Jim. I always keep it in the sheath, so that nobody can cut his fingers by accident.'

'Well, then!'

'But listen. Abu couldn't have taken the blade out of the sheath while he was here with me; I watched him too carefully. He couldn't have taken it afterwards. Just before I went out of this office, I looked in a mechanical kind of way at my desk. There was something wrong, something missing. But I couldn't think what until a couple of seconds later, when I turned round at the door and looked back inside. The knife wasn't in the sheath.'

'Are you sure of that?'

'Positive. The handle always shines when the desk lamp's on; you notice it. That's the evidence, Jim; I could swear to it. Abu couldn't have taken the knife if it wasn't there to take. Therefore somebody got it beforehand, to kill Abu with it.'

Jim surged to his feet.

'Wait, now! Wait!' he urged. 'When was the last time you remember seeing the knife in its sheath?'

'About two hours before then.'

'Did you have any visitors besides Helen? And Abu?'

'No.'

'Very well. Could anyone have sneaked in here, nicked the dagger, and slipped out again without being seen?'

'I don't see how.'

'Then what in blazes are we arguing about?' Jim, who foresaw more trouble for both of them than Hugh had ever dreamed of, tried to hold him with a hypnotic eye. 'If you'll calm down for a second, old boy, I'll give you a clincher. After you left Abu, you were practically hanging to the doorframe outside. Did you keep an eye on him?'

'Yes, except when you went on ha-ha about this being a hoax!'

'And I was standing on the other side of you, in front of my own door. Now think! Could any—any murderer have slipped past both of us, into the room, without either of us seeing him?'

'No, of course not!'

'When we rushed in, was anybody here? Or hiding here?'

'Certainly not. There's no place to hide.'

Jim, who thought he had won the argument, exhaled a deep breath.

'Then there you are, Hugh. Nobody *could* have killed the blighter. For some reason he stabbed himself, just as . . .'

Jim Vaughan stopped, because of the new notion which had so clearly sprung into his friend's eyes. Hugh, who would have been handsome but for the severe lines from nose to mouth, looked far from severe now. His grey eyes glittered with excitement as they surveyed the fireplace, surveyed the body, then crept round to the two windows in the south wall.

Quickly he stalked over and examined the catches on both windows. He swung round, studying the room again, and nodded.

'Besides,' he said abruptly, 'why should Abu of Ispahan have committed suicide when he wanted so desperately to tell me something first? The man was terrified. He *said* he was frightened for his brother; but he hesitated before he said "my brother". He was frightened for himself. And I'll bet you a five . . .'

Back he went to the fireplace, trying to squeeze himself into the narrow space between fender and grate. One sheet of the newspaper had been burnt up and curled black. The other few sheets were gritty but untouched on the hearth-tiles.

Remembering that his right hand was still wet with blood where a dying man had grasped it, Hugh picked up the newspaper with his left hand. He shivered as he stepped across Abu of Ispahan's body. But, still using his left hand, he spread out the paper on the sofa and feverishly turned over its pages.

'And what,' Jim inquired almost calmly, 'is the idea now?'

'I only hope it wasn't on the page that was burnt. I've got to find the page that lists the entertainments at the theatres and cinemas.'

'That's fine. That's very helpful. What we need now,' said Jim, 'is a nice movie with a lot of corpses in it.'

Hugh didn't hear him.

'Got it!' he said. His finger travelled down the page, hesitated, and stopped. 'Got it again!' he added. 'It couldn't have been anything else.'

Then, a figure of inspiration in overcoat and bowler hat, he straightened up and took up the handle of his brief-case in his left hand.

'Jim,' he said, 'your facts are quite correct.'

'Glad to hear it. If you're at least sane enough to agree this is suicide . . .'

'Nobody,' Hugh interrupted, 'could have slipped past us, at the doorway, without being seen. Nobody is hiding here, or has been hiding here. The chimney-flue is too narrow to admit anyone. Both windows, if you look at 'em, are solidly locked with catches on the inside; and, anyway, in cold weather they're so stuck you can't move 'em. And yet, my lad, somebody *did* get in and out unseen.' His voice rose. 'I can't help it, Jim: this is murder in a sealed room.'

There was silence.

'Hugh,' remarked the other in an offhand tone, 'do you know what's the matter with you?'

'Well?'

Despite his bulk Jim made a very quick dash at the lowest drawer of the steel filing-cabinet. He yanked open the drawer and held up a detective novel.

'This!' he said. 'And this! And this! And this!'

Each time he said 'this!' he would hold up another novel and hurl it down with a bang on the floor. Dust puffed up; luridly coloured jackets flapped wide; the pile was accumulating when Jim, pink-faced, lumbered across and seized Hugh's arm.

'And now,' he snapped, 'I am going to take you into my office and tell you the facts of life.'

Despite Hugh's protests (they were shouting at each other as they had done when they were boys), Jim marched him into the other room. It was colder here, in every sense colder

25

and murkier. Hugh banged down his brief-case on the desk, side by side with Jim's own battered brief-case.

And Jim, badly frightened though he wouldn't show it, put his fists on his hips.

'For some reason,' he said, 'this flying-carpet wallah killed himself on the premises here. That's very poor publicity, as a beginner. We're strictly a family firm; we don't touch criminal cases or divorces. Have you thought what your uncle is going to say about it?'

This, admittedly, was bad. Hugh remained silent.

'In the second place,' Jim roared, 'we've got to dial 999 and get the police. They're going to ask why we didn't do it sooner. And, if we tell this scatty story about an impossible murder, they won't believe one word we say!'

'I know.' Hugh drew a deep breath. 'That's why I'm clearing out of here.'

Jim's heavy hand accidentally fell on the desk telephone, which clanked and jingled.

'*Clearing out?*'

'Yes.'

'You're doing a bunk, are you? And leaving me to hold the baby?'

'No, no, no!' said Hugh, pounding his fist on the desk. 'Who said anything about running away? Give me five minutes' start; then ring the police. I can be back here by the time they've arrived.'

'But where the devil . . . ?'

'To Patrick Butler, just as I'd intended. Can you think of a better man to help us in a situation like this?'

Jim hesitated, mouth open and glassy blue eyes roving. His hand went up and rubbed the side of his cheek.

'But we can't brief him, Hugh! There's nothing to brief him with!'

'We don't need to brief him. Just let me tell him this story; he'll jump at the chance to help us, and you know it. It's meat and drink and life to Butler.'

Still Jim hesitated. 'If he's got old Dr. Gideon Fell to back him up, I admit . . .'

'In this case, he hasn't. Dr. Fell's in Madeira or Majorca or somewhere. But what difference does that make?'

'Difference?' shouted Jim, pounding the desk in his turn. 'Listen! Who actually solved the problem in the Renshaw poisoning case? In the Bragley murder? In three or four others I could mention?'

'Jim, that doesn't make the slightest . . .'

'Oh, yes, it does! Without Gideon Fell, Butler's ten times crazier than you are. Seriously, now; he's too arrogant. He won't take a word of advice. Hugh! For God's sake! Come back here!'

But it was too late.

Hugh, snatching up brief-case and again impressing on Jim that he must ring the police in five minutes, was already running down the passage. With some difficulty he wrenched open the outer double-doors to a tile-paved landing.

The lift, a very narrow one in a steel cage, had not worked for about five months. Despite the profane complaints of the building's tenants, it still lurked in defiant fashion half-way between the second and third floors. Hugh plunged down the tile-floored stairs which surrounded it.

His brief-case had flopped open, apparently as he ran. He snapped shut its catch. On the ground floor the fog-ghosts were thicker. But, in the ceiling of the vestibule, somebody had switched on a very bright light in a glass dome. It illumined the stone stairs leading down to the pavement; even the pavement and the area-railings loomed clearly in a visibility-distance of ten or a dozen feet.

Hugh threw open the glass-panelled door, raced down the stone steps—and cannoned straight into a policeman.

The policeman, majestic in black waterproof, had swung to his left as he heard clacking footfalls dash down the stairs. Hugh struck him head on. They did not both go sprawling; Hugh's right hand gripped the law's left arm, extended from under the waterproof, as instinctively as the policeman's seized Hugh's left wrist.

They staggered, swayed, and then looked at each other. But Hugh felt his heart jump up into his throat.

'Er—sorry, officer.'

'Now, then!' began the policeman, and stopped.

On the fingers and back of Hugh's right hand, as he jerked it away, glimmered undried blood. The policeman looked at this, at his own left sleeve, and at the smears round the catch of Hugh's brief-case.

No chemist stood there to pronounce that these were blood-stains. But one glance at Hugh's guilty expression was enough. Some distance to the right, from the direction of Holborn, swung round the blurred yellow lamps of an approaching car; driven, undoubtedly, by one of those who think they can put on speed in a quiet square at any time, fog or no.

The policeman, eyes widening, opened his mouth to speak. Hugh, quicker of thought and action, politely said, 'Excuse me,' and bolted across the road in the path of the approaching car.

Its headlamps leaped up. The car swerved, skidded in a screeching of tyres, and missed him by three inches. But that black flying missile, which somehow righted itself and bumped on, obscured Hugh's backward glance.

He expected the policeman would dash after him. He expected, at least, that the law would take out a whistle and blow it. But the constable, of course, did neither. Having carefully memorized Hugh's description, he hurried up the steps to find out what had happened in the building.

On the opposite pavement, suddenly conscious of bitter cold on his body and of mist stinging his eyelids, Hugh stood panting. He caught a glimpse of the constable going up the steps, and guessed what was in the latter's mind. Then he ran down the broad paved walk, towards the centre of the spacious garden in the middle of Lincoln's Inn Fields.

Up to this time he was convinced he had been doing the wise, sensible thing. True, there had been misgivings. He pictured his Uncle Charles—fat, pettish—coughing with 'flu in an overdecorated house at Hampstead. He pictured his dark-haired and temperamental sister, Monica, who was engaged to Jim Vaughan but whose marriage had been postponed twice because Jim was broke from playing the horses.

These were minor misgivings. But now . . .

Now the police were chasing him in good earnest. And it wasn't adventurous, and it wasn't funny.

When you dialled 999, or rang the operator for the police, most people believed the call went to a main-divisional or sub-divisional police-station. Hugh Prentice knew it didn't. Your call was put straight through to the Information Room at Scotland Yard; and, without fuss or flurry, they flung out a net with very few meshes.

'Easy!' Hugh thought. 'No panic!'

In the middle of the garden at Lincoln's Inn Fields, which in summer was murmurous with green trees and the thud-thump of tennis-balls on hard courts, there stood a summer-house. Hugh, in cold and fog, took refuge in the summer-house for a moment to think.

'And the worst of the cursed business,' he declared aloud, 'is that I've got the clue!'

Who *was* Abu of Ispahan? What was his character, his background, his living and breathing entity, before it had been drained away by a dagger-stab? He, Hugh Prentice, believed he could find the answer to all these questions, if only—for an hour or two, anyway—he could avoid the grip of Scotland Yard.

Well! Six or seven minutes' rapid walking would get him to Patrick Butler's chambers. On the way he must stop only to wash the blood off his hands, and to telephone Helen. Helen would back him up whatever happened; and, in the plan already taking form in his mind, he needed Helen badly.

Out of the summer-house, Hugh cut southwards and to the left on a paved path which brought him out close to Serle Street on the Gray's Inn Side. From Serle Street he turned left again into Carey Street. A little way down on the left was a famous pub, the Seven Stars, where he could wash. Across the street, behind the bulk of the law-courts, were no less than four public telephone-boxes.

The Seven Stars was closed and dark. Either (incredibly)

29

it couldn't yet be half-past five, or else the pub did not open until six.

He stood in an unreal world. Ahead on his left, for a few feet, pavement and low-built houses were fairly distinct. Beyond hung a white wall, merging mysteriously into smoky blackness smudged by a few light-glows. But among these were the oblong-framed panels of the telephone-boxes.

All were empty. Hugh slipped inside one, miraculously found three pennies in his pockets, and dialled the number of Helen's flat in Knightsbridge.

While the ringing-tone buzzed, he examined his stained right hand. He put down the receiver on its metal box. From his overcoat pocket, where he had thrust them away after the murder, he drew out his gloves and put them on both hands. The blood-stains would be hidden; what else mattered?

'All my troubles have been caused by your gloves.'

And, just as insanely:

'My brother, who is a magician, has been *escroqué*.' What in blazes *did* that word *escroqué* really mean?

At this point Hugh snatched up the telephone-receiver again. Still its ringing-tone buzzed interminably, without answer. But Helen, who would have gone home by Underground, must surely have reached her flat by this time? For some reason she had been angry, yes. But she couldn't have been angry enough to refuse answering any 'phone-call! She couldn't—

Then Hugh went hot and cold with relief.

'Yes?' inquired a familiar voice, adding something which blotted out as he pressed Button A and the pennies clanked down inside the box.

'Helen!'

There was a pause.

'Oh,' Helen said coolly. 'So it's you.' Another pause. 'Do you know,' she added, 'that you've got me out of the bath? I'm sopping wet and I've only got a towel round me. Really, Hugh! Even if you do think I'm childish . . .'

Then that was it!

That was what she had been brooding about. For the life of him he couldn't remember calling her childish; but he must have done so; *she* wouldn't have forgotten.

'Helen, this is serious. I'm in a 'phone-kiosk in Carey Street, on my way to Mr. Butler's. The police are after me, and I need help.'

Another pause.

Though she might be miles away, he could see the expression on Helen's face as clearly as though she stood beside him. In an instant she would have forgotten that he had called her childish; or, indeed, called her anything worse. The brown eyes would soften, the mouth change to that sympathy which had almost the power to burn.

'Oh, Hugh, why didn't you tell me? I—I thought it was some of your detective story nonsense. What's happened?'

'There isn't time to tell you now. But that Persian bloke's been . . . well, he's dead. And there's trouble.'

'Never mind, darling. What do you want me to do?'

'First, I want you to pack two suitcases without initials or anything to identify them. Then—'

This time it was Hugh who paused, abruptly, in a rush of realization.

'Some of your detective story nonsense', Helen had said. And she was right. In contriving his beautiful plan to go after the murderer, he had been acting blindly and without any thought of the consequences. This blood was real blood. That constable, marching up the steps to number 13 Lincoln's Inn Fields, already would have set off the alarm to Scotland Yard.

Hugh cleared his throat.

'Sorry,' he said. 'I've been a fool. I can't involve you in this.'

'Hugh!'

'I'll ring you later, my dear. Good-bye.'

'Hugh! Wait! Don't put down the telephone!'

Tortured, indecisive, he hesitated. It was as though Helen were stretching out her arms to him. The faint soft voice, infinitely beloved, pleaded with him.

31

'I don't know what this is about,' Helen said, 'and I don't care. But what good am I, what am I for, unless I can help you? If you love me at all—'

'You know I love you. That's why I can't involve you in this. Good-bye.'

The telephone went down with a decisive click. Intimacy was cut off; appeal and persuasion vanished.

Hugh caught up his brief-case, shouldered out into the cold, and turned right down Bell Yard towards Fleet Street. If an image of Helen accompanied him, this only added a fiercer tenderness. Jim complained that he didn't make enough fuss over her; no doubt Jim was right; this could be remedied, though he must forget her now.

But he couldn't forget her. Helen's image went with him into shrouded Fleet Street, through a density of traffic crawling home. Buses suddenly loomed up, like red and lighted houses; then they stopped, as everything seemed to stop, amid squalling motor-horns. Nothing hurried except white-faced, fighting-faced pedestrians who swept him off the pavement.

Hugh squirmed past bumpers or tail-lights, and dived under the arch of the Temple across the road. Here, with the mud-smell in his nostrils and the fog-cough in his throat, he was compelled to grope his way. Helen's image had not quite faded even when he entered an ancient building in Brick Court, East, and ascended bare stairs between walls white-tiled like a lavatory.

'Mr. Prentice, Mr. Prentice!' a thin old voice said reproachfully, as Hugh opened the outer door to Patrick Butler's chambers.

A little chiming-clock, on the mantelpiece of the outer office, was tinkling out the notes of a quarter to six. Hugh glanced past it to the door of Butler's lair. This door was closed; or, as the barristers liked to say, sported. Behind a tidied desk sat little old Mr. Pilkey, Butler's clerk for many years, and continued to shake a snuff-coloured head which would never turn grey.

'Mr. Prentice, Mr. Prentice!' he repeated.

'He's—he's gone, I imagine?'

'Yes, sir.'

Pilkey could have pointed out that Hugh was three-quarters of an hour late. But Pilkey was as unlike most barristers' clerks as the Great Defender was as fiendishly unlike most barristers.

'I am afraid, sir, that Mr. Butler left at four o'clock.'

'Four o'clock? He left here at four o'clock?'

'Yes, Mr. Prentice. He conveys his apologies. You see, the young lady . . .'

'Oh. A client. All the same—!'

'No, sir.' Pilkey put his finger-tips together. 'Not a client. A young lady, I may say, in whom Mr. Butler takes a particular and personal interest.'

Astonishment jarred Hugh out of his correct attitude.

'But he's married, isn't he? Didn't he marry a widow, a Mrs. Lucia Renshaw, about seven years ago?'

'No, Mr. Prentice. This is a *new* young lady,' said Pilkey, apparently emphasizing the high polish on the article.

'Pilkey,' Hugh said desperately, 'I've got to find him. It's vitally important. Do you by any chance know where he is?'

'Yes, sir.'

'Well! If I could ring him . . . ?'

Pilkey took pity on his desperation. He had always liked young Mr. Prentice for Hugh's inflexible honesty; whereas, in private, Pilkey had always considered Hugh's uncle a fat-jowled old crook.

'Under the circumstances, sir, it might be difficult to reach him by telephone. On the other hand, he is not far away. You could find him quite easily if you cared to go there.'

Hugh's gasp of relief was loud in the bare office.

'Oh! That's better! Where is he?'

'Mr. Butler, sir, is at Scotland Yard.'

Chapter 4

WHEN Hugh Prentice marched straight up the stairs at New Scotland Yard, he had decided his course was far less foolhardy than it seemed.

And this knowledge was inspired by one word, an accidental word, in his conversation with Pilkey.

'You see, sir,' Pilkey had explained comfortably, 'the circumstances are unusual. Mr. Butler is not altogether popular with the police. But he wanted this young lady to see the Metropolitan Police Museum.'

'You don't mean that place with all the gruesome exhibits? The one you're not supposed to call the Black Museum?'

Pilkey inclined his snuff-coloured head.

'And was that his idea of amusing her?'

'Lady Pamela, sir, is a scion of the aristocracy. She is blasée. That's the word: blasée. Also ennuyée, if I may say so. In all this broad city, I doubt that there is a young lady so languid, so bored with all customary . . .'

'Thanks,' Hugh said quietly. And he left the office with confidence in his heart and a blaze of realization in his mind.

City! City of London!

He had forgotten that Lincoln's Inn Fields lay within the domain of the City; technically speaking, it was not in the Metropolitan area at all. The City of London had its own police force, its own organization, and dealt with all crimes in its borders; in fact, it jealously guarded these rights. News of a murder, of a man fleeing with blood on his right hand, would be reported to City headquarters, wherever they were; for the moment, at least, it would not even reach Scotland Yard.

And he would be safe in the very lair of the enemy.

Hugh got to Scotland Yard, by way of the Temple Gardens and the Embankment, in a very few minutes. Tall iron railings, once gilded, showed their teeth round an open archway surmounted by the Royal Arms. Beyond glimmered a black paved courtyard. On either side a massive building, once red-and-white brick but now soot-darkened to menace, towered up into mist.

There was foggy illumination under an enclosed arch on the right, where stone steps led up to broad glass doors, and a wall plaque said: *Metropolitan Police—Commissioner's Office*. Not without a qualm, Hugh strode up the steps and pushed open the glass doors.

In a spacious foyer, with cream-painted walls, a solitary policeman stood motionless and looked at him.

That was all. A very broad corridor, having an arched roof and shut off by glass panels, extended away towards his left; and another such corridor straight ahead, beyond the bulky policeman. Otherwise the building seemed deserted.

Hugh's footsteps clacked, amid echoes in the slight haze, as he approached the policeman.

'Good afternoon!' he said with false heartiness.

The constable nodded, but did not speak.

'My name is Prentice,' Hugh announced, with unnecessary loudness.

Again the constable nodded, but did not speak.

'I'm a solicitor. Actually, I'm here to find a barrister named Butler'—easy! He had almost said a butler named Barrister —'whose clerk says he's being shown round your museum. I don't suppose I could go and see him there?'

At long last the big constable came to life, and even smiled.

'Oh, I don't think there'd be any trouble about that, sir. You'd have to get permission, though.'

Hugh, acutely conscious of the blood-stains under his right glove, smiled falsely in return. 'Permission? From whom?'

'From Mr. Lee. Or Mr. Hatherton or Mr. Wirt.'

'Who are they?'

'Mr. Lee is the Assistant Commissioner. Mr. Hatherton is the Commander of the C.I.D. Mr. Wirt is the Relations Officer. Oh, ah! There's Mr. Wirt now.'

The constable nodded past Hugh's shoulder. The door to an office, close to the main entrance, was thrown open. Out bustled a lean, straight-backed man with clear-white hair and shell-rimmed spectacles, fussing with a button of his tweed coat. The policeman, without hurry, sauntered over for a silent conference with him.

This accursed place was getting on Hugh's nerves. It was too much like the entrance to a schoolroom or a church.

But the term 'Relations Officer' had a reassuring sound. Hugh was still further relieved when Mr. Wirt came bustling over with a cordial if rather strained smile.

'Mr. Prentice? You'd like to see the museum? Yes, yes: glad to have you! Inspector Basilisk is taking a party over it now.'

'Thank you. Er—do I need a pass or something?'

'Pass? No, no! Take you myself. No, no trouble at all!' Mr. Wirt gestured hospitably towards his office. 'Care to leave your overcoat? Hat? Gloves?'

'No, thanks!'

'Just as you like. Can't take too much time, you know,' observed Mr. Wirt, glancing at his watch. 'This way. Come with me.'

Hugh found himself hustled into the broad corridor beyond the policeman. What seemed to be a glass partition opened and swept him through. Then he stood in an alcove, in front of a door with the metal numeral 31. The tongue of its spring-lock held the door slightly ajar.

'Ah!' said Mr. Wirt. 'Haven't got the key myself. Down you go.'

It was much warmer as they descended wooden stairs into an even deeper hush. In the long, high museum there were flat glass-topped cases and tall glass-fronted cabinets. The tall cabinets, topped by what looked like discoloured busts, divided the museum into a series of 'rooms'. Its own school-room atmosphere, at first, was disturbed only by a faint shuffling of feet on concrete as an unseen Inspector Basilisk led his unseen main party through a far room.

But there was another and unexpected sound.

36

This sound burst out from close at hand, where two of the visitors had decided to remain behind in the first room amid flat-topped cases and glass-fronted cabinets of burglars' tools. The sound caused Hugh Prentice, at the foot of the stairs beside a hat-stand loaded with overcoats, to start and swing round. It made even Mr. Wirt open his eyes wide.

It was the loud, unmistakable, ringing slap of a man's hand against a woman's posterior.

'Oh!' said a voice.

A tall, stately girl, with a mink coat carried over her arm, walked away from her companion in outrage. She stalked to a table on which lay a hideous plastic-or-rubber death-mask of Heinrich Himmler. There she paused, back turned and aristocratic head raised haughtily.

'You struck muh!' she said.

Her companion also drew himself up, and folded his arms.

'Madam,' he replied, 'I did.'

The handsome Mr. Patrick Butler assumed his best eighteenth-century air. Long ago his enemies had said that he would grow stout and florid-faced. Yet Butler, though forty-seven years of age, looked no older than Hugh Prentice.

His fair hair gleamed under soft light on the burglars' tools. His arrogant nose was offset by a wide humorous mouth, his intellectual contempt for others offset by a twinkling blue eye. If he had not been genuinely kind-hearted, and free with money to a point of idiocy, there might have been many who hated him.

But there was no twinkle in his eye now. His rich, rolling voice filled the museum as it filled a courtroom.

'Much as it grieves me, madam—'

'You *struck* muh!'

'The point, madam, is conceded. Your expiring languor I can tolerate. Your bad manners, with difficulty, I can at least endure. But butcher the English language you shall not. And, when I hear this museum described as "most frightfully too-too", I am bloody well fed up.'

The tall girl whipped round to face him.

'*You* struck muh,' she cried tragically, and burst into tears.

37

'Oh, bejasus!' roared the Irishman, becoming instantly and guiltily contrite.

Hugh cast a quick glance at Mr. Wirt. But Mr. Wirt, as though scenes like this occurred every day at Scotland Yard, merely showed a mild-mannered interest and did not speak.

For Patrick Butler's contrition lasted only for a moment.

'My dear Pam,' he said grandly, 'I apologize. But is it possible you're really a human being after all?'

'Yes! Yes! Yes!'

'Then these ethereal airs of yours, when you float away like ectoplasm—?'

'You scare muh,' Pam said simply. 'You scare muh most ohfully.'

Again Butler's mood changed. He was a product of Westminster and Christ Church, Oxford. But often, very deliberately, he would inflect his speech with a tinge of Dublin accent which the English called a brogue; they loved it and fell for it.

'Sure, now, me dear, and 'twas only me way! You'd not hold it against me, surely?—Come here.'

'Sha'an't!' sobbed Pam, holding her head high. 'You struck muh.'

'Acushla! Come here.'

'We-ell . . .'

This time Mr. Wirt did intervene. Dragging Hugh by the arm while the latter removed his hat, Mr. Wirt hurried over to the others. Patrick Butler, in his fine Savile Row suit, instantly towered up with full suavity.

'Ah, Commander,' he said.

'Sorry to intrude,' apologized Mr. Wirt, hastily consulting his watch. 'But I believe this gentleman is a friend of yours, Mr. Butler; he wants to see you. Now please excuse me. I must tell Inspector Basilisk he's here.'

And away he rushed out of sight.

'My dear fellow!' exclaimed Butler, radiating charm as he gripped Hugh's hand. He genuinely liked Hugh, because he knew how much Hugh admired him; and for this particular

38

solicitor he would have done anything. 'What are *you* doing here among the manacles and murder-husks? Oh! I don't think you've met Pam. May I present Mr. Hugh Prentice: Lady Pamela de Saxe?'

What Hugh couldn't understand was how every trace of tears had gone from Pam's make-up, apparently by magic. Seen close at hand, she seemed even more ethereal or spiritual. Her bright blonde hair was swept back, showing a good deal of cheek and neck. Her grey eyes were wide-spaced. She was very fashionably if not warmly clad. Though tall and slender, she also displayed a good deal of bust and hipline.

'Mr. Hugh Prentice,' roared the exasperated Butler, while Pam inspected the newcomer, 'Lady Pamela de Saxe!'

Pam murmured that she was ravished, but ravished.

Patrick Butler shut his eyes. His right hand, palm open, began to swing in a thoughtful manner.

Instantly Pam sprang at Hugh, hurled her arms round his neck, and kissed him on the mouth. It was not a casual kiss. It went, so to speak, all the way down. Then Pam released him and drifted back, her mink coat still over her arm.

'The-ah!' she announced, with innocent-eyed triumph. 'But he's nice!' she protested, meeting Butler's look. 'He's *ohfully* nice!'

Again Butler closed his eyes.

'Indeed,' he said politely. 'Then I shudder to think, my pet, what might have occurred here had you fallen in love with him at first sight. Look here, old boy: Wirt said you wanted to see me . . . ?'

Hugh hastily got out a handkerchief and wiped the lipstick off his mouth.

'Just a minute!' he begged. 'What did you call that white-haired bloke who keeps rushing about like the office-boy? Who is he, anyway?'

'Oh?' inquired Butler. 'And just who or what do you think he is?'

'I thought he was some kind of superior clerk. They call him the Relations Officer.'

39

'They do. He is also Commander John Wirt, V.C., the head of the Special Branch.'

'Oh, crikey!'

'Yes,' agreed Butler. 'For God's sake be careful in this renowned institution. They're a deceptive-looking crowd.'

'It's this "Mr." business among the V.I.P.'s," groaned Hugh. 'If they'd only give 'em a good walloping title, as they do in the stories, you could tell whether you're talking to the Assistant Commissioner or to the man who sweeps the floors. Why did Commander Wirt keep looking at his watch?'

'Because visitors are supposed to be turfed out of here by six o'clock. And it must be well past six by now; usually they begin at four, and show you the Map Room and the Information Room. But I repeat: what do you want with *me*?'

Hugh looked round and lowered his voice.

'For one thing, because the police are chasing me.'

'*What?*'

'Sh-h-h! Mr. Butler, I can't offer you a brief . . .'

'And why should ye, pray?' asked the Great Defender, contemptuously sweeping this matter aside.

'But I can offer you a murder mystery. To my certain knowledge, a man was stabbed to death in a sealed room where no one could have approached him. The murder, apparently, must have been committed by a pair of gloves.'

Hugh glanced at his companion, for signs of derision. But the Great Defender alone showed no indication of doubt or scepticism. He showed only a kind of ecstasy.

'Oh, bedad,' he whispered. 'Tell me about it!'

'Here?'

'And why not?' demanded the other. 'Can you think of a place more poetic to plot damnation to the spalpeens than in the sink of their own iniquity?'

'Hoy!' muttered the conservative Hugh. 'Do you realize you're talking about the police?'

'Naturally.'

'Then you'll help me?'

Butler drew himself up. 'Sir, I will more than help you. I will solve your mystery for you.'

40

'But . . . suppose you're wrong?'

'I am never wrong,' said Patrick Butler.

He did not say this arrogantly, you understand. Butler, six feet two inches tall and proportionately broad, with an agreeable smile on his handsome if somewhat ruddy face, merely stated what seemed to him a simple fact.

And there was at least one solicitor, Hugh Prentice, who had implicit faith in it.

'Now the details, please,' Butler added.

'But Inspector Basilisk will be back here with his party at any minute! And where's Commander Wirt? He can't have taken all this time to tell the Inspector I'm here!'

'The details, please.'

'All right!'

Hugh spoke in a low voice, rapidly and concisely, beginning at his debate with Helen and the entrance of Abu of Ispahan. Pam immediately intervened to ask who Helen was; Hugh explained before Butler shushed her.

Through this concrete cavern, with its light-painted wood and the death-masks of hanged men on the cabinets, they could hear a very faint sonorous voice—presumably Inspector Basilisk's—explaining the mechanism of a crooked gambling-wheel at a fair-ground. Hugh's quiet tones swept on.

As he piled detail on detail—the watched door, the windows locked and stuck fast, no other way of entrance or exit, a dying man squirming on the hearth-rug—he could sense the excitement gathering in both his companions. He ended with his flight down the stairs at Number 13 Lincoln's Inn Fields, and his collision with the City policeman.

Butler's eyes were shining, moving from right to left as he considered.

'*I* think,' Pam said mistily, 'you were simp-lah wonderful.'

Again she drifted towards Hugh. Butler, without noticing her, put a powerful hand round her neck and yanked her back.

'Mr. Prentice, we must have a conference at my house. It's not far away, and my car is outside. But continue! What happened then?'

'On my way to your office, I 'phoned Helen, and asked her to pack two suitcases . . .'

'Why?'

'You see, Mr. Butler, I wasn't sure this was the kind of affair you'd care to handle—'

'You think so, eh? Ho!'

'Because it's partly a tracking job and may turn into a chase. I'm not even certain who Abu was or where to find his associates, though I think we can deduce it from the evidence. Hence my plan.' About to rush on, he stopped. 'By the way! What does *escroqué* really mean?'

'It means swindled, of course.'

'Swindled?'

'Yes, yess!' hissed Pam, with bursting and hazy excitement. 'And, Patrick! About the pooah man's last words . . . !'

'Balm of my soul, shut up.'

'But, Patrick—'

'We are faced, madam, with a criminal case in which the interference of woman must not only be deplored but even discouraged by the palm of the right hand. Gods of Babylon! If this is to be a chase, let it be a chase to make the town ring! Prentice and I will deal with it.'

'And I,' Pam said simply, 'will go with you.'

Butler turned and gave her what is described in fiction as a long, slow look. From somewhere Pam had taken up a handbag; now, her blonde head held back, she was studying her lips and working them round for better effect.

'Oh, yes, I will,' she added, breaking off in the act of applying lipstick. 'Else I shall tell Daddy. And *he* will tell the Home Secretary, and the Commissioner of Police, and—oh, almost anyone who could do the most frateful things. So theah.'

'God save me from all women!' shouted Butler, who would have been in a bad way if the Deity had taken him at his word.

'And I shall go with Mr. Prentice,' said Pam, giving Hugh a languishing look.

'Madam, you are a spoiled brat of whom it may be said

that only your intelligence is virgin. Will you kindly permit me to question my client, so that all of us may not land prematurely in chokey?' He swung towards Hugh. 'Look here! You washed that blood off your hand, of course?'

'Well . . . no. There wasn't time.'

'And, after all you've told me, you walked straight into the middle of Scotland Yard?'

'What else could I do? Your clerk said you were here. And after all, I'm in no danger.'

'Oh? What makes you think you're not?'

'But I told you!' Hugh retorted. 'The City of London police investigate the crimes in their own area. And that copper was a City policeman!'

Butler shook his head.

'I greatly fear,' he answered, 'that you have been guilty of confused thinking. You may be in much more danger than you imagine.'

'What's that?'

'It is quite true,' Butler continued, 'that the City police handle their own crimes. But, when it's a question of summoning a car or chasing a fugitive, the Metropolitan police cover the City as well. They don't have two sets of cars, you know. Unless you've been very lucky, your number's already up at the Information Room here.'

Through the museum, distantly, spoke a jocular and hearty voice.

'Well, gentlemen,' said Inspector Basilisk, 'I think that's everything. Would you come this way, please?'

A gritty stamping of shoes, a mutter of fascinated voices, swelled up as the visitors approached along a lane of cabinets towards the wooden staircase leading upwards.

And, at the same moment, Commander Wirt materialized on the lower steps. Hugh could not imagine how he had got upstairs and then down again without being seen. But there he was, with the light on his big spectacles. His head was turned towards the three conspirators in the first room, and he looked at them steadily.

43

Chapter 5

HUGH, who had felt a premonitory twinge of dread at the way in which Pam kept regarding him, was now conscious of far more pressing dangers.

But Patrick Butler, as usual in the presence of trouble, became even more calm and bland.

'Have no fear, my dear sir. My small talents are entirely at your service.'

'But Mr. Wirt!' Hugh whispered fiercely. 'He's probably known all the time!'

'No. No, I don't think so.'

'Why?'

'It isn't his department. True, he took Pam and myself down to the Information Room in the sub-basement . . .'

'Information Room!' groaned Hugh.

'But he didn't stay there. Besides it's the quietest room at the Yard.'

'And I hope you think that comforts me?'

Both of them were speaking ventriloquially, without moving their lips. Butler, though still agreeably smiling, gave Hugh a dirty look.

'I said it, young man, because they don't rush about or shout into telephones. They never say what is happening, or what reports have come in. When a car is sent out, somebody with a neck-'phone slips over to one of the map-boards and drops a red ring round a counter marking a car. That's all.'

'Listen. What the hell am I going to *do*?'

Butler raised his eyebrows.

'Do? Nothing whatever. Say little, do nothing, and mingle with the others as we all go out. Steady!'

'The others' had already appeared. They consisted of three Scottish mayors, one honorary ex-police-official from Malaya, and a detective-story writer who had annoyed

44

Inspector Basilisk by knowing more about celebrated crimes than the Inspector did. Ahead of them sauntered Inspector Basilisk, a plump well-dressed man with the air of a schoolmaster on holiday.

Yet seven pairs of eyes, including those of Commander Wirt, were turned curiously towards Butler and his companions.

Butler saw it, and met the situation. Taking Pam's mink coat from her arm, he draped it over her thin shoulders with an air of soothing tenderness.

'There is nothing, Lady Pamela,' he declared loudly and formally, 'which need frighten or alarm you or trouble your lovely head. They have done their best to scare you. They have failed. It is over now.'

Pam swung round, her soulful grey eyes lifted in anger.

'But I *was* scared!' she cried with obvious honesty. 'You struck muh!—On the behind,' she added passionately. 'And I won't be treated like a child! I won't I won't!'

Butler ignored this.

'Is it surprising, gentlemen,' continued his ringing oratory, 'that a young girl of fragile sensibility and delicate nervous system should have been upset by the parade of horrors shown here? Indeed, I am amazed that such things are exhibited to young ladies by our so-called guardians of the law.'

The men, who hitherto had been hiding grins, showed changed faces. Sheepishness turned to awkward mutters of sympathy and even an angry growl.

'Well, well, Lady Pamela,' soothed Inspector Basilisk, giving Butler such an indecipherable glance that he didn't even observe Hugh as he strolled over, 'Mr. Butler brought you here. And it's not as bad as all that, is it? We never show the photographs to ladies. Allow *me* to escort you, Lady Pamela.'

'Oh, th-thank you!'

The result was that Hugh, in a crowd struggling to retrieve overcoats and hats from the hat-stand, went upstairs without being noticed at all. Much as he feared some

45

Machiavellian craftiness from Commander Wirt, it became clear that Mr. Wirt only wanted to get these nuisances out of here as soon as possible.

Totally invisible amid three Scottish mayors, Hugh was borne along the corridor and across the foyer. The group gabbled and gabbled, as people will after going through the Metropolitan Police Museum. Much was made of Pam who, now stately and somehow imagining herself a persecuted heroine, greatly enjoyed herself. Ahead went the magnificent voice of Patrick Butler, descanting on the iniquities of the police.

Hugh was within two steps of the front doors, and breathing freely again, when disaster overtook them.

Commander Wirt, a conscientious man, wished to make sure he had done his duty.

'You're all right, Lady Pamela? Excellent, excellent! Goodbye, Mr. Prentice!'

That name, Prentice, rang out in the quiet foyer.

An immensely tall and somewhat burly man in his shirt-sleeves, who had been crossing the left-hand corridor with a file in his hand, stopped short. He turned round, showing heavy black eyebrows, and made an almost imperceptible sign. Commander Wirt, whose eye could follow lightning, sauntered towards him.

And Butler spoke in ventriloquist fashion to Hugh.

'The tall bloke,' he said, 'is Commander Hatherton of the C.I.D. Get to blazes out of here! No; don't run!'

'But—'

'Pam! Go with him and show him where the car is. Stay there until I've adjusted the matter. I'll join you in two minutes.'

As one man the crowd pushed open the glass doors, carrying Hugh and Pam with them.

Under the hooded arch of stone steps down to the court-yard, bitter-cold air swirled up at them. Hugh stumbled on the top-most step. Mink-clad arms locked round his left arm; a mink coat pressed against his left side.

'Dahling,' Pam whispered below his ear.

46

At the foot of the steps the visitors, as usual with strangers who don't quite know how to take leave of each other, lingered and talked. Pam slid her arms up round Hugh's neck; once more she drew close, implanting on his mouth a kiss of even more soul-searing quality.

('And here,' Hugh thought despairingly, 'we go again.')

The fascinated spectators stood dumb. Pam moved her lips a few inches away from his mouth but not from his face.

'This *fiancée* of youahs,' she murmured disdainfully. 'This Helen person. Why did you ask her to pack two suitcases?'

'Look! I—'

'You wished to run away with her. And live in sin. Didn't you?'

'Great Scot, no! I never thought of,' Hugh gulped, 'sin.'

'Oh, de-ah. But you must. I ohlways do.'

Back went her mouth again, her arms pressing in tighter grip.

Hugh had no interest in the accursed woman, being concerned only with his Helen. But there are some challenges which no gentleman ever can or should resist.

'All right!' he thought, and seized Pam in a way which all but swung her legs from under her.

'*Hugh!*' interposed the voice of another girl.

Not for nothing are we given, even long ahead, these premonitory stabs of dread. It is no contradiction in terms to say Hugh knew who had spoken even before she spoke. Yanking Pam's arms from his neck, he spun round.

In the fog, not four feet away from him on his right, stood Helen. She carried a big suitcase, obviously packed, in either hand.

Helen did not say anything, which is a bad sign. It is possible that her face, more pretty than Pam's in a heartier and more vital way, grew slightly red and then slightly pale. Helen set down the two suitcases. She glanced at Hugh, then casually looked away.

'Well . . . now!' Hugh began.

Pam moved back, looking ethereal, and then spoiled the whole effect by leaning her head against Hugh's chest and giggling. Helen's face went a shade whiter, but still she did not speak.

'Well, now!' Hugh began again more heartily, without any notion of what he was going to say.

Fortunately, it was not necessary.

Behind him, at the top of the stone steps, the glass doors opened and closed. Patrick Butler ran down, a swaggering and striding figure silhouetted against misted yellow light, and stood on the lowest step. There he let his voice roll out, to the whole group, full-charged with menace and doom.

'*Run, everybody!*' he shouted. '*There's trouble! Run!*'

Subtle, mighty and disturbing to the calmest nerves, is the very atmosphere of New Scotland Yard.

It is sober fact that three Scottish mayors, a blameless gentleman from Malaya, and a relatively blameless writer of detective novels, turned and bolted in all directions like fowls in a chicken-run. The detective-story writer ran hardest of the lot.

For an instant Butler stood there like Henry the Fifth, enjoying the noble figure he presented. Then, divining Helen's identity by faint remembrance, and seizing one girl by each arm, he himself pounded away into the fog. Hugh had no choice but to pick up the suitcases and run after them.

Bang! went the glass doors, opening and shutting again. The police-constable on duty in the foyer, with instructions to detain Mr. Hugh Prentice for a few questions, ran down the steps and stopped in bewilderment.

It was impossible to identify Hugh Prentice, much less detain him. In a courtyard banging to the stamp of heavy-soled boots, about fifty persons seemed to be flying away both east and west. The constable, swearing under his breath, hurried back up the stairs for further instructions.

Butler had not departed by the Embankment side. The fog, astream with criss-cross blurs of car-lamps, showed him swinging his two female charges in the other direction: between the soot-darkened buildings, through the western gate towards Derby Yard and Whitehall. Hugh was only three

48

steps behind when, outside the gate, he turned left into a tiny lane.

Here was parked a long sleek black limousine. A uniformed chauffeur sprang out to hold open the rear door.

'Johnson!'

'Sir?'

'Sling this gentleman's suitcases into the seat beside you. Then get home as fast as you can in this weather.'

'Very good, sir!'

Butler uttered brief if flowery apologies to both girls. Afterwards he picked up Pam bodily and hurled her into the car, where she landed squealing at the far side of the back seat. Helen, treated with more ceremony, was merely jerked up under both arms and deposited with a thump on the near side. Butler, in his fashionable overcoat and soft grey hat, dived in and sat between them.

Hugh, stumbling after him, was left to one of the pull-down seats facing the others. Doors slammed like pom-pom guns; the car nosed out into Derby Yard.

'Ah, now!' said Patrick Butler, breathing hard but with the air of one who preens himself and awaits a compliment.

'Look here!' protested Hugh, also gasping for breath. 'What was the game in doing that?'

Butler, taken aback, could only stare at him.

'Doing that?' the barrister roared. 'Don't you understand Hatherton wanted to detain you?'

'I know; but . . .'

'So I bade him a polite good-bye, slipped out, and created a diversion which ensured your escape. By God! Have you no sense of gratitude at all?'

'Yes, yes! I only mean: won't they chase us?'

'No. They think rational and responsible persons, such as you and of course myself, can be found whenever they want 'em.'

'And if you happen to be wrong?'

'I am never wrong.'

Hugh clutched with both hands at the brim of his bowler hat.

49

'Of course,' Butler added, 'if you care to stop and explain matters to the nearest policeman . . . ?'

'No! No, not for anything!'

'Very well. Then pay heed, my boy, and show proper thanks.' Butler reflected. 'It may comfort you to learn, however, that there's someone they want far more than they want you.'

'Oh? Who's that?'

'Your partner. Mr. Vaughan.'

This time Hugh could not believe his ears. It was as though the whole limousine had suddenly lifted into the air and floated away like something out of science fiction.

'*Jim* Vaughan?'

'Yes. Who else?'

'But Jim had no more to do with the murder than I did!'

'Yes; so I gathered from your story. That is purely irrelevant. They are now pursuing him all over London in the biggest wanted-for-questioning search since they went after Christie.'

'But why?' What happened after I left my office?'

'Kindly remember,' Butler said with a touch of hauteur, 'that I talked to Commander Hatherton for less than two minutes. He tells you what he wants you to know; not a word more. Still! I did gather . . .'

'Yes, yes? Go on!'

'Well! You may recall the City policeman with whom you collided during your dramatic exit? Tut, tut! Such a disrespect for—'

'Tell me!'

'The bobby, it appears, took a little time to inspect three floors before finding a corpse on the fourth. Meanwhile, your friend Mr. Vaughan had dialled 999. The Information Room people at Scotland Yard weren't unduly impressed. After all, they get on an average of twelve hundred 'phone-calls a day, mostly duds, including twenty or thirty reports of sudden death.'

'Are you seriously telling me there are twenty or thirty murders a day?'

Up went Butler's eyebrows, crushing resistance.

'Now who spoke of murder, if you please?'

'But you said—'

'I said "sudden death". That may mean anything from a motor-smash to an octogenarian dying in bed. Much as I have spoken against the pestilent Peelers, they have a certain magnificence that nobody ever knows or talks about.

'Bedad!' he exclaimed, as all his Irish sympathies flew in the other direction and he slapped his knee. 'They listen patiently to every call, and deal with it. They listen to their lunatic regulars, who ring up almost every night, and soothe 'em to sleep. They listen to some poor devil who's going round the bend. And God knows how many suicides they've prevented by sending a car in time.'

Hugh Prentice was growing desperate, as the car hooted and manœuvred through dense traffic in mist.

'Mr. Butler, I've got nothing against the police! I was only asking about Jim Vaughan. You say he dialled 999 . . . ?'

'Ah, yes.' Butler recovered himself, a little embarrassed. 'Well, I repeat: they weren't unduly impressed. But out went old Nine A . . .'

'Who's he?'

'He's a police-car from the City area. (Stop these digressions, can't you?) The car, with a sergeant and two men, arrived just as the City policeman entered the offices of Prentice, Prentice, and Vaughan.'

'And then?'

'Your friend Vaughan explained you'd got blood on your hand when the dying man grabbed your wrist. He said you'd run out of there only to fetch the police . . .'

'Didn't they think that was a trifle strange? When I smacked straight into a policeman without mentioning the murder?'

Butler nodded thoughtfully.

'Yes; they pointed it out. Mr. Vaughan turned slightly green. He said, apparently with much sincerity, that you were rather scatty—'

'I know! Jim honestly believes it.'

51

'He next told them the true story of the murder, just as you told it . . .'

'And they didn't believe him?'

'Precisely. Not a word. Furthermore, the City sergeant dug up some entirely new piece of evidence—'

'What evidence?'

'How should I know? Do you imagine Commander Hatherton would tell me? This evidence, for some reason, indicated that Mr. Vaughan himself might be the murderer.'

'Oh, God!'

'Calm yourself,' Butler assured him, with a negligent wave of his hand. '*I* will prove his innocence. Nevertheless! By this time your friend, not unnaturally, was more than rattled. *He* bolted out of the office.'

Hugh, putting his head in his hands, groaned aloud.

'And yet,' mused Butler, 'I can't help admiring Mr. Vaughan. He charged straight through four City coppers, dashed down the stairs without his overcoat and minus one sleeve of his jacket, and disappeared in the fog.'

'They haven't found him?'

'No, but the whole Metropolitan and City Police are trying their best. By Jove! Common civility suggests that we retrieve him, and . . .'

Butler paused, as though remembering some monstrous incivility of his own. He glanced at Helen. Gallantry, even tenderness, swelled through him.

'Madam!' he pleaded in his warmest tones. 'You will forgive me, I hope, for removing you from a difficult scene with so little formality. But I am sure we have met, or at least seen each other, before this?'

'Y-yes,' stammered Helen. It was the first word she had spoken there.

'Ah!' said Butler. 'You are Miss Helen Dean? And engaged to be married,' his gesture indicated Hugh as though the latter were about fourteen years old, 'to my young friend here?'

'I *was* engaged to him,' she said.

At this last devilishness, piled on top of all the others,

Hugh was stung to fury. Only Butler's look kept him silent. Butler glanced quickly between Helen and Pam.

'Madam, listen to me!' he said. Seizing Helen's chin, he yanked her face round so that she was compelled to look up at him. 'We are deep in rather a desperate business. We have no time for feminine tantrums now.'

'Will you *please* let me go?'

'No, madam, I will not. Let me see if I can deduce the cause of this particular tantrum.'

Helen's undignified attempt to kick him in the shin was forestalled.

'He asked you, as we know, to help him by preparing two suitcases. Then, because his conscience wouldn't let him involve you in a murder-case, he told you to forget it: doubtless having informed you already he was on his way to my chambers.

'But you, madam, wouldn't have this. Obediently, heroically, you packed the suitcases and rushed to my chambers in the Middle Temple. You would show your devotion even though you had been begged not to do so.'

'*Will you kindly . . .!*'

'No, madam. At my chambers, no doubt, Mr. Pilkey told you he was on his way to Scotland Yard. Against all obstacles you raced to Scotland Yard. At the door, I deduce, you found him being embraced by a young person who would make passes at a stuffed mummy. And this, you thought tragically, was the reward of all your devotion! So you blew up. Is this true, madam, or is it not?'

It was true.

In fact, it was far too true. If you guess to a hair-line what is in a woman's mind, she is apt to get ten times madder than she was before. But Patrick Butler, relentless, gave Helen no time to cry that it wasn't true.

'Madam,' he said sternly, 'you are doing this young man a grave injustice. Is it his fault if he is attractive to other women? Should fair arms be flung round his neck, would you have him stand there like a priggish stick-in-the-mud, not even touching her and pretending nothing is happening?

53

In your heart you know you wouldn't. Finally, I would remind you that he is in great danger.'

Helen's chin ceased to struggle in Butler's grip.

'D-danger?'

'The very gravest, if they find him.'

'That's s-silly! I don't believe it! You're joking!'

And now Butler's voice would have scared the ears off any group listening to a ghost story.

'He will be hanged by the neck,' intoned the barrister, looking straight into Helen's eyes, 'until he is dead.'

Even Pam looked alarmed. Throughout all this Pam, either from prudence or mere vacancy of mind, had said no word; now, after spending the time in repairing her make-up and admiring herself in the compact-mirror, she glanced round.

Patrick Butler released Helen's chin. He dusted his hands. He sat back.

'Madam, I have done,' he said.

Outwardly, at least, Helen did not relent. None the less her brown eyes strayed towards Hugh, intimating that she would love to forgive him if only he said it was all his fault. Hugh, on the other hand, was so angry and confused by injustices that he sat bolt upright, arms folded.

'Hugh!' Helen said softly.

But the impetuous Mr. Butler, who swept through life like a whirlwind, gave them no emotional rest.

'You!' he continued, pointing his finger in Hugh's face. 'Suitcases! That reminds me. You said you had a theory which might solve, or at least help to solve, the whole mystery. It's probably of no importance . . .'

'It isn't, eh?' Hugh yelled.

'No! But what can you tell us?'

'I can tell you,' shouted Hugh, 'who "Abu of Ispahan" really is. I can tell you—'

He paused. The limousine came to an abrupt stop, jerking him backward. Automatically he grasped Helen's knees.

'Continue in a moment,' said Butler, 'before the fire in my library. Out you go, all of you!'

Johnson was opening the rear door of the car. They had stopped in front of Butler's sedate house in Cleveland Row, off St. James's Street. As they struggled out, the door of the house was opened by an elderly, wizened little woman, who in misty outline appeared to be blinking hard at a telephone note-pad.

'Mrs. Pasternack!' said Butler. 'You'll catch your death in this weather. Go back inside at once!'

'Very good, sir,' meekly replied Mrs. Pasternack, without moving. 'Sir, are you acquainted with a Mr. James Vaughan?'

Hugh, clutching the handle of his brief-case, strode forward. Butler was ahead of him.

'I have not met the gentleman, Mrs. Pasternack; but the name is all too familiar. What about him?'

'Well, sir, he's been ringing up here every fifteen minutes for the past hour. He seems to be in rather an excited state of mind.'

'Where is he?'

'That's it, sir. He won't say. He says that all he wants to do,' Mrs. Pasterneck peered more closely at the note-pad, 'is to murder a Mr. Hugh Prentice.'

Chapter 6

In the small back-library, where white-painted bookshelves stretched up to the ceiling on every wall except one, Butler and Helen stood with their hands outspread to a roaring log fire under the hood of an Adam mantelpiece.

Helen's glossy light-brown hair shone by firelight and soft lamps. Her more than admirable figure was set off by a tight-fitting dinner-dress which caused Pam, sprawled out in one of the deep leather arm-chairs before the fire, to narrow her languid eyes.

But Helen was looking up at a framed sketch hung above the fireplace. It was a black-and-white sketch of a girl's head, which for some reason faintly disturbed the whole room. It was not precisely beauty in the pictured face, but a haunting quality in the eyes and the slight enigmatic smile.

'She's lovely,' breathed Helen, still looking at the sketch. 'May I ask who she is?'

Patrick Butler, his hands stretched out to the flames, did not raise his eyes.

'Her first name was Joyce.' he spoke shortly. 'She's the only woman I ever honestly loved.'

'"Was?"' repeated Helen, her quick sympathies touched. 'I'm awfully sorry. She's dead, then?'

'No. The jury found her guilty but insane. She's serving a life-sentence at Broadmoor.'

Silence. Nobody knew what to say.

The fire threw shifting, lurid-yellow lights. Books, too, have their own atmosphere. To one who loved books, as Hugh did, this great crime-library exuded an air sinister and even evil: like the threshold across which they seemed to have stepped.

Butler swung away from the fire. He eyed a dictaphone standing beside one of the leather chairs.

'Arrah!' he snapped, momentarily in one of those black

56

moods during which he cursed the whole world. 'What's the odds? That was years ago. I usually tell people it's the sketch of a Victorian actress playing Rosalind with short-cut hair. Why the devil do I tell *you*?' He hesitated; then smote his hands together. 'Never mind. To business. Prentice!'

'Well?'

'Tell me the story of Abu's murder.'

'*Again?*'

'Yes. Again. The rushing about in that museum wasn't conducive to good thought.'

'And I haven't heard it, you know,' observed Helen, turning round and looking Hugh in the eyes. For some reason she kept her hands behind her back.

'I'll do it gladly,' Hugh said, 'if you'll show me a place to . . .'

Though he had doffed overcoat and hat, his hands were still gloved. He held out his right hand, pulling at the glove-fingers. But the glove was stuck; it wouldn't come off.

'The blood's dried,' he said thoughtlessly, with marked effect on Helen and even on Pam. 'And,' he added with some haste, 'do you mind if I use your 'phone? I've got to reach Jim Vaughan.'

'Vaughan?' exclaimed Butler, beginning to forget his black mood. 'Man, the whole police force don't know where he is. How do you know?'

'I don't; but I think I can guess. Jim wouldn't be foolhardy enough to go home. He's engaged to my sister; I'll give you five to one he's gone to ground at Monica's flat. Besides, until we hear about this dangerous "new evidence", we're stymied.'

Butler nodded towards a door enclosed in bookshelves.

'Across the passage,' he said. 'Washbasin in a cupboard under the stairs. The 'phone's in the dining-room: first room on your left at the front. Hurry!'

Hugh hurried. It was difficult to get the glove off. But he scrubbed his hands in water, almost boiling, with much soap, and thrust the gloves into his hip pocket.

57

Afterwards, hurrying along the narrow eighteenth-century passage with its black-and-white marble floor, he wondered why the whole narrow house seemed sinister. He supposed it was because the last scene of a famous murder-case, as well as the penultimate scene of several others, had been played here.

The dining-room was dark. The glass prisms of a chandelier tinkled to his step. Snapping on a light-switch beside the door, Hugh found the telephone table in a corner. An ormolu clock on the mantelpiece said that it was nearly half-past seven.

Monica's flat was at Hampstead, not far from his uncle's house. With a stumbling hand Hugh dialled HAM 5975.

Again the ringing-tone seemed to buzz interminably, as it had done at Helen's. But it was answered at last.

'Yes?' inquired the cool, unmistakable voice of his younger sister, Monica.

'Monnie, this is Hugh. I've got to speak to Jim, if he's there. Is he?'

'What number did you want, please?'

Clearly he could envisage Monica, dark-haired and handsome and rather haughty in a pale way. She would have been a warm human being, he considered, if she had not become private secretary to some pompous Whitehall executive whom Hugh cordially detested.

'Monnie, it's Hugh! Your brother! The police don't know where Jim is, and I'm only making a guess! But I think . . .'

'You must have the wrong number.'

As Hugh pictured her there, in that hesitating second before a 'phone is put down, it seemed to him the difference between success or failure, perhaps life or death.

'Monnie! If you think some crafty detective is imitating my voice, let me tell you a few things nobody but your brother could know. When you were about eleven years old you had a damn'-silly doll named Caroline Jane. You used to give that doll a lorgnette made out of wire, and had one yourself. I landed a cricket-ball slap in the middle of the table, when you were giving a tea-party where everybody had to wear a lorgnette and take a name out of Debrett, or you got furious.'

'Don't be utterly absurd,' said Monica. But her tone had changed; it was repressed, but angry and a little panicky. 'Just one moment.'

In the background there was a whispered, scuffling argument. Then somebody, male, breathed very heavily through the receiver.

'*My friend*,' said Jim, in a voice beyond description.

'I'm sorry, Jim! I couldn't help it. But you shouldn't have run away from there.'

This was an error. The pause, doubtless open-mouthed, was caused by Jim's sheer stupefaction at such cheek. Hugh hastened to rectify it.

'Wait; I didn't mean that! I know it was my fault for running away at the beginning,' Then he spoke just as quietly. 'But listen, Jim! If this whole mess isn't cleared up by to-morrow, I'll give myself up for the murder.'

More hard breathing; afterwards, a voice less thick.

'You mean that?'

'Yes!' retorted Hugh, who meant every word. 'I'll even put it in writing. But what happened at the office?'

'I warned you, didn't I, what would happen if I told the coppers the truth?'

'Yes, you did. Yes! I mean, why did you have to cut and run?'

'Have you looked at your brief-case recently?'

To Hugh the words meant nothing; they were gibberish.

During a silence—when he could only imagine Jim, freckles and slight corporation and all, sitting on the fashionably uncomfortable blue sofa in Monica's sitting-room, with his tie undone and one sleeve torn from his jacket—every coherent thought seemed sponged from Hugh's head.

'Brief-case?'

'It's not your brief-case, you somethinged somethinged thus-and-so! It's my brief-case! Get that? *My* brief-case! Don't you remember?'

'Wait! I seem to . . .'

'After old Hashish died, you carried your brief-case into my office. Its catch was shut. You put it down on the desk beside my brief-case, which was open and empty. In the excitement of the moment, I admit I didn't notice it when you grabbed my brief-case and dashed out. If you've got the case there, have a look at it.'

'Stop. Hold the line a second.'

'But—!'

In the background Hugh distinctly heard Monica's voice say, 'Oh, God!' in a way which summed up her view. Even as he ran out into the passage, he had already remembered.

The cases, old and battered, looked very much alike. But the case he snatched up from the desk in Jim's office was open. He remembered closing it, thereby getting blood-smears from his own fingers round the catch, as he ran downstairs at number 13 Lincoln's Inn Fields.

In the dim-lit passage at Patrick Butler's house, the case lay on top of two suitcases. One close look at it told Hugh it was Jim's and not his. He opened it; it was empty. It made him shiver to think he had marched into Scotland Yard with blood-smears round the nickelled catch; but they had dried, and might have been rust or mud.

Back he ran to the 'phone, where Jim poured out the story of the police's entrance, and the questioning which seemed to make out Jim a prince of liars.

'Look!' said Jim. 'I don't know what was bothering 'em so much. But they couldn't seem to find any fingerprints on the ivory handle of that knife. They hauled me into my office for more questioning. I don't mind saying J. Vaughan was in a state.'

'But what has the brief-case got to do with . . . ?'

'If you'll listen, you incarnadined traitor, you'll understand!'

'Jim, keep your shirt on!'

'Keep my . . . never mind. It wouldn't have been so bad if they hadn't been so incarnadined polite. Up and down prowls this sanguinary City sergeant. Doesn't seem even to see my desk. Stops by it, all the same.'

'Well?'

'"This your brief-case, sir?" Casual as kiss-your-hand. God help me, I said yes. "Mind if I open it, sir?" "No; go ahead."'

Hugh's hand was sweating on the 'phone.

'Jim, there was nothing in that case except the Matheson brief: the one I was taking to Butler!'

'There wasn't, eh?'

'I tell you, the Matheson brief—'

'Yes; that was there. So was a pair of white cotton gloves, one of 'em heavily stained with blood.'

Gloves again.

Once more he could hear Monica speaking to Jim, in the background; and this time with icy calmness.

Well, Hugh decided, you couldn't object if Monica blamed everything on her brother. Monnie wanted Jim to settle down; to find, after marriage, what she called a 'suitable' house, say at Sunningdale; to be elected to a 'good' club and join a 'good' golf-club where he might find 'useful contacts'.

And, Monica being a woman, that was understandable too.

Yet Hugh's sizzling wits put all those words into inverted commas because they stood for everything he despised and held in contempt much as Patrick Butler did. 'Useful contacts, begod!' Patrick had once said, in the members' enclosure at the Garrick Club. 'If a man can't succeed by his own abilities alone, it's the poor weak success he deserves!' Those words had been Hugh Prentice's motto ever since.

But there was no time to think of this. He could think about only a nightmare of gloves and a crackling telephone.

'Jim, is it any good telling you I know nothing about these white cotton gloves? That I can't even imagine how they got into my brief-case?'

Jim's voice changed to a cold tone he had never before heard.

'Now get this, Hugh. I didn't give you away. I broke out of there before they'd got over their surprise. But enough's enough. *You* were the only one who could have killed Abu, and you know it.'

'Yes,' Hugh agreed, after a pause. 'Apparently that's so.'

'*You* were the only person alone with him. *You* said he was alive, sitting on the sofa, when you left your office; who else can say that? *You* owned the dagger. *You* started all this talk about a sealed room—'

Hugh held the 'phone away from his ear. Every syllable, though not loud, crackled and shrilled clearly in the chilly dining-room.

'—*You* ran away. *You* substituted brief-cases. *You*—'

'It's no good going on with this. My offer still holds.'

'To give yourself up and confess?'

'Yes.'

'When?'

'That's just it. I'm at Patrick Butler's house now, but I can't say where I might be for the rest of the night. But I ask one thing: I have twenty-four hours before I give up?'

'No!' said Monica, apparently snatching away the 'phone.

'Yes!' said Jim, snatching it back. 'I can hang on till then.' His voice wavered. 'Look, old horse. I'm certain there must be some explanation . . .'

'We've made our bargain,' said Hugh, and rang off.

For a little time he sat there, without thinking, staring at the telephone. The clock ticked on the mantelpiece.

He was roused by a kind of physical awareness. Helen, in her dark-blue dinner-dress, stood in the doorway as though wondering how much to let him know she had heard. Her pink lips were parted, her face pale.

'Helen,' he said, jumping up from the chair by the telephone-table and forestalling her before she could speak, 'do you want *me* to make useful contacts? To play golf decorously and butter up my prospective clients? Or would you like me, as in the rhyme, occasionally to burst from my cell with a hell of a yell, and do something idiotic for no reason at all?'

Helen's eyes widened.

'Yes! No! Yes!' she whispered incoherently, and threw out

62

her hands. 'I mean, didn't I tell you, only this evening, I couldn't endure it if you turned into a stuffed shirt?' For some reason she was trembling badly. 'I mean, with golf and an eye to business and never bursting out?'

'Helen, have I ever told you just how much I love you?'

'No, but you could try,' said Helen, running into his arms. 'I don't mind listening.'

Up behind her towered a tall, stately figure with flaxen hair. The impressive figure tapped Helen on the shoulder.

'Whereas I, on the other hand,' intoned Patrick Butler, 'have strong æsthetic objections to hearing amorous drivel. This objection does not apply, I need scarcely say, when the amorous drivel is uttered by myself.'

Whereupon Butler's whole expression changed.

'You have been given an ultimatum, then?' he asked grimly.

'Could you hear?'

'Sir, the whole house could not help hearing. They have given you an ultimatum?'

To Hugh, suddenly glancing at Butler's face, it occurred that he would not care to have the Irishman for an enemy in any kind of contest.

'Well—yes.'

'So!'

Helen's soft body went rigid in Hugh's arms.

'If you think you'll be allowed to confess to a crime you didn't commit,' Helen said with her lips against his neck, 'then you'd better think again! I hate her,' Helen added. 'Your own sister!'

'Helen, Monica didn't mean any of that! I know her too well. She's only upset and frightened for the moment, that's all; and she loves Jim. And Jim, in his heart, wants respectability as much as she does.'

'I hate her!'

'Besides, what choice had I? In doing what I did, I probably ruined the firm, prevented Monica's marriage, and shoved Uncle Charles out of the next Honours List. He's expecting a knighthood.'

'Whereas your true and sole offence,' observed Butler, not without majesty, 'lay in seeking *my* advice at a time of crisis? Indeed. Now come to the back-library,' he snapped, 'with no more nonsense. Come!'

In the back-library, Pam stood tall and thin with her back to the fire, seeming less bored or languid than deep in pondering some abstruse problem.

'I'm hungry,' she stated.

For a second Hugh quite seriously thought Butler would pick up the Shorter Oxford Dictionary and hurl it at her.

'Food!' he said, as though shuddering at thought of a painful poison. 'At a time like this! Food!'

'You're *mean*,' said Pam. 'You're fratefully, fratefully *mean*! You said we were going to the Caprice.'

Butler pointed to a distant chair. He spoke in a deep, shaking voice.

'Woman, sit down there and shut your potato-trap. Otherwise, so help me—!'

Pam, hastily protecting her posterior with her hands, did as she was told. 'Now!' said Butler to Hugh. 'Your whole story again, if you please. Omit no detail.'

The yellow firelight writhed and crackled, the enigmatic face of the girl in the sketch looked down, as Hugh told it again.

Butler strode up and down under the walls of books. Helen, seated on the edge of a leather chair, kept her eyes fixed on Hugh's face until the latter, in sickened reaction, had ended. Butler stopped and turned.

Quite unconsciously Butler's head went back. His hands sought his coat-lapels, as though holding the edges of a black silk gown in court.

'A question or two, if I may detain you. When you left Abu in your office, you are certain he was alive?'

'For the last time, yes!'

'You are sure there could have been nobody hiding in the office at the time?'

'Yes, quite sure. Where could anybody have been hiding?'

Butler opened his mouth to speak. But, with his eye on a corner of the ceiling, he changed his mind.

'At the doorway, fearing your client might in some fashion have vanished or got away, you turned and looked back?'

'I've said so at least twice.'

'He was sitting on the sofa, his back turned. He was too small for his face to be seen in the mirror over the fireplace. You are still sure he was unharmed?'

'Yes, yes, yes! He was turning over the pages of that newspaper, and talking to himself. Besides, there wasn't time for anybody to have got at him. Yes! I'm sure!'

'During the brief time you glanced in at Mr. Vaughan's office, could any murderer have entered your office, stabbed Abu, and got away again?'

'No.'

'Well! While you appear to have been clinging to the side of the door outside, do you consider it likely our hypothetical assassin could have slipped past you?'

'No. It's definitely impossible.'

'Well, well, well.'

In that library, redolent of tobacco smoke and murder, it made Hugh's scalp crawl to see Patrick Butler smile narrow-eyed at a corner of the ceiling.

'It would indeed appear,' the barrister agreed, 'to be one of our more classic locked rooms.' He made a mesmeric pass at Hugh. 'A final question! Why should this famous theory of yours help us with regard to Abu of Ispahan?'

Hugh thrust out his head.

'Because his name wasn't Abu of Ispahan! I've only got twenty-four hours' grace. If we know who he really was, and why he came to my office, won't it help to find his murderer?'

Chapter 7

HELEN sprang up from the arm of the sofa. Butler's gesture made her sit down again.

'You may proceed,' he said.

'Just before he walked in, as I've explained,' Hugh went on, 'Helen and I were having an argument about detective stories. She invented, or thought she invented, a character called Omar of Ispahan. When "Abu" entered, both Helen and I realized she couldn't have invented a name so close to the original; she must have seen or read it somewhere, probably recently.'

'But I still don't know where!' Helen protested.

'Never mind; I do. Little Abu (we'll still call him that for clearness' sake) was frightened out of his wits. Practically his first words were about his so-called brother. "My brother, who is a magician, has been swindled." I didn't know then the word meant swindled, or a lot of things would have been clear.'

'Yes?' prompted Butler, who had taken out a cigarette-case.

'Let me quote several things!' insisted Hugh. ' "Unless you help me there will be a murder." "Who is going to be murdered?" Hesitation; then, "My—my brother." He stumbled all over his own tongue, even speaking French, when he talked about this brother.'

'Then, in other words . . . ?'

'Nobody could have been so frightened as he was about his brother or anybody else. Either he hasn't even got a brother, or else no brother figures in the matter. That little bloke was talking about himself.'

Butler spoke drily.

'The point,' he said, juggling his cigarette-case, 'had already occurred to me. Is that all you have to tell us?'

'No! Not by a jugful! When Abu said his brother was "a

magician", he didn't mean a story-book magician who appears when you rub a lamp. He meant a stage-magician, perhaps with an elaborate stage-show of the sort you don't often see nowadays except at Christmas. I guessed then that "Abu" himself was the magician.'

Butler, taking out a cigarette and lighting it, closed the elaborate silver case with a snap. A flat gust of smoke, with an up-and-down jerk to it, was released from one corner of his mouth. His face became arrogant again.

'You have evidence for that?' he demanded.

'Yes. I don't insist on the bloke's theatrical overcoat with the astrakhan collar. Or on his music-hall suit with the white tie. Or even on his mannerisms and modes of speech. But,' said Hugh, tapping a forefinger into the palm of his left hand, 'I do insist he was a genius at pantomime.'

'Pantomime?' echoed Helen.

'At gestures without words.' Hugh looked at Butler. 'By George! When those snaky hands of his began to describe how much money had been swindled out of him, I could *see* the cash piling up, in silver and banknotes and bonds, until it reached the ceiling of the office.

'Now that's a quality,' Hugh added swiftly, 'which must be possessed by a stage-magician who doesn't speak much English. Don't you recall the old-time Chinese, or supposed-to-be Chinese, magicians who never spoke? Their whole effectiveness was in gestures and the use of music. They conjured up almost more than the imagination could bear. Then the cymbals crashed; the lights dazzled on; the lady had vanished.'

It was at this point that Pam, like a figure in one of the illusions, floated to her feet in rapture.

'How lov-leh!' she breathed. 'Oh, how lov-leh!'

'Woman,' said Butler, 'sit down.'

'Finally,' Hugh swept on, 'have you got a newspaper? Any newspaper, morning or evening, for the past week or so?'

Patrick Butler strode over to a wooden stand, stuffed with books and old magazines, beside one of the leather chairs.

67

From this he fished out a two-day-old copy of the *News Chronicle.*

Hugh, catching it as it was flung over, leafed through the newspaper sheets, found what he wanted, and folded them back.

'Here,' he continued, pointing to an item as he handed the paper to Helen. 'It's a list of the attractions at the various West End theatres. Read that item.'

Helen took one look at it, and jumped to her feet.

'Of course!' she exclaimed. 'How could I have been so stupid! I saw—'

'Read it! Aloud!' Hugh insisted.

'OXFORD,' began Helen, with her own style of drama. 'Tem. 0006. Evgs. 7.30 . . .'

'Never mind the damn' telephone-number! Read what's playing at the Oxford Theatre.'

'OMAR OF ISPAHAN. Miracles and magic for all. Mats. Wed. Sat. . . .'

Again Lady Pamela de Saxe evinced a kind of pre-Raphaelite rapture.

'Patrick!' she breathed, seizing Butler's arm. 'Daddy took me to see a magician. It was lov-leh. Couldn't you take muh to see this one? Couldn't you?'

'No. He's dead.'

'Who is?'

'My pet,' said Butler, lowering his head as though to cool it, 'there is no time to explain this matter's complexities to your already overburdened brain. Kindly keep out of my hair for just one moment, won't you?'

And Butler, with smoke jetting past the cigarette in one corner of his mouth, drew himself up with a loftiness verging on the sulky. Hugh was to learn that Butler always looked lofty when Hugh was right, and always looked bland or benevolent when Hugh was wrong.

On this occasion, Butler went over and yanked at an eighteenth-century tapestry bell-pull beside the fireplace.

'Granting,' he said, 'granting for argument's sake that your client may have been the Omar of Ispahan at the Oxford

Theatre—which we can prove or disprove at once—does it tell us why he came to your office?'

'Yes! And much more.'

Butler made a courteous gesture for him to continue.

'For a starter,' said Hugh, 'I know that type of man. He loves wildcat speculations, especially in non-existent gold or oil; he's the confidence man's joy. Somebody swindled him, probably for quite a lot. Then what did he do? He went straight to a solicitor to discover what legal action could be taken.'

Hugh hesitated, and swallowed hard.

'But that's the trouble,' he went on. 'That's why I couldn't involve Helen! That's where we run into danger, and perhaps touch the horrible.'

'Danger?' Butler repeated quickly. There was a soft gleam of anticipation in his eye. 'Why?'

'Well, did you ever hear of a confidence trick just like that? The confidence man isn't a killer or a thug. When he's milked his victim, as a rule, he's only too glad to run from the police. This is a new one.'

'Meaning exactly what?'

'Our excitable little magician, greedy for profits, made a deal with somebody who's dangerous, somebody who's powerful, somebody who wouldn't hesitate to shut Abu's mouth for good if he complained. And the Opponent did; four walls and a watched door couldn't stop Abu from being stabbed before he talked. Do you see what we may be fighting?'

'By Jove!' murmured Butler, with a soft whistle of pleasure.

The door of the library opened. Mrs. Pasternack, in response to the bell-pull, made patient appearance.

'Mrs. Pasternack!' said Butler, flipping his cigarette into the fire. 'Please be good enough to 'phone the Oxford Theatre.'

'Very good, sir.'

'Where the devil's that newspaper? Ah! The telephone number is Temple Bar 0006. Their show begins at seven-thirty; it's ten minutes to eight now. All the same, ask whether you can book four front stalls for the performance tonight.'

'How lov-leh!' said Pam, 'Oh, how lov-leh!'

'We are not going to the show, my patient Grizelda,' snapped Butler, giving Pam a curious glance Hugh could not interpret. 'Mrs. Pasternack! If they say the performance has been cancelled, ring off. If they say anything else, ask whether Omar of Ispahan is appearing, or whether someone else is taking his place. You understand?'

'Yes, sir,' replied Mrs. Pasternack, who didn't.

'Now!' said Butler, whirling towards Hugh as the door closed behind his housekeeper. 'Do these deductions of yours have anything to do with your original plan for tracking down the murderer?'

'Yes! A hell of a lot!'

'How?'

'Well, Abu didn't speak much English. He couldn't have had many associates. Yet there must be somebody, English or at least English-speaking, close to him and knowing all about him. Then where do we investigate his murder? I'll tell you: back-stage at the Oxford Theatre. And where, by the way, is the Oxford Theatre?'

'Seven Dials,' said Butler. 'Yes, that's it! Seven Dials!'

There was an uneasy pause, while the fire cracked and snapped at them.

'Seven Dials?' exclaimed Helen. 'Do you know,' she added, 'I've been hearing about that place for years. But for the life of me I can't tell you where it is.'

In Hugh's imagination, with almost intolerable vividness, images reared themselves against the soft dusk. He saw the red-glowing electric sign of a hotel, high above seven floors of a concrete façade. He saw soft lights in a theatre-foyer, with the shadows of people passing and repassing inside. He saw a dim blue glow inside the window of an antique-shop . . .

Never mind.

'Seven Dials,' he answered, 'is a very small area between

the top of Shaftesbury Avenue and the top of St. Martin's Lane. Seven small streets come together, like wheel-spokes, into a tiny little square. On one corner is the Oxford Theatre. On another is the Buckingham Hotel. On a third there's an antique-dealer's ... well, I can't remember the lot. But my scheme centred round the Buckingham Hotel, which is a good one and a modern one.'

'Why did it centre round the hotel? My dear fellow, don't chew your mouth and twist about! Why?'

Hugh made an impatient gesture.

'There's a friend and client of mine named George Darwin; lives at Thames Ditton. He and his wife have often put up at the Buckingham, though George says the management and even the clerks don't know their faces; only their names. Well! My idea was to take Helen there, pretending to be Mr and Mrs George Darwin ...'

He did not look at Helen; he flung the words at them.

'Don't you see? The secret of all this, I repeat, can be found back-stage at the Oxford Theatre. Even with the police after me, I could investigate all I liked. A theatre has two entrances, front and back. According to the newspapers, this fog will hold for several days. If a policeman or a detective did see me, I could be away in a second—'

Here Butler smote his hands together; but nobody else observed it.

'—and who'd suspect me of bolting to a hotel only a stone's throw away? Even if anyone did, or made inquiries, they wouldn't think of me as putting up there. In the register they'd find only the names, well known there, of a blameless husband and wife from Thames Ditton. That's all.'

Again in the midst of dead silence, Mrs. Pasternack opened the door.

'Yes, Mrs. Pasternack?' asked Butler.

'I am sorry, sir. There are no seats at all for tonight. Mr. Omar of Ispahan is himself indisposed ...'

Butler and Hugh exchanged glances.

'That's the very word for it, you know.' The barrister nodded. 'He's indisposed, right enough. On a morgue-slab.'

'Don't say that!' cried Helen.

'Anyway,' said Hugh, a little weary and dispirited, 'that was the plan. It doesn't matter now. Go on; tear it to pieces. I suppose it *was* foolish and idiotic.'

He could not get used to these queer, abrupt silences. Moodily looking down at the carpet, wondering why the whole problem seemed to turn on pairs of gloves, he realized that three pairs of eyes were fixed on him. He raised his head.

'Now who,' demanded Patrick Butler, 'who said your plan was foolish or idiotic?'

'Yes! Who even thinks that?' cried Helen.

'Foolish, indeed!' scoffed Pam, giving him a yearning look.

Sheer excitement was sweeping the library like a blowing wind.

'Hugh!' protested Helen. 'You're wanted by the police. Your own sister and your closest friend are so scared they'll give you up in twenty-four hours. Yet all *you* can think of, darling, is avenging the murder of a total stranger and offering to confess if you don't. You're so wonderfully mad I'll go with you anywhere! In fact, I already—'

Here Helen stopped, suddenly putting her hands behind her back again. It was not before Hugh had glimpsed something hitherto unnoticed. On the third finger of Helen's left hand, above the engagement-ring he had given her, was a white-gold wedding-ring he had certainly not given her and had never seen before.

Helen's face went pink.

'All right!' she said, tossing her head mysteriously. 'All right!'

Butler, deep in thought, was striding up and down.

'I, of course,' he announced, 'shall go with you and book a room at the same hotel.'

Mentally, Hugh reeled.

'But why?' he asked. 'Nobody's chasing you, or wants to arrest you. You're as free as fog.'

Butler drew himself up. 'Do you object to my presence, sir?'

'No, no! Of course not!'

'Then consider the matter settled.' Butler relaxed his haughty look and resumed pacing. 'You,' he continued, 'will be Mr. Darwin of Thames Ditton. Obviously I cannot be Mr. Huxley of Hampton Court. The jest is stale. But I must be somebody.'

'Oh, good heavens,' Helen burst out, 'why must you? Why can't you simply be yourself? Or do you love playing an actor's part as much as that? You may be a great barrister, but you're an absolute *child*.'

This time the pause was deadly.

Butler stopped and merely looked at her.

'Evidently, madam, it has not occurred to you that the police may evince some curiosity if they find *me* at a hotel where they are looking for *him*. Your common sense, I fear, is not at its best. However! There may be much in your suggestion. I am Patrick Butler.' He bowed. 'I shall remain Patrick Butler, though it may cause your *fiancé's* arrest.'

'But wait! I didn't understand . . . !'

'The question, madam, has been decided by you.' And Butler waved a negligent hand, dismissing it.

'Hugh! Tell him what I meant!'

('Easy, Helen!')

'Mrs. Pasternack! One moment, if you please.'

'I am still here, sir.'

'Oh. Yes. So you are. Mrs. Pasternack, kindly 'phone the Buckingham Hotel. Its number will be in the book. Reserve a room (no, a suite) for Mr. and Mrs. George Darwin. Also reserve a suite . . .'

'And I, Patrick,' Pam interrupted placidly, 'shall be *youah* wife. Oh, and don't say you won't take muh!'

'Otherwise, I presume, you will 'phone the hotel and tell them the most frateful things about all of us? As you please, then!' said Butler, giving Pam another of those indecipherable glances. 'Mrs. Pasternack, you may reserve a suite for Mr. and Mrs. Patrick Butler.'

'Very good, sir.'

'Stop! I forgot!' Butler spun round. 'You said, if I remem-

c*

ber, that the Omar of Ispahan was indisposed; but there wasn't a seat to be had. Is someone else doing the part?'

'Yes, sir. A French lady, Madame Feyoum. She is Mr. Omar's wife. Excuse me, sir.'

'A Frenchwoman, eh?' muttered Butler, as the door closed. 'You know, Prentice, you may have been right the whole time! Omar's wife! That's our source of information, and she may complete what we can (I hope?) already deduce.'

'Yes,' Hugh urged, 'but go easy!' He wanted to add, 'No histrionics', but substituted, 'Nothing spectacular.' And then: 'This may turn into an ugly business. What's more, if the police are at the theatre . . .'

' "If" the police are there?' inquired Butler drily. '*Sancta simplicitas!* Instead of making all these deductions, didn't it occur to you to go through the dead man's pockets when you had him there?'

'No.' Hugh shuddered. 'There are some things you can't do.'

'Well, the police aren't so squeamish. They'll have been at the theatre for some time. Curse it, we must hurry!'

To Hugh it seemed only a few minutes, though actually it was a much longer time, before they were in Butler's car with the stolid Johnson at the wheel.

The delay was caused by a long argument between Butler and Pam. Pam said she simp-leh must have clothes, and couldn't they drive round by way of Park Lane? Butler calmly said no, and did she think she was spending three weeks at Cannes? But he ordered a suitcase packed for himself; and this sent Pam into a fit of hysteria which the barrister watched with much relish.

Helen offered clothes to Pam: though a little doubtfully, since Pam was over three inches taller and of a somewhat different shape. These Pam refused. But she refused them with overwhelming gratitude and affection, clasping her arms round Helen and causing the latter more than a moment of alarm.

Worst of all, to Hugh, was the cold, sinister gulf between

74

Helen and Butler. When they addressed each other at all, it was with exaggerated politeness. But they seldom spoke, and pointedly ignored each other.

In this worked-up atmosphere, with Pam drying her tears, the limousine glided off through cold and fog towards Seven Dials. Hugh, once more balanced on a pull-down seat, was in despair.

Now why, he was thinking, why must people get into these emotional states over a wrong word or nothing at all? Why couldn't they act as calmly, as rationally, as he did himself?

'And,' he addressed himself silently, 'unless I can think of a solution, I must confess to the crime because it's the only way of saving Monica, saving Jim, even saving Uncle Charles. Besides, if I stabbed the fellow when I was alone with him, there's no locked-door problem.

'But, even if I do confess, will anyone believe me? The police don't want convictions; they want the truth. Where's my motive? Why should I up and stab a total stranger for no reason at all? Admittedly, in law, the Crown aren't obliged to show motive. That's only another legal fiction. Unless they do show motive, no jury will ever convict.

'Clearly Butler sees or guesses something I've completely missed. What in blazes is it? He's already done enough to get him disbarred by his Inn, to say the very least. If he keeps silent too long, we shall all be over the cliff.'

The three faces in front of him were only blurs with shut teeth.

Johnson, taking the shortest route, drove by way of Pall Mall, round the top of Trafalgar Square, and up into Charing Cross Road. They avoided most of the traffic, which went by in hooting distortion. They slipped past several streets away from the crowds and vari-coloured light-illusions in Leicester Square.

And yet, once they had passed Long Acre, the whole air subtly changed. Sounds seemed muffled in a thicker smoky dark.

It was Helen herself who spoke first.

'Seven Dials! Why didn't I remember?'

75

Her words had been meant for Hugh; but they were spoken, involuntarily, to Butler.

'Isn't it a dreadful kind of slum or something?'

Butler smiled a tolerant smile which might have driven any woman mad, and nearly had that effect on Helen.

'Sixty or seventy years ago, madam, your information might have been correct and up to date.'

Helen shivered but said nothing.

'In mid-Victorian times,' pursued her informant, with rich urbanity, 'it was the vilest of slums. Noted chiefly for poverty, fights, gin-shops, harlots, and ballads.'

'Ballads?' repeated Hugh.

'Street-ballads, yes. When there was a truly sensational event, when a tallow-chandler murdered three mistresses at once or a noted housebreaker seated a City merchant on his own fire to discover where he kept his money, it was celebrated in a stream of songs known as penny-yards. They were even less literate, though far more interesting, than the products of Tin Pan Alley today.'

Butler, leaning forward, was peering out of the left-hand window.

'And that,' inquired Hugh, 'was the Victorians' notion of amusement?'

'The hanging was, anyway.'

'But the slums?'

'Oh, they destroyed the slums when they opened Shaftesbury Avenue and Charing Cross Road in the middle eighteen-eighties. Seven Dials may not be the most fashionable district in town. But it's as respectable as Kensington Gardens. In fact, you couldn't find a safer, more—'

Abruptly Butler paused.

He snatched up the speaking-tube communicating with the chauffeur beyond the glass partition. His voice, though not loud, made his listeners jump.

'Johnson! Pull up at the kerb! Here! Where you see the shop window with the little blue light inside!'

The car, which had been crawling through murk, stopped dead.

'What *is* it?' blurted out Pam.

'Nothing, sweet Jezebel. Johnson! There's a cardboard sign propped up just inside the window of the antique-shop; I can't quite read it. If you've still got the big electric torch, switch it on.'

They were in Seven Dials itself. The antique-dealer's, which Hugh had remembered as being on a corner, was ten yards from the end of the tiny street. But he had been right in one sense. The long, dusty window, with *J. Cotterby* in white enamelled letters, was kindled by a gas-mantle burning inside a long-fringed shade of dirty blue silk hung low over a counter.

Dimly they saw Johnson scramble from the driving-seat across to the offside window, opening the glove-compartment as he moved. A brilliant, wide beam of light sprang out across the pavement.

'Higher!' said Butler. 'The sign in the window! Got it!'

He said this, but he said no more at the moment.

The sign, a large piece of grimy white cardboard, bore a message done in block capitals and in thin black paint drawn by a shaky hand. Yet it had a kind of prim, ultra-refined correctness as the light picked it out.

DEAD MEN'S GLOVES
Historical Curiosities for Connoisseurs
Enquire Within

Chapter 8

PATRICK BUTLER was out of that car in about five seconds. Hugh went after him, leaving the door open. Yet Butler, about to attack the premises of J. Cotterby (they'd be closed, wouldn't they?), stopped and looked round him.

Despite their apparent isolation, there was a sense of life everywhere beyond the fog barrier.

Diagonally opposite, above the glass doors to the Oxford Theatre, the letters *O* and then *R* glimmered in a smudged yet fiery green with fragments of the ISPAHAN; narrow green lights, because the theatre appeared triangular in shape to fit between two streets. Slow-moving shapes, smoking cigarettes, moved ghostly in a foyer.

Straight ahead, some thirty or forty yards away, the Buckingham Hotel carried spectres of lighted windows high above them. Its scarlet-glowing sky-sign was all but invisible. But a porter's taxi-whistle shrilled and thrilled.

Someone unseen walked across the little square with hollow, muffled steps. An invisible car, advancing and backing, ground its gear-teeth and seemed to curse. Only the blue-lit premises of J. Cotterby, antique-dealer, were deserted.

DEAD MEN'S GLOVES
Historical Curiosities for Connoisseurs
Enquire Within

'Johnson!' Hugh heard Butler say.

'Sir?'

'Come here. I have an errand for you. And switch off the torch.'

A car door opened and slammed. The stocky Johnson, now all eager and human, hurried up to them.

'You see the theatre over there, Johnson? There's an act-interval now; probably the only act-interval. Go over and mingle with the people in the foyer. Your chauffeur's uniform is a passport anywhere; act as though you were looking for somebody.'

'Who am I looking for, Mr. Butler?'

'No one. Listen to what they're saying about the performance, whether it's going well or badly. It's been taken over at short notice by an understudy named Madame Feyoum. She may be making a mess of it, or she may be scoring a hit. In either case, come back and tell me.'

'Yes, sir.' Johnson's curiosity fought him. 'Excuse me, sir, but might I ask—?'

'No, old son. You may not ask why I want to know. Hop it, now! No, stop! Before you go, you might back up the car about twenty-odd feet so that it's not standing in front of the antique-shop.'

Johnson did so, with Butler following to watch. Butler peered in at the open rear door.

'You will be quite safe here, ladies,' he announced.

It was evident that neither Helen nor Pam liked this at all. But he closed the door with a kind of polite slam, and joined Hugh outside the shop. Hugh, meanwhile, had been staring at the glass-panelled door to the left of J. Cotterby's long window. A small sign, dangling on a string from a blind, bore the word *open*. On the wooden part of the door, below the letter-slot, another name was painted in white letters; but it was so close to the pavement, and in so much shadow, that Hugh couldn't read it.

'And now,' said Butler, 'for the dead men's gloves.'

'Any special reason for going into the place?'

Butler halted with his hand on the knob of the door. He was biting at his lip, all indecision.

'Quite frankly, I'm hanged if I know. But, when in doubt, follow a coincidence or dive into a blind alley. It's all you can do.'

'You're bothered by the gloves too?'

'Bothered by them?' the barrister exclaimed. 'There are too many pairs of gloves; they seem to have no meaning at all. But they must have a meaning or we retire to Bedlam.

79

In fact, they're almost the only feature in this affair I can't understand.'

'Including the sealed room?'

'Oh, the sealed room!' Butler said impatiently. 'The explanation of that is simple.'

And he opened the door and shouldered in.

Just inside, they faced a wooden door, closed: it gave on to what was clearly an enclosed staircase leading upwards. Hugh imagined, wrongly, it must lead to the antique-dealer's living-quarters.

Otherwise the shop had the stale, sour smell usual in such places. It was bitterly cold. There was only one unusual feature: a short counter, built to the right of the enclosed staircase. The lamp with the dirty blue shade, swung on a long cord from the ceiling, hung with its fringe almost against the counter.

Its dim, squalid light showed that the 'antiques', in wild profusion, were mostly rubbish. Hugh saw much china, much glass, bad paintings time-darkened and in elaborate once-gilded frames, an eighteenth-century clock without hands.

'Hallo!' called Butler, and rapped his gloved knuckles on the counter.

The gas-mantle hissed inside its blue-silk shade. Hugh, looking round, received a slight shock.

Behind the counter, its back against the enclosed staircase on the left, stood the wax dummy of a woman dressed in a fancy brown-taffeta gown of Edwardian cut. Then Hugh realized why the dummy seemed so odd even at first glance. The dummy's head, with real hair and glass eyes, was a modern head; it had bobbed hair and a nineteen-twenties' smile above the Edwardian gown. But head and gown alike were dusty.

'Hallo!' Butler repeated.

Somewhere towards their right, a tower of Japanese bells jingled in haste. A picture-frame flopped over. Somebody of heavy body bustled out, and behind the counter.

'Ah!' said a heavy, husky voice, clearing its throat.

The man must once have been very powerful, and was now only fat. His spaniel eyes had a hangdog look under sparse white hair. Sagging jowl-flesh nearly covered his hard white collar and made-up tie. He exuded a sweat of gin. Putting big hands flat on the counter, he tried to look affable.

'Good evening, Mr. Cotterby,' said Butler with much heartiness. 'It *is* Mr. Cotterby, I assume?'

Butler, when he chose, could charm a totem-pole into smiling. Mr. Cotterby visibly brightened.

'That's me, sir. Your very good 'ealth, sir!' he added, as though Butler had just stood him a drink.

And yet, even as he said it, it sounded all wrong. The fat old man was either very frightened or very angry: perhaps both. It exuded from him like the aroma of gin. It added uneasiness to this queer shop, where a macabre wax dummy smirked at nothing.

For some reason, Mr. Cotterby cast a quick glance at the ceiling.

'Now I dessay you're wondering, sir,' he said, firing off the question rather too quickly, 'why I've got my shop open at this time?'

'Well—no. It didn't occur to me.'

'Ah! But it's the theatre-crowd, sir. They like a nice antique to decorate the 'ome. I dessay you're from the theatre, sir? You and the other gentleman?' Mr. Cotterby's hangdog look included Hugh. 'Or maybe from the meeting of the S.A.S. at the 'otel?'

'From the theatre. As a matter of fact, I wished . . .'

'A nice clock, sir!' The big man seemed to jump at him, throaty-voiced. 'I can show you a genuine antique Looey Cans clock, just the thing!'

'No, thank you.' Deliberately Butler raised his voice. 'I was intrigued by your sign about dead men's gloves. Your historical curiosities for the connoisseur.'

Again Mr. Cotterby glanced at the ceiling. Again terror or wrath sweated from him. But he fought both, and wouldn't give in.

'Them, sir? Just as you like.'

Reaching over to another cord of the lamp, he first turned up the gas and then raised the lamp to a point high above his head. The light, from blue, changed to a bright, watery yellow-white, accentuating the dust.

Hugh stifled a whistle. On a short wooden wall, well behind Mr. Cotterby, hung a big wooden-framed square of shabby velvet in which were embedded, in a circle with points inwards, twelve longish knives.

As Mr. Cotterby bent down to get something from under the counter, Butler glanced at the knives. Then he looked at the counter.

'Now, sir,' continued Mr. Cotterby, raising himself up with a heavy breath and holding two sets of objects each wrapped in tissue-paper. He spoke very loudly.'I wonder what you'd think of *these* gloves? Eh?'

Wheezing, he put both wrapped-up pairs on the counter. Hugh hardly looked at them.

The knives were of no great value. But, instead of being Apostle-spoons, these were Apostle-knives. Each handle, of some metal painted to resemble silver, was carved into the likeness of one of the twelve Apostles.

They were polished. They had inexplicable fascination. They gleamed wickedly in their circle against squalor.

'Frankly,' Butler was saying in a disappointed tone, 'I don't know much about gloves. These two pairs, for instance. Can you tell me anything of their history?'

'Ah! You might be surprised, sir!'

'Never mind, for the moment. Have you any others?'

Suddenly inspiration seemed to seize Mr. Cotterby and ooze from him.

'You bet I 'ave, sir! In me back parlour. Stop a bit! Go and fetch 'em. Excuse me.'

Blundering, lumbering, Mr. Cotterby hastened behind the counter towards the right. Hugh could not forget his piteous eyes. The Japanese bells jangled wildly as he went past. Butler, head bent over the counter, hissed at Hugh and beckoned him close.

Somebody was walking about, pacing up and down, in the room above.

Butler's whisper was so soft that it barely reached Hugh.

'Prentice. Can you hear me?'

Hugh nodded.

'If there should by any chance be a rough-house . . .'

The same quick whisper went back. 'Rough-house?'

'Yes. Can you take care of yourself?'

Butler's whisper stopped. In a second it commenced again, more soft but charged with bitterness.

'Somebody asked me that question. Years ago. I was a fool. Said I wouldn't lower myself to use my hands against scum. Learned to use 'em since. Can you?'

'Yes. Commando stuff. It's fast and it's quiet.'

'Good! Better still!'

'What's up?'

'Bad trouble. Coming soon—when Cotterby returns, talk to him. Say something; say anything. I want a good look at these gloves.'

The whispers darted. The circle of knives gleamed. Upstairs, someone was still pacing up and down.

'You see, these gloves . . .'

Bl-lang! clashed the Japanese bells, rather with the effect of gongs. Mr. Cotterby kicked over a statuette of the goddess Diana, which rolled out into the shop. But the proprietor gasped his way back, carrying a shoe-box.

'Now, gentlemen! As I was saying.'

He put down the shoe-box. Beside it he placed a torn-off scrap of paper on which he had scribbled two words. Noiselessly his forefinger tapped the paper.

The two words were *get out*.

More than Mr. Cotterby's hideously raised eyebrows in his big dejected face, that tapping finger cried danger. Hugh unbuttoned his overcoat, reaching into his inside waistcoat-pocket for a pencil. On the same scrap of paper he wrote *Why?* and turned it round.

Butler had pushed the two pairs of gloves to one side. Hugh glanced at them. Except that both pairs were wafer-

83

fragile with age and in perfect condition, he could see little of importance. The first were a man's gauntlet-gloves, once grey or white: delicate, for small hands, with embroidery down the fingers. The second, though larger, had clearly belonged to a woman; they were of elbow-length kid, faded nearly to grey from their original colour of black and crimson.

'I'll tell you what, Mr. Cotterby,' Hugh said in a loud voice. 'There's something here that interests me a good deal. Those Apostle-knives.'

Mr. Cotterby's entire expression changed. Even his throaty voice was different.

'No!' he said, backing up and raising a thick arm as though to shield the knives. 'Oh, no, you don't! Not them!'

'Sorry! I only . . .'

Again the dealer's expression altered in a flash.

'And I'm sure *I'm* sorry, sir,' he replied with much dignity, 'if I spoke up sharp. But they're not for sale. Not the throwing-knives.'

'Throwing-knives? Who threw them?'

'*I* did,' said Mr. Cotterby. 'On the 'alls. Before Nellie left me. Me and Nellie, now . . .'

The whole past, for a second or two, was mirrored in his eyes. Then, suddenly, another inspiration seized him.

'Don't believe me, do yer?' he demanded, with an affectation of fury. 'Watch!'

Before Hugh could protest, Mr. Cotterby's unwieldy hands darted up. What happened was like a conjuring trick. In his left hand appeared a fan of three knives, handles upwards and spaced exactly apart. In his right hand, gripped thumb and forefinger by the point, materialized another knife.

'Just watch the Figger,' he suggested.

He nodded towards the wax dummy, which stood with her back to the thin wooden wall enclosing the staircase. Mr. Cotterby, facing her, backed away ten and then fifteen feet beyond the counter. The dummy continued to smile between dusty wings of bobbed hair.

'I call her the Figger, sir, 'cos Nellie wouldn't let me give

84

her a proper name when I practised at 'er. Said she'd be jealous, Nellie did. Nellie was like that. But she left me all the same.'

His right arm whipped back and up. Hugh took a step forward.

'Here! Go easy!'

'No call to be alarmed, sir,' said Mr. Cotterby, with an even more dignified smile. 'When I've 'ad me first nip o' gin of an evening, this 'and is as steady as it ever was.' He frowned. 'Not that it's the 'and so much, like what people think. It's a kind of knack. See?'

Thud!

Hugh saw no flash. But the knife, with the figure of the Apostle Paul quivering and gleaming, stood out above the middle of the dummy's head without shearing a hair. The thin wooden partition rattled and shook to its impact.

Mr. Cotterby spoke under cover of the noises.

('Father Bill wants yer,' he said.)

Thud!

('Clear out before 'is boys—')

Thud!

(—'get you. They're late.')

In the air-rush as Mr. Cotterby's arm swung over, the lamp above him was swaying back and forth. Its gaslight, blue and yellow-white, threw wild shadows. Two more knives stood out, one against either side of the dummy's cheeks.

And someone was coming down the enclosed stairs. They could all hear the footsteps.

To Hugh that incongruous name, Father Bill, meant nothing whatever. But Patrick Butler, as soon as he heard it, put down the gloves and turned round.

Mr. Cotterby, sweating, whipped back his fourth knife to throw. At the same moment, the door to the enclosed staircase opened wide against the far wall. A youngish, thinnish man stood against it, looking at them.

Either the gin did not aid Mr. Cotterby's hand, or he was frightened or upset, or his fingers slipped. The knife flashed

85

and flew wild. Its point thudded into the door not three inches from the neck of the man who stood against it.

Silence, except for Mr. Cotterby's hard breathing. The blue-white light swung and steadied. The newcomer spoke in a voice neither harsh nor soft, neither quite pleasant nor definably unpleasant.

'That's a foolish thing to do, isn't it?' he asked. 'Throwing knives when you're past the age or sobriety for it?'

'Ah! Maybe it is,' retorted Mr. Cotterby, between cringing and open defiance, 'or maybe it ain't. You're a educated man, Mr. Lake. You'd know, eh?' He looked at Hugh and Butler. 'Mr. Lake's got 'is office upstairs.'

Without comment the man called Mr. Lake wrenched the knife out of the door and took a few steps forward.

His dark hair was cut very close, as though he could not be troubled with the nonsense of having it cut too often. His thin face, not ill-looking, held eyes eager yet composed. His brown suit was not good, nor yet was it altogether bad; it simply hung on him, as though he could not be troubled with this nonsense either.

The whole look and air of him might be summed up in the word utilitarian. *He* was utilitarian: squeezed-up, cut out, his ambition for use and service alone. There was a folded newspaper thrust into his coat pocket.

'Yes,' he said, balancing the bright Apostle-knife in his hand, 'my name is Lake, Gerald Lake. You may have seen my name painted on the door outside. I am a solicitor.'

'A solicitor?' Hugh repeated sharply.

Gerald Lake regarded them with a full stare, yet without favour or disfavour.

'Men like you,' he observed, 'are surprised that a solicitor should have his premises outside certain well-understood areas.'

'Indeed?' said Patrick Butler.

Butler stood very straight, his courtroom manner wrapped round him like the cloak of a Regency duellist.

'There are poor people,' said Lake, 'in need of legal advice. They get it, at a very small charge, from one almost

86

as poor as themselves. The ignorant, the foreign, must be told what to do with their money. Some are without hope. Why, I could show you statistics . . . !'

Momentarily Lake's dark-brown eyes shone with intensity. Holding the bright knife under one arm, he dragged the folded newspaper from his pocket and spread it out.

It was a copy of the *Daily Worker*. Butler went even more rigid. Seeing his face, Lake put down both knife and newspaper on the counter.

'Never mind,' he said, with a weary sigh. 'You don't know poor people exist at all.'

'No, my friend? I have defended more of them than you have ever advised, and with no charge at all.'

Up went Lake's eyebrows.

'You think that's to your credit? Don't talk nonsense. You could afford to do it.'

'And how could I afford to do it?'

'You received an education. Did you pay for that education?'

'You received several pairs of gloves,' said Butler, tapping the counter. 'Did you pay for those gloves?'

Lake, ignoring the question, turned and spoke over his shoulder.

'Come up to my office, both of you. It's my duty to tell you something that will help both you and Mr. — your friend there.'

'One moment!' snapped Butler.

Lake only partly turned. He was looking out of the window. So was Mr. Cotterby, who sweated and made secret gestures of warning.

'I was fascinated,' Butler continued in an agreeable tone, 'by the placard advertising historical curiosities. You wrote it, of course?'

'No.'

Butler laughed.

'Come, how your kind love to quibble. Let us say you composed it, and our friend Mr. Cotterby copied it. With all respect to him, I doubt he could manage "connoisseur" or

87

even "curiosities".' Then the Irishman's tone changed. 'But did you need such elaborate bait, by God's beard, just to lure me into this shop and up to your office? A telephone call, with any insulting challenge, would have brought me soon enough.'

'A 'phone call or a message,' sneered Lake, 'might not have reached the great Mr. Patrick Butler. And yet what, after all, have you achieved?'

'When a young man asks for my achievements,' smiled Butler, 'he had first better state his own.'

Now Lake did turn round, his eyes aglow.

'I've done a little good, I think. Yes! More than a little good, in a world that needs it. And I've done no harm.'

'No harm?' shouted Butler. 'No harm?' He nodded towards Mr. Cotterby. 'You have frightened an old man nearly out of his wits, you and your damned Father Bill. You shall pay for *that*, my hypocritical friend, if we ever meet again.'

'Take care, Mr. Butler!'

'Now of what?' asked the Irishman, looking him up and down.

Whereupon, in leisurely fashion, Butler buttoned his overcoat, fitted on his own leather fur-lined gloves, and glanced at Hugh.

'Ready to leave, me lad?'

'Quite ready,' said Hugh, though his curiosity had simmered and sizzled to boiling-point. 'But what's all this talk about historical gloves? What are those things on the counter, anyway? Whose are they?'

'Those? Oh! Each pair, worth a small fortune at the very least, aren't Cotterby's to sell or Lake's to use as bait. They were probably supplied by Father Bill, as big a crook as exists today; and *he* stole one pair from the London Museum. They set a trap for us, with the curious notion it would work.—Come along.'

'I warn you, for your own good,' said Gerald Lake, 'not to go out of that door.'

Butler, with Hugh at his elbow, shouldered past him. Butler opened the front door. Haze and icy air coiled into

Hugh's lungs as he went out. He stood on the pavement, facing outwards, eyes moving right and left. Butler, closing the shop door with a loud bang, moved out and stood at Hugh's left a little distance away.

'Get ready,' he muttered out of the side of his mouth. 'Father Bill's mob won't be long.'

They weren't.

The visibility-distance was still about a dozen feet at best. Slowly, very slowly, the forms of three men took shape out of haze. Their shoes made no sound on the asphalt. Their eyes were fixed on Hugh Prentice and Patrick Butler. They stopped about ten feet away, and a little snicker of amusement ran among them.

Chapter 9

PATRICK BUTLER unbuttoned and tore off his overcoat, throwing it to the left on the pavement and making himself twice as active. Hugh did the same, slinging his own coat to the right.

Another snicker rippled among the three men in front of them.

Behind Hugh and Butler was Mr. Cotterby's big shop-window, stretching within eighteen inches of the pavement. Its watery gaslight showed them their enemies not clearly, but with less than illusion.

The man on the extreme left, with a bowler hat pulled down above a flattened nose, was as tall as Butler and much burlier. The man on the extreme right, though a good deal shorter, had immense shoulders and a steady stare; his head was uncovered, and mist-drops glistened on his flat yellow hair.

But Hugh's attention was caught, as though by the scent of evil, on the weedy youth in the middle.

This weedy youth, whom Hugh mentally christened Snake-face, wore no overcoat as his friends did. His face, upper lip lifted, was shaded by a hat with a very wide brim. His coat was long and narrow; it showed no waistcoat: only a tie with an exaggerated knot, yet thin and narrow. But his look was more repellent still.

'Now!' he said.

Then, to the shock of his friends as well as his adversaries, he slid his hand inside his coat. It came out holding a squat revolver with a short barrel.

The burly man with the bowler hat twitched his head sideways. So did the shorter man with the yellow hair. Their voices hissed in the fog.

'Ar, yer so-and-so! No noise!'

'No noise! Want the scotches on us?'

'In this smoke?' jeered Snake-face. 'Get 'wayeasee!'

The ring of the revolver muzzle swung not towards Hugh, but towards Butler.

'Two in the belly,' Snake-face said, 'for luck. Take it, chum.'

His finger began to squeeze the trigger.

Something whistled past Hugh's ear and flashed at the corner of his eye.

The point of the Apostle-knife, hard-flung from ten feet back, struck Snake-face just under the right collar-bone and pierced through to stand out above his back. Its impact spun him round, staggering, to face them again.

He lurched, but did not fall. He stood swaying, mouth open and a stupidly surprised look on his face. Hugh, who shouldn't have risked it, nevertheless cast a quick glance behind and to his right.

'*That's* me answer to Bill,' said Mr. Cotterby, with throaty fury. 'You see 'e gets it, eh?'

Mr. Cotterby, driven past endurance and all but insane, shook big and flabby in his own doorway. His hands were now empty. There was no sign of Gerald Lake in the blue-lit shop.

'See?' yelled Mr. Cotterby.

Snake-face, with the figure of the Apostle Luke below his collar-bone, didn't see. Like most men struck by steel or a bullet, he didn't yet understand what had happened. The shock killed even pain. But the revolver dropped from his hand and clattered on the road.

That sound stung to life both Bowler-hat and Yellow-head. They looked at Mr. Cotterby, who had no more knives in his hand. Their victims seemed wide open.

From the corner of his eye Hugh saw Bowler-hat charge at Butler, swinging a left-lead. It was all he had time to see.

Yellow-head, big shoulders lowered, had drawn a razor. It was a razor with a fixed handle; the blade could not move or slip. He held it before him in his right hand, moving a little. Not forgetting he must jump up on the pavement, Yellow-head ran, leaped, and lunged straight at Hugh.

Afterwards, even in deep thought, Yellow-head never knew what happened. He lunged at an adversary who wasn't there.

A left hand cracked down on his right wrist, and jerked. His legs were kicked from under him. As he sailed forwards, largely through the weight of his own charge, the edge of Hugh's right hand chopped like a hatchet two inches below Yellow-head's right ear.

He was unconscious, still flying, when his head struck the big plate-glass window. The glass smashed from top to bottom, in a bursting and falling crash. Yellow-head pitched through and lay face down, motionless, with his feet out over the wooden coping.

To Hugh, cold with horror because he had thrown Yellow-head too far, the world seemed raining, showering, deluging with jangling glass whose noise must cry alarm to every policeman within half a mile.

He whirled round, with a glimpse of Yellow-head's razor fallen on the pavement.

It must be a dream, he thought, that he saw both Helen and Pam, not eight feet away and to the right. But he heard the thud and slither of the fight between Butler and Bowler-hat, stamping very close.

At this moment Snake-face woke up and uttered a scream. With his fingers touching the Apostle-figure he stumbled and ran blindly away into the mist.

A gloved fist smote flesh. Hugh saw the back of Bowler-hat's overcoat, now split up the middle. He saw Butler hit him with a left, then a right. Hugh dodged away and to one side. Bowler-hat, very much full of fight, was nevertheless rocked by that last blow. He reeled two steps towards the empty window. Butler, lips drawn back from his teeth, crowded in and hit him again.

'*Look ou . . .*!' The warning died in Hugh's throat; it was given to the wrong man.

The calves of Bowler-hat's legs bumped that low wooden coping. His arms flew wide as he lost his balance and pitched backwards.

Hugh saw his face, astonished and blood-smudged from a cut over the right eye, before Bowler-hat landed inside. His back crunched on breaking china. One side of his head whacked a marble statuette of the goddess Diana, which had rolled too close to the window. He lost all interest.

And two of Father Bill's boys, one on his face and one on his back, lay witless inside the empty window, with both their heads on a grimy placard advertising dead men's gloves. And, in the background, the unwieldy figure of Mr. Cotterby capered and wheezed for joy.

For a brief space of time, a blessed, soothing, unbelievable quiet comforted Hugh Prentice's heart and nerves.

But Patrick Butler, though panting hard, would not let anyone remain soothed for very long. He snatched off his hat and held it up high.

'*In pace requiescant!*' he said, choking for breath.

'*In pace* my eye!' said Hugh. 'Let's clear out of here!'

'Right!'

Butler jammed on his hat again. He raced into the road, picked up Snake-face's short-barrelled revolver, and raced back. Stepping inside the window, he placed the revolver in Bowler-hat's hand, fitting his fingers round it. Then he caught up the razor and put it in the hand of Yellow-head, whose finger-prints were already there.

'Come on!' snapped Hugh, who was dragging on his overcoat. 'That noise . . . the police . . . !'

'No hurry, me bhoy. Sure and 'tis aisy!' carolled the exalted Butler. 'First make certain . . .'

He stopped. Distant footsteps, pounding heavily through the fog at a run, as much choked Hugh with alarm as Butler was choked for lack of breath.

But it was only Johnson, returning from the theatre-foyer. Johnson took one look at the damage; his face all but crumbled to ruin.

'I missed it!' he said tragically. Johnson then lost his head and jumped up and down. 'Oh-me-behind! Another of the governor's fights, and I missed it again!'

'Johnson!' said Butler, instantly all dignity.

'Sir?'

'Nip down to that car and start the engine. We must make a very stately entrance at the hotel.'

Pulling on his overcoat, Butler found his left-hand glove stained with Bowler-hat's blood, and stuck both into his pocket. Next, beckoning Mr. Cotterby to the door, he pulled out a wad of five-pound notes and pressed them into the dealer's hand.

'You 'elped me!' protested Mr. Cotterby, hurt and recoiling. 'I don't want no money. You *'elped* me!'

'No; please keep the money. But listen to me carefully. Listen! Do you understand what I say?'

'Yessir!'

'When the police get here—'

'Which will be any second now,' said Hugh. 'For God's sake, no lecture!'

'—when the police get here, say nothing whatever about the knife you threw at the man in the appalling clothes. It's the slightest of wounds; but it'll hurt him very beautifully. Even if the police pick him up, which isn't likely, you have two witnesses to say you threw only because he'd drawn a revolver to kill.'

'They'd 'a' killed me too, them and 'is 'ighness Gerald Lake, if it hadn't been for you and t'other gentleman.'

'Do you understand what I'm saying?'

'Yessir. Got it!'

'If you must say Mr. Pren—Mr. Darwin and I were here, be careful to give wrong names and wrong descriptions. Got that too?'

'Can't remember yer names, sir. Or what yer looked like.'

'Finally, hide those gloves and don't show them to anybody. Don't worry about Father Bill; I'll settle *his* hash. That's all.'

Grotesquely, tears appeared in Mr. Cotterby's eyes.

'God bless yer, sir. You can trust me.'

Off went Hugh and Butler, running towards the car, only to fetch up against Pam and Helen. The two girls had not moved. Whether or not they were completely bereft of speech, a condition sometimes satisfactory in dealing with the feminine species, they were whirled up and swept into the car.

The engine throbbed softly. Johnson, discarding the formality of holding open the back door, slipped into gear as the door closed.

In the ensuing scramble, mysteriously, Hugh found himself in the back seat with Pam sitting on his lap. Familiar mink-clad arms wound round his neck; a familiar voice whispered at his ear.

'Dahling,' said Pam, completely unruffled by anything she had seen, 'you were simp-leh mahvellous. But whatevah did you do to that ohful man? You simp-leh touched him. And he bowed to you and dived through the window.'

'It wasn't quite as simple as that. And it was all my fault. I was out of practice; I missed him.'

'You *missed* him?'

'I pitched him too far. That broken window might have ruined everything. As it is—'

Scuffling noises, and the sound of a cold angry voice on his right, made him work his eyes above Pam's arm. There Helen sat on Butler's lap, writhing. But Hugh, who knew her, was aware Helen was far less angry than she tried to sound.

'Mr. Butler. Will you *kindly* let me go and take your arms from round me?'

'Faith now, me dear, and isn't it surely the time ye called me Pat?'

'Well . . .'

'Ah, bejasus!' breathed Butler in ecstasy. 'And wasn't it the foine beauty of a fight and all and all?'

'It was disgusting and revolting!'

'And that grand young man of yours, now—!'

'I have often thought,' said Helen, 'that Hugh has in his nature a streak of cruelty, even sadism. Yes! Once, when a cousin of mine tried to say (quite harmlessly!) that the Commandos were not so very much after all (which they aren't!) that sadistic brute landed my Cousin Andrew face-down in a manure-bed. I don't believe he's normal, some-times.'

Though Hugh knew Helen talked like this only because she was upset and unstrung, he tried to work his head free and make a protest.

'Well, well!' clucked Butler. 'Sadistic or not, he's the lad I'd have at me side in a dust-up. And there may be another, if Father Bill strikes back.'

For some reason Pam abruptly tightened her arms round Hugh's neck. But the latter spoke none the less.

'I *will* know,' he yelled in muffled fashion, 'something about this mysterious master criminal you call Father Bill. And who owned those gloves you said were worth small for-tunes? They're seventeenth or even sixteenth century; that I could swear. Otherwise . . .'

'Whist!' said Butler in a warning voice. 'Here's the hotel!'

Their arrival before the revolving doors of the Bucking-ham Hotel was not perhaps as stately as Butler had com-manded.

Johnson leaped out. A tall street-porter in cap and long grey-and-gold uniform coat, saluting as he opened the door, hastily averted his eyes as he saw the tangle inside.

It did not matter. Butler, after depositing Helen on the floor, emerged like a Roman Emperor leaving his pleasure-barge at Capri.

'Good evening,' he said.

'Good evening, sir!' said the porter, instantly at salute again.

'We—ah—have reservations, I believe.'

'Ah! That's just as well, sir,' heartily said the porter, help-ing Johnson to get three suitcases from the back, and beck-oning another porter. 'Tonight's the annual general meeting of the S.A.S. They occupy three whole floors: to say nothing of the Banqueting Room, of course. (S-t-t! Burton! Get these bags inside!)'

Whereupon Hugh, following Pam and Helen through the revolving doors to the foyer, received another shock.

It was not merely that the big foyer was packed with guests. Or that the guests were formally attired: the men in white ties and tails, the women in evening-gowns.

So much might have been expected. What daunted him was the whole air and tenor of the surroundings. There must have been, and undoubtedly were, people here under sixty years of age. But most of them appeared at least in the seventies and some considerably older. They moved slowly, their talk a frail whispering with a spectral smile or nod as though to show they were alive.

But worse was to come.

First went the under-porter, with three suitcases, writhing towards the reception-desk. Next marched Butler. Then followed Pam and Helen, with Hugh in the rear.

He saw three clergymen, one of them a bishop in full gaiters. He saw two famous barristers, noted for the dry sting of their wit. Finally, he could have sworn he saw the withered features of Mr. Justice Stoneman, Butler's deadliest enemy among the judges, who was talking to a daughter in her early fifties.

Hugh hunched down into his shoulders and hastily averted his head. One of the clergyman laughed heartily. (Oh, God, this was worse than a police-convention!)

Behind the reception-desk, two well-dressed young men scurried about on apparently no errand whatever. The impressive figure of Patrick Butler was instantly noted by the better-dressed of the clerks, a very thin young man with sleekly brushed hair.

He moved up to the counter.

'Yes, sir?'

The barrister, superbly unconscious of a slightly grimy face, a cut lip, and a dusty overcoat, looked round haughtily.

'My name is Butler,' he remarked.

'Mr. Butler? Of course, sir!' The clerk's smile became vastly cordial without being too subservient. 'Very happy to have you, Mr. Butler. There must be many of your friends here tonight.'

'So I have observed. Yet it surprises me, I confess, that you would admit so ignorant and stupid a swine as Sir Horace Stoneman.'

Butler, who meant every word he said, let his voice ring out in full bass resonance.

The clerk, deciding this was a joke, smiled nervously.

'Er—yes, sir.' He lowered his voice. 'I regret, Mr. Butler, that due to the unusually large number of guests tonight we can offer you and your friend Mr. . . . Mr. . . .'

'Mr. Darwin,' Butler supplied sharply. 'Of course you remember your old client Mr. George Darwin?'

'Of course!' smiled the clerk, who didn't. Yet it was clear that Hugh, who tried to look lofty and even sadistic, had shot up many degrees in the clerk's opinion. 'As I was saying, Mr. Butler, I regret we can offer you only the Royal Suite and the Bridal Suite, both on the top floor. I think you will find both satisfactory. You, sir . . . ?'

'The Royal Suite, I think.'

'Yes, Mr. Butler.' The clerk hesitated. 'May I ask, sir, whether *you* are a member of the S.A.S?'

Butler's tone abruptly changed.

'Now look here,' he said. 'I'm not more curious than anybody else. But what *is* this S.A.S., anyway?'

'Forgive me, Mr. Butler; but you don't know?'

'No!'

'Ah! I was only about to suggest that the dinner begins in ten minutes; you might wish to hurry and change.—Naturally, sir, they must meet in this district. We are always happy to greet them. It is a joy to watch Archdeacon Crowleigh with "The Hangman's Daughter".'

Patrick Butler shut up one eye.

'I have no doubt,' Butler replied, 'that his behaviour would be even more spirited with the curate's aunt. But just what the hell *is* it?'

'Officially, sir, it is known as the Society of Ancient Sins.'

Pam, uttering a gurgle of pleasure, pressed herself against the desk.

'Oh, how love-leh!' she exclaimed. 'Do they know more things than we do?'

Helen, scarlet-faced, silenced her with a terrible glare. Pam, radiating seraphic innocence, looked bewildered. Butler, his elbow on the desk, turned and slowly surveyed the assemblage. A very elderly gentleman made some spectral joke to his wife, who replied with noiseless mirth. The hum of conversation floated up faintly.

'And these,' inquired Butler, 'are the sinners?'

'In a manner of speaking, yes.' The clerk smiled. 'The title, of course, is facetious. It refers to the ancient ballads, composed and printed in Seven Dials, which once were so celebrated. "Shed Tears for the Fallen Woman" is one. Your—er—your friend Sir Horace Stoneman prefers to sing "The Lay of the Roaring Girl".'

'"The . . ." *Old Stony sings that?*'

'Er—Mr. Justice Stoneman, yes.' Again the clerk smiled and turned round a large ledger. 'If you will sign, Mr. Butler?'

With a flourish the barrister wrote, 'Mr. and Mrs. Patrick Butler'. He added an address so powerfully impressive, Castle Something-Something-Something in Ireland, that Hugh wished he would exercise some artistic restraint. It was not until long afterwards Hugh learned that Butler really owned the place, and had been born there.

'Thank you, sir. Now if you and Mrs. Butler would . . . ?'

The clerk's eyes moved hesitantly between Helen and Pam.

Suddenly, with a sense of horror and doom upon him, Hugh Prentice felt mink-clad arms press tightly round his left arm, and a slender body pressed against his left side while lips brushed his ear.

'Oh, no!' cooed Pam, lifting adoring eyes. '*I* am Mrs. Darwin. It will seem strange to occupy the Bridal Suite, aftah so many yeahs. Sign for us, Hugh, won't you?'

Chapter 10

STANDING at one of the windows in the sitting-room of the Bridal Suite on the seventh floor, staring down and unable even to see the Oxford Theatre except for vague green glimmers of its sign, Hugh revolved bitter memories.

Oh, memory!

Somewhere behind him, Pam was speaking to a telephone and ordering a vast meal.

Never in his life, Hugh decided, would he forget the expression on Helen's face when Pam had uttered those words at the reception-desk.

Nor would he forget Butler's bland, 'Come along, my dear,' as he put a hand under Helen's elbow and urged her gently towards one of the lifts. Helen had not spoken; she had only breathed.

What is more, Hugh had overheard the quick, brief conversation between Butler and Johnson, looking like a chauffeur in M.I.5, as Johnson reported matters in the theatre foyer and made this affair (if possible) even more preposterous and puzzling. It was just before the lift soared upwards.

Finally, they had all underestimated Lady Pamela de Saxe. They had thought Pam a beetle-wit, a dandelion-clock. (Or had Butler really thought so, despite his outer pretences? Why those curious glances at her?) Anyway, when four unmarried persons who pretend to be husbands and wives approach a hotel-desk, and one woman firmly claims a definite man as her husband, you can't sing out and say he isn't. You are caught. You are trapped as inexorably as though by one of Butler's own tricks in court.

'—and, for muh husband,' Pam was now murmuring to the 'phone, 'the same as for me. I will repeat it. Half a dozen Whitstable oysters, *filet de sole Jean Bart, un châteaubriand très bien cuit . . .*'

At long last Hugh broke his forbidding silence.

'No!' he raved. 'Rare! Never a steak well done! I can't eat it. Rare! Very rare!'

Pam gave him a meek yet reproachful look from her beautiful grey eyes.

'*Très, très bien cuit*,' she cooed to the telephone, 'with the same vegetables. For a sweet? Oh, yes! For him, too, a *pêche Melba*.'

Hugh stoked his fury by taking another look at the sitting-room. Though the rest of the hotel had been decorated with quiet good taste, some lunatic had been given a free hand with the Bridal Suite. It was overstocked with allegedly voluptuous furniture in strange colours; it had hangings of soft quality; it looked like something out of Hollywood.

And Hugh gritted his teeth.

'*Cheese!*' he said. 'Do you think I can swallow a sickeningly sweet concoction like a *pêche Melba*? Cheese! Stilton, if they've got it. Cheese!'

Pam shuddered delicately.

'You hev taken note,' she murmured to the 'phone, 'of the wines I oahdehed with each course? Ve'y well. Coffee of course, with Armagnac brandy. Oh! You had bettah bring the bottle of Armagnac. *C'est entendu? Bon! C'est tout, merci.*'

With a fragile hand she hung up the 'phone. Then, her blonde head lowered, she looked up at Hugh.

'Dahling!' she said. 'You'll feel much bett-ah, you know, when you're just a bit tight.'

'But I can't get tight! Don't you understand that?' He pointed to one of the windows overlooking Seven Dials. 'As soon as we hear from Johnson that the performance is over, Butler and I have got to slip across to the Oxford Theatre.'

'Hugh.'

'Yes?'

'Don't you like muh?'

'Er—yes! Of course!'

(That was the trouble. She *was* attractive, in her way. Curiously, this attraction increased when you realized that

101

Pam hid quite an acute intelligence under that load of affectations. Hugh's conscience, his stern Calvinistic conscience, was already making him writhe at his own thoughts.)

'I suppose,' murmured Pam, looking away, 'you think I behave like this with oll men.'

'Candidly, yes.'

'Well, I don't!' retorted Pam, flinging up her head with sudden spirit. 'What hev they told you about muh?'

'Nothing at all. I never heard your name until Butler's clerk mentioned it late this afternoon. He said you were a "scion of the aristocracy".'

'Daddy's peerage,' said Pam, 'is *oll* of two yeahs old. He bought it to please Mummy and *ooo* what it cost him. Do you know what I am? I'm as coarse and vulgah and common as Daddy himself. But I'm just as forthright and determined when there's anything or anyone I want.' Unexpectedly she looked haughty. 'As for this woman of youahs . . .'

'Woman!' exclaimed Hugh, stricken. 'Just a moment!'

'Hugh! Where are you going?'

'Not far; back in a second!'

He rushed over to the heavy mahogany door opening on the passage outside. He opened and closed it behind him. The Bridal Suite and the Royal Suite, opposite each other on either side of a broad and heavily carpeted corridor, occupied the front of the top floor in a hush of subdued lighting.

There must be telepathy in these matters. At the same moment Helen opened the opposite door, closed it behind her, and faced him. As against his look of guilt, Helen appeared outwardly calm.

This may have been deceptive. When Horatio is describing to his overwrought friend Hamlet the expression of the latter's Father's Ghost, Hamlet demands to know whether its countenance is red or pale. When Horatio replies, 'Nay, very pale,' both think this solves the question.

And yet, by some inexplicable body-alchemy, the face of a pretty girl in a rage may be both very red and very pale at the same time.

'Yes?' murmured Helen. 'And what are you and your blonde doing now?'

'Nothing! She's just ordered dinner.'

'Oh? Why couldn't we all have had dinner together, in your suite or in ours?'

'I suggested that. But she howled the place down. And we mustn't attract attention.'

Helen lifted her head and looked him in the eyes.

'Hugh. Don't you *dare*.'

'Don't—dare—what?'

'*You* know what I mean!'

'Lord, Helen, can't you think about anything except that?'

'No. And neither can she, for that matter. I wouldn't trust that blonde with St. John the Baptist, let alone you. Whereas Pat . . .'

'It's "Pat", now, is it? Have you fallen for him?'

'I haven't,' Helen answered rather too quickly, 'and you know quite well I haven't. I—I admit I may have misjudged him before this. He's not arrogant, really. He's worried, horribly worried. All he does is pace up and down.'

'I said you were wrong about him, didn't I? And Pam . . .'

All the red had gone from Helen's face. It was sallow white.

'Yes. You and Pam.' Then her voice went shrilling up. 'You arranged this whole change of suites between you, didn't you, so that you could be together? Oh, don't deny it! Take a look at your own face, Mr. Hugh Prentice, before you dare say anything at all!'

Helen was frantically fumbling at the third finger of her left hand: with some difficulty, since she had wedged someone's borrowed wedding-ring above the other.

'Well!' she cried. 'If you want to see something in the first skinny, washed-out, made-up blonde bean-pole who makes oh-such-Victorian eyes at you, Mr. Hugh Prentice, and *if* you're so passionate about her just because she's got money and I haven't, then it's perfectly satisfactory to me! But you'd better take this engagement-ring back until you find a real woman, which I doubt you or anybody like you will do in a hundred years!'

Hugh, a patient man, studied her with his head on one side. But too much is too much.

He seized Helen by the shoulders, and shook her so violently that moisture blurred into her eyes and every tooth rattled in her head.

'Now hear this,' he said, like a battleship's loud-speaker in an American film. 'I appreciate your standing by me when I was in trouble; never think I don't. But there are certain things about *you*, my precious pet, which I can't take and I won't take any longer.'

Still he shook her until her hair flew.

'You are not going to pretend anger when you're not angry at all, so as to make me climb down or beg your pardon. If I like detective stories, you are not going to roar with laughter at my alleged pompousness, as you did in my office this afternoon. If I say something that offends you, then explain so that I can apologize or explain; but don't march out of my office, as you also did this afternoon, without a word one way or another. Now keep the engagement-ring or give it back; I don't give a whistling damn which it is. But don't call yourself a real woman until you can act like one.'

And he flung her with a bump against the wall.

'Oh!' whispered Helen, when she could get her breath. And then again: 'Oh!'

Though Helen could not have known it, since she was not there, her tone sounded like that of Pamela de Saxe when struck on the posterior in the Metropolitan Police Museum. It was not the act in itself; it was the indignity and outrage.

She tore off the wedding-ring, flinging it one way. She tore off the engagement-ring, flinging it another way. She ran at Hugh, to slap his face. Hugh pitched her off. That gentleman, in a boiling mood which appears like utter indifference, calmly picked up both rings, flicked them up in the air with a careless gesture, and let them fall where they would.

At this moment Patrick Butler, dressed in full evening-clothes, opened the door.

'Tut, tut!' he remarked, lifting his eyebrows. 'Such behaviour!'

Helen lifted a trembling forefinger and pointed in the general direction of Hugh.

'That man—' she choked, like one who begins an indictment for high treason.

'Ah, yes. So I heard. You deserved every word of it.' Butler glanced at Hugh. 'Come, you are not dressed?'

'Dressed? Why should I be?'

Butler considered this, his forehead heavy and troubled.

'To be quite honest, I am not sure. But I have always thought it the appropriate and proper gesture, like putting on armour for battle. Come inside, both of you.'

Helen would have refused, out of mere instinct, if she could have thought of anywhere else to go. Always, always Hugh had been patient and quiet-spoken. Almost, she had sometimes thought with faint derision, a little too patient. And now . . .

So Helen, only inwardly screaming, ran into the sitting-room of the Royal Suite. There was a heavy slam as the door of the bedroom closed behind her.

Butler paid no attention. Hugh was at the moment too angry to care.

Besides, Patrick Butler's attitude added to his uneasiness. The lunatic decorator, having filled the sitting-room with gold, white, and a glass chandelier too ornate for Buckingham Palace itself, had left comparatively little space to move.

Nevertheless, Butler seated himself in a gigantic gilt chair like a throne. But for some reason it suited him.

'Johnson,' he said, consulting a thin watch in the pocket of his white waistcoat, 'should report very soon, just before the performance is over. You heard what he told me, before he went up in the lift?'

'Yes?'

'Our Madame Feyoum is scoring a smash-hit. Johnson describes her as "a looker, all Frenchy, with curves".'

'Did he see her?'

'No. But photographs of her are all over the foyer. Omar of Ispahan, it appears, spoke very seldom. Madame Feyoum talks all the time, in an accent which the audience seems to find irresistible. Should an illusion go wrong, she simply laughs uproariously; and the audience applaud harder still. Prentice, I don't like it.'

'Why not?'

'Well! The end of the show will undoubtedly mean the police; we were prepared for that. But word of a success spreads instantly. It will also mean the press: in droves, and with cameras.'

Hugh said nothing.

'I take it,' the barrister peered up, while his fingers tapped and tapped on the arm of the chair, 'you heard the news relating to yourself?'

This, to Hugh, had been the most inexplicable devilment.

'Yes! But I still don't believe it! My Uncle Charles?'

'Nevertheless, Mr. Charles Grandison Prentice was sitting in the foyer, smoking one of his obnoxiously large cigars, and lording it in his customary objectionable way at social functions.'

'Mr. Butler, that's impossible! Uncle Charles is at home with 'flu! Johnson must have been mistaken.'

'Johnson is rarely mistaken. He knows, by sight at least, almost as many people as I do. However, those need give us no trouble. The police or the press?' Butler snapped his fingers with contempt. 'Your uncle?' He snapped his fingers with a personal dislike and contempt. 'Our real difficulty is different. You see . . .'

Hugh glanced surreptitiously towards the door leading to the bedroom.

Beyond that door, he imagined, Helen would be sitting in quiet haughtiness. As a matter of fact, she was lying face down on one of the beds, crying her eyes out and hammering at the coverlet with her fists in hopeless misery. Hugh did not even guess this, or he would have gone haring through that door in an instant.

Besides, something in Butler's expression held him dumb.

'Yes?' he prompted.

'You see,' said Butler, 'I may have been wrong.'

Dead silence, except for a heavy murmur of voices on the floor below.

Butler tried to say this very lightly. He looked up, with an attempt at a careless smile, in his armour of evening clothes and with the long line of 'miniatures', representing decorations, across the left breast of his coat.

He had always seemed at least ten years younger than his actual age. Hugh never before observed the crooked blue veins at his temples.

'W-wrong?' Hugh echoed.

'I imagined your locked-room problem was comparatively simple.' Butler's fingers became a heavy fist. 'Now tell me. Not long ago, in Cotterby's antique-shop, you saw that old man throw three knives at a dummy figure. Yes?'

'Yes. Well?'

'Did you actually *see* the knife in the air when he threw it?'

'No. He was too fast. His arm came over; the knife jumped up in the wall.'

'Now picture again the scene of Omar of Ispahan's murder, as you described it to me. You are clinging to the left-hand side of your office door. Your friend Jim Vaughan is to your own left, in front of his own office-door. If someone had thrown a knife from the broad *and* dark corridor behind you, would either of you have seen it?'

Again the scene took form. Hugh saw Jim, with waistcoat unbuttoned and the beginning of a corporation. He saw the door, which he had pushed still farther open. He saw the sofa, its back to the fire . . .

'That might be,' he admitted. 'But it still won't work.'

'And why not?'

'The man was stabbed from in front, and with a downwards blow. Granting a thrown knife, do you know anybody who can throw one so that it turns round in the air like a boomerang, and kills a victim sitting with his back to the thrower?'

107

'Again—oh, sacred simplicity!'

'Why so?'

Again Butler smote the arm of the chair.

'Once more,' he almost pleaded, 'you don't remember, or at least see no meaning, in a scene played before your eyes in the street. It would answer the objection you've just made. If one of Father Bill's associates should be behind this after all . . .'

He stared at the carpet.

'I—I am sometimes an arrogant fool. We Irish often are. I've once or twice said (I don't know whether you've noticed it, my dear fellow?) that I am never wrong . . .'

'Well,' muttered Hugh, also staring at the carpet, 'here's one unimportant lawyer who thinks you aren't.'

'Thanks.'

'It doesn't matter. I only . . .'

'No, by God!' roared Butler, and sprang to his feet. 'They're not going to laugh at me. They say I can't succeed at a murder mystery unless I've got Gideon Fell to back me. Don't they?'

Jim, to tell the truth, had said so. But Hugh only garbled something unintelligible.

'Well, we shall see! Even if I am wrong, I have nearly twenty-two hours to redeem your pledge and prove I am right. In fact, my dear fellow . . .'

There was a short, quick knock at the door. Without waiting for a response, Johnson slipped into the sitting-room. He looked far from easy.

'Better hurry, sir!' he hissed. 'The show'll be over in six minutes, and you'd best get across there.' Again Johnson hesitated. 'But I don't know how you'll get out, sir; it's a fact I don't. The whole hotel is full of cops.'

Chapter 11

IT took only that to do it.

Patrick Butler was instantly a different man. He stood straight-backed, easy, a smile of enjoyment on his face, with the light shining on his fair hair.

'Admirable, admirable!' He rubbed his hands together. 'The Minions of Evil, eh? We shall deal with them. Metropolitan or City-of-London?'

'Metropolitan, sir. But they're led by a plain-clothes City-of-London Scotchman, Inspector Duff.'

'Ah! And is it after chasing myself they are, now?'

'No, sir. But your name's in the register. I don't think it took 'em long to twig who was with you.'

'But, even if they made inquiries all over the district,' protested Hugh, 'how did they find me so soon?'

Johnson, uneasily shifting his cap from one hand to the other, regarded Hugh in some accusation.

'Well, sir, I think you signed the ledger "Charles Darwin" and not "George Darwin", and you gave your uncle's address at Hampstead. I think you must 'a' been a bit upset, like, by the young lady with the fair hair. Even so, if it hadn't been for Mr. Butler's name written as big as a Guinness sign ...'

'Tut, tut!' beamed Patrick Butler, not at all displeased. He nodded towards the bedroom door. 'I told your good *fiancée* this might happen if I gave my real name. Still, she would have it.'

'Governor, for gossake hurry!'

'Calm yourself, Johnson,' said his employer. Butler swept up a great black cape from a near-by chair, fitted it round his shoulders with a silver clasp at the neck, and put on a rakish soft black hat with a D'Artagnan air. 'Er—Johnson! You already left my card at the stage door, I trust? Not my

109

real card: the card we customarily leave on such occasions? And you had the flowers sent as I instructed?'

'Long ago, sir! Madame What's-her-name's got 'em long ago. But—'

'Excellent. Come along, my dear Prentice.'

'But I haven't got my coat and hat! I . . .'

'Tush!' said Butler, slapping Hugh affectionately on the back. 'What need have you for a hat and overcoat? We are merely going across the street. Hurry!'

All three of them ran out into the heavily carpeted, softly lighted corridor. Butler glanced sharply right and left as they went past a cross-corridor.

'Never trust lifts, my dear fellow,' Butler advised Hugh in a low voice. 'All policemen have a child-like passion for riding up and down in lifts. But I thought I saw a staircase at the rear of the floor. Yes, so I did. Here.'

The staircase, with a long window heavily muffled in curtains at its top, had also a broad and carpeted set of steps which descended beside the wall; then, at a landing, it turned at right-angles to descend to the floor just below.

Butler ran lightly down the first set of steps. Then even he got a shock. He stopped, pressing his charges behind him against the wall.

A harsh, stern voice, evidently in argument with someone just as stern, arose from the floor below just at the foot of the stairs.

'—I've shown ye my warrant-card,' someone said loudly, 'and I'll no' show it tae ye again. My name is Duff, Inspector Duff. And I'm askin' ye . . . eh, ma Goad! What's yon?'

Inspector Duff might well ask.

It is observable that no group of persons can form a club or society, with more joy and for some utterly useless purpose, than a group of highly cultured and well-bred people from the middle-aged to the very elderly. While this admirable habit still exists, there will always be an England.

From time to time Hugh had noted, by the heavy murmur from the floor below, that this must contain the Banqueting Room. There was no doubt of it now. A piano smote three

110

crashing chords. Two fiddles joined in. The music sank to a
sad, plaintive note as a hundred and fifty voices, which afore-
time Hugh had considered soft or frail, rang out together in
deep and all but tearful solemnity.

> Shed tears for the fallen woman! She 'as gorn to 'er
>   lonely grave;
> For she lost 'er 'eart to a sailorman, and the dirty dog
>   was a knave!
> 'E ruined 'er! 'E ruined 'er! Oh, the 'orrible, dreadful
>   gin—
> For she lost 'er flahr in an evil 'ahr, and sank to a
>   life of sin!

Butler, Hugh, and Johnson could not see Inspector Duff or
his companion, because of the right-angled turn of the stairs.
But they could hear the former's voice.

'I'm askin' ye,' he bellowed above the din of the second
verse, 'what's *yon*?'

'That, Inspector,' coldly replied the voice of the head-
waiter, 'is the Society of Ancient Sins.'

'Sins, eh? *I'll* gie 'em sin!'

'Kindly remember, Inspector, that you may not pass
beyond those doors. The chairman, Mr. Justice Stoneman
himself . . .'

'Oh, radiancy of glory!' whispered Butler, with a light in
his eye as of one who sees Heaven's gates opening. 'Do you
think he'll nab Old Stony for singing lewd songs in public?'

'Sir! Sir!' hissed the maddened Johnson. 'How do we get
out of this one? They'll be up here in half a sec!'

'Ah, yes. To be sure.'

Butler swung round, his eyes darting. Instantly he ran
back up the stairs, with the others following. Butler flung
open the heavy curtains shrouding the long window.

'Fire-escape, of course,' he said with some hauteur.
'There's always one on a landing.' Not without noise, which
was drowned by the singing below, he wrenched at the full-
length window and sent it screeching up. 'You see?' he
added, pointing out.

111

Unfortunately, this time, there wasn't any fire-escape.

'H'm,' said Butler.

They were above the heavy fog, which made whitish-black clouds underneath, but otherwise they saw only a faint haze which did not impede sight. At their feet, along the back of the hotel, ran a stone ledge only eighteen inches wide. True, it might be said in one sense that there was a fire-escape; but it was thirty feet away towards their right along that narrow stone ledge.

Up rose the voice of Inspector Duff.

'I'm no' askin' ye that noo! I hae no authority. I'm askin' ye aboout—'

> I sing the lay of the high-way-man,
>   And his flying, galloping ma-are!
> For he was a wreeth on Hounslow Heath
>   And of bar-kers he'd one pa-air!
> His gal was Sal of Buttercup Lane
>   In the parish of Mary-le-boh-ne—

'The Bridal Suite, Inspector, is on the floor above this. It is number 2, at the front . . .'

Hugh Prentice has always since declared that, if Patrick Butler says a thing exists, then in his own mind it does exist.

'A fire-escape, you see?' remarked Butler. 'Follow me, both of you. Close the window, someone, and draw the curtains. Now!'

And, without the slightest hesitation, he stepped out of the window seven floors above the street.

Hugh's first impression, that Butler really thought he saw a fire-escape there and had taken this unusual form of committing suicide, was corrected immediately. The Irishman swung to the right on the eighteen-inch ledge, his face to the wall and his hand on it, while he shuffled along towards the actual fire-escape.

Nevertheless, Hugh's insides had done a kind of flip-flop. He was as mad as a hornet when he swung out on the ledge and himself hastily shuffled along sideways with his hands up. Behind him Johnson, kneeling perilously on the ledge with his face to the window and his legs out over a fog-gulf, was yanking shut the curtains. But Johnson nearly toppled over backwards before he closed that tight-fitting window.

Hugh, who had done this sort of thing in war-time, was steadier than he had imagined he would be. And all were helped because they could not see down to the street; a heavy blackish-whitish carpet lay nearly on a level with the ledge.

But imagination can play ugly tricks when there are no windows, no hand-hold at all in front of you.

And, when they were more than half-way to the fire-escape, Butler stopped dead.

Hugh, imagining there must be some obstruction beyond him, tried to peer past his shoulder. Instinctively he leaned backwards. A nerve jerked in the calf of his leg; his balance took him swaying out, and panic surged up in his vitals before he steadied himself and straightened up, remembering not to claw at a smooth concrete wall.

'What's wrong?' he demanded.

'Eh?'

'I said, what the hell's wrong? Why are you stopping?'

'Oh, I was wondering. I mean, what happened to the roaring highwayman and his girl from Buttercup Lane?'

'I can tell you what'll happen to all of us,' yelled Hugh, 'if you stop to philosophise about street-ballads when we're hanging sixty-odd feet up in the air. Get on with it, can't you?'

'A-i-sy, me bhoy! Let not your English temper rise. We're almost home.'

And, in a second or two, they were.

A beacon guided them: chinks and glimmers of light, flowing out from between the heavy but not-quite drawn window of another hotel-suite. This was also a long window; it was pushed up, so that a stirring of hazy air made the light fairly clear on the fire-escape.

It was set against the wall about two feet up from the window. The metal slats of its floor glimmered wetly; they

113

could see the silhouettes of its upright supports and the iron hand-rail round it.

Butler, leaning out, gripped the hand-rail and vaulted over it with his long black cloak flying out like Count Dracula's. What he forgot was the noise he would make.

His feet landed on the metal slats with a crash and clang which must have cried 'burglars' to anyone inside the window. There was worse. On that slippery surface he immediately skidded to the right. He staggered, lost his balance, and tumbled through the curtains of the open window. Then he landed upright on the floor inside.

Hugh, vaulting over the rail and landing as lightly as a cat, closed his eyes and waited for disaster. He heard Butler's voice roll out.

'Madam,' said the barrister, 'pray accept my assurance that this intrusion was entirely accidental. Or, if you must scream (which I beg you not to do) I *will* first say that a finer figure and a better pair of legs I never set eyes on.'

'Oh, gord,' moaned Johnson, who was breathing on Hugh's neck. 'The governor's at it again.'

'Very well, very well!' softly called a woman's voice. 'But get out of here! Please! My husband—'

'Ah, there is a husband? I feared as much. Some soulless brute from the Stock Exchange . . .'

'*Please!*'

Butler's head appeared through the curtains and outside the window, his left foot high on the fire-escape.

'I go,' he said. 'But, like a certain celebrated general, I shall return.'

The gallant effect of this was somewhat marred by the fact that his left foot was almost as high as his waist; and that Hugh, with a powerful heave, whisked him up out of sight on to the fire-escape. Butler straightened up.

'There was no need for that.' He spoke with much severity. 'Now follow me, both of you. Kindly try to make as little noise as possible.'

The fog closed round them in full density as they descended, groping and turning each time the fire-escape

114

turned. One floor, two, three, four, without another window open or uncurtained.

Car-lamps flickered below. Faint noises drifted up: mostly strange, intense oaths from people trying to extract ordinary-sized cars from parking-places which might have held a baby Austin.

One more dark floor went past. The fugitives, vaguely seeing Butler throw up his hand for a halt, could discern a line of iron steps projecting straight ahead and parallel with the street high above it.

'Now listen!' said Butler. 'When we three step out on that ladder, and our weight carries it down to the pavement, I will begin shouting, "Officer! Officer!" before we even land there.'

Hugh's brain reeled.

'I see,' he said. 'But don't you think we've got enough policemen after us as it is, without you leaning over the rail and yelling for more?'

Butler clucked his tongue.

'My dear fellow,' came that unruffled voice, 'where is your sense of strategy? Inspector Duff, if he happens to be a good policeman, will already have stationed a man at the foot of the fire-escape to cut off an obvious line of retreat.'

'*Another* cop?'

'Naturally. What else did you expect? But, if we begin calling in agitation for his help before he thinks we can even see him, he won't suspect us of being fugitives. Now will he?'

For the first time it struck Hugh Prentice, and forcibly, that there was far more method in Butler's apparent madness than he had ever dreamed.

'Right!' he agreed. 'What do we tell the constable when we've got him?'

'It's very simple. We tell him a handsome woman with practically no clothes on (which is true) is being strangled by her vicious husband in a suite on the seventh floor. If that doesn't send him up the fire-escape like greased lightning, the Force isn't what it used to be.'

115

'It strikes me,' said Hugh, 'that you and I have already created a two-man crime-wave. We have burst our way out of Scotland Yard, we have wrecked an antique-shop, knocked out two mobsters, and got a third stabbed under the collar-bone. Now you want to have an innocent man arrested for strangling his wife.'

'Very well. You think of a better one.'

'Never mind; I can't. Let's go!'

Together they charged out on the metal steps, all three of them, holding hard to the side-rail. The fire-escape shot downwards with unexpected velocity. Butler had only three times bellowed for a constable before the steps struck the asphalt with a thump and a clang.

They jumped off. Slowly, sedately, the stairs rose up behind them and vanished into fog.

But there was no constable. And nobody else paid the slightest attention to them.

There was only a thicker blur of car-lamps, heavier revvings of engines and gear-grindings. Two infuriated gentlemen, the front and rear bumpers of whose cars had become inextricably locked together, stood in the street and shook their fists under each other's noses.

'Come!' muttered Butler. 'I am disappointed in Inspector Duff. Never mind. We can run now; we're free. Straight ahead; then first right down the street past the east side of the hotel.'

Side by side they raced through the fog, Johnson running ahead with his arm out to stiff-hand anyone who tried to stop them. They whirled round the side of the hotel and flew on.

'Let me repeat,' Butler panted as they ran, 'I am disappointed in Inspector Duff. *I* should have corked up that hotel like a bottle. If I am ever on the side of the law . . .'

'Which isn't likely?'

'Which isn't likely, as you say. Do I detect a slight disapproval of my methods?'

'Great Scott, no! But, just between ourselves: does learned counsel always carry on like this?'

'*I* do. That is why, if I may venture the remark, I am unique.'

'Agreed.'

'Solicitors,' continued Butler, raising an admonitory finger as he ran, 'solicitors often swear when I tear up their briefs as useless, and go out and get witnesses for myself. Most barristers hate my guts. Let us consider a barrister of the so-called old-time or stiff-necked school, who is supposed to defend some poor devil on a charge of murder but won't even talk to the client in case it should "prejudice" him.'

There was real hatred in the Irishman's soft, panting voice.

'May he fry in the everlasting bonfire, as he will. He's failed his client; he's failed himself. What's his job, anyway? It's to get his client acquitted, by fair means or foul, no more and no less. That's my conception of the law, bejasus; and let those sneer at it who can match me record.'

'But aren't they all waiting and eager to catch you out in something?'

'Oh, yes. And one day they will.—Stop!'

They had emerged into the fog-bound square of Seven Dials. The show at the Oxford Theatre was not only over; they knew it had ended long ago. Faint footsteps clattered away in droves; most of the cars had gone; the foyer was deserted.

'Sir!' gulped Johnson, again apprehensive. 'Hadn't I better scout ahead to the stage door? And make sure no cops are there?'

'Yes; by all means. Though I don't think you'll find any.'

Both Hugh and Butler stopped to glance over their shoulders in the direction of Mr. Cotterby's antique-shop. They could see quite literally nothing. The fog, Hugh thought, would not completely have shut out lights had there been any at all; but the whole side of the street appeared dark, with not even a sign of the omnipresent law.

Butler scowled. About to make some remark, he made an impatient gesture instead. They hastened down a narrow street, whose name Hugh never learned, just beside the

117

right-hand side of the theatre as you faced it. The stage door entrance was at the back, immediately round the corner.

There they stopped in something like consternation.

The theatre crowd had gone. There was nobody who even remotely could have been a policeman. But the stage door premises, very small, were packed and resounding with a vociferous little mob of admirers. Behind the window of a cubicle on the right, a bald-headed man in his shirt-sleeves was going crazy as he dealt with them.

'No!' he was yelling. 'You're not a friend of Madame Feyoum's; *I* know you! No, and *you're* not from the *Daily Express*, either; the press has been and gone. No! No more autographs tonight! No more . . .'

The voices of the small mob drowned him out.

'Johnson,' Butler observed, swinging off his dark cloak and throwing it across his arm, 'I can abide many things. But never a crowd. This calls for another of the useful-cards.'

Pronouncing the last two words as though they were one, he drew out a card-case. From this he drew out a visiting card, inscribed: *The Most Hon. the Marquess of Dunwich*. Gravely he handed the card to Johnson, who received it just as gravely, saluted and then, with shoulders down like a bull, butted into the mob.

'Shocked at my methods once more?' asked Butler. Yet there was little life in his tone. His eye strayed up the street, clearly with the antique-shop in mind. His expression had grown dark and uneasy.

'Forget your method,' Hugh said quietly. 'Out with it! Why do you doubt yourself?'

'Eh?'

'Up to the time we went into Cotterby's place, you were certain you had the solution of the problem on a plate. And yet, as soon as you studied those old-time gloves and heard the name of "Father Bill", it shook you badly. Why?'

For a moment or two Hugh believed Butler would not reply.

'No!' bawled the stage door keeper. 'Sixteen years old, you! No mor'n a boy. And you want to . . .'

118

Then Butler spoke clearly amid the clamour.

'You recall the first pair of gloves? Grey or white gauntlet-gloves, for a man with rather small hands?'

'Yes, of course I remember. What about them?'

'They were worn by King Charles the First,' replied Butler, 'when he met his death on the scaffold.'

'. . . *you want to meet Madame Feyoum, eh, 'cos she's a good-looker with a figure? If I was your dad . . .*'

An elusive-burning street-lamp, the veiled light from the stage door, shone on Butler's grim face even as Hugh blurted out his question.

'Are you serious?'

'Yes, yes, yes!—Sorry; mustn't lose my temper. The second pair are still older; sixteenth century. They were worn by a very famous woman when *she* was executed in the hall at Fotheringay Castle.'

The light, on the fog-screen, threw weird moving shadows of heads in the mob. Hugh stood motionless.

'You're not talking about—?'

'Yes again.' Butler nodded. 'If you care to look at *The Trial of Mary, Queen of Scots,* which is in my library, you'll find an eye-witness account of her execution. Those gloves, originally vivid black and crimson, matched her costume then.'

'*No! No! That's final! Here, you in the chauffeur's uniform . . .*'

Butler squared his shoulders.

'The second pair, I seem to remember, went up for auction at Sotheby's about eight months ago. They were knocked down to a Bond Street dealer; but he was acting, in secret as usual, for some very wealthy man whose name didn't appear. Now, then! From all this, what follows?'

'Go on,' said Hugh. 'You lead; I'll try to pick it up.'

'First,' said Butler, 'the trap was set by somebody with a devil of a lot of money. Second, by somebody who can pick up such rarities at very short notice. By the way, you don't doubt it was a trap?'

'No; I don't doubt that. But a trap for which of us?'

'For both of us, obviously!' Butler retorted. 'Look here. If you had been passing the shop alone, and saw that sign, would you have gone in?'

'Yes. Immediately.'

'Why would you have gone in?'

'Because,' Hugh said simply, 'of the reference to "historical curiosities for connoisseurs". I couldn't have resisted it.'

'Neither could I. Third, then,' snapped Butler, 'it was a trap set by somebody who knows us, knows our tastes, and, above all, knows we're working together. Very well; we're working together on what case?'

'The murder of Omar of Ispahan!' Hugh said quietly. But, for all he was shivering without an overcoat, hot excitement ran in him. 'So that—fourth, as you would say—those "historical gloves" can't possibly be a coincidence. Our somebody knew all about the dying reference to gloves; he knew about the blood-stained white-cotton gloves I haven't even seen; and, as a kind of elaborate flourish, he used more gloves for the trap.'

'Exactly.' Butler threw out his arms. 'But, if that's so, my whole theory collapses in ruin.'

'Why?'

'Because we know who our "somebody" is. It's Father Bill. That's certain. And yet, if Father Bill's organization killed Omar and then arranged to get us killed or badly beaten up as a warning, then I'm so wrong as to be completely half-witted. Half-witted, damn it! And I am never wrong.'

'For the last time,' said the maddened Hugh, 'who *is* this Father Bill?'

'Nobody knows. I think *I* know. But that's because more grasses come to me, with secret information I can use, than ever whisper a word to Scotland Yard. I pay better, for one thing.'

'All right! But I'm still asking . . . !'

'Father Bill?' And Butler gave his companion a curious glance. 'Outwardly, he's one of the biggest bookmakers in the country, with sixty-odd branches in many cities. The bookmaking part of it is quite honest, though heaven help you if you don't pay up. Even there, for obvious reasons, Father Bill won't let his name appear. But underneath that cover there's a whole nest of profitable rackets, some of them so vicious that even I don't care to talk about it.'

Against the hazy light a part of the small crowd surged and swayed outwards, amid snarls or squeals, as somebody fought to get out. Again Butler glanced in that odd way at his companion. Carelessly he added:

'You've guessed, I hope, that Pam de Saxe is Father Bill's daughter?'

Chapter 12

THERE are mental blows in the face which stun the brain worse than any physical impact. It was not the last Hugh was to receive in this affair, but so far it was the worst.

Of course he hadn't guessed. Butler, who was showing off again, knew he hadn't. And yet, as Pam's image rose up in his reeling mind, together with certain remarks she had made about Daddy, his conception of her altered its line without changing in the least.

'Her father?' Hugh said mechanically. 'You don't mean,' he groped for the title, 'Lord Saxemund?'

'I do.'

'But isn't Lord Saxemund known for his charities and good works?'

'Certainly. Why shouldn't he be?'

'But a peer—!'

'Tut, tut! You English always take the romantic view. Certain noble lords, for instance, derive their incomes from the vilest slum-properties. Isn't the fine old profession of book-making, which will last as long as sporting blood remains or I have a good thing for the 3.30, far more honest?'

'Yes, yes, but I'm not making myself clear! I mean: as the notorious Father Bill, a gangster with a bodyguard . . .'

Now Butler was really impatient.

'My dear Prentice,' he said, towering high in the impressiveness of his evening clothes, 'you have been reading too many thrillers of the alleged tough school. What do you mean, the "notorious" Father Bill? Had you ever heard of him, before tonight?'

'Well—no.'

'He isn't a gangster; he is merely a man who can pull strings behind the scenes, as others can. What the devil would he do with a bodyguard?' Butler looked thoughtful. 'You might, with some trouble, prove he's the power behind the bookie-business. But what if you did? Nobody would care. As for the number of ugly rackets he controls underneath it, you'd never prove that in a million years. He could have me up for slander if I mentioned it in public; and he would.'

Three figures, two large and one small, loomed up beside them. A voice was speaking loudly, even hoarsely. A hand plucked at the barrister's arm. But neither Hugh nor Butler, each immersed in the violence of his own emotions, paid the slightest attention.

'All the same,' Butler muttered, with a gleam in his eye, 'it may soon be necessary for me to have a show-down with that tough old sinner.'

'About this murder case?'

'No. He made some remarks about me; they got into the press; they shall not be forgiven him. I thought at first I might learn much from a little judicious questioning of his daughter.'

'Then you and Pam . . . that is . . . ?'

Butler stared at him. 'Gods of Babylon, man! You didn't think I had any designs on Pam's virtue? Always assuming it exists?'

'By this time, so help me, I don't think *anything*. I can't!'

'No, no, no, no!' exclaimed Butler, a little offended. 'My dear fellow, I like 'em mature. No woman knows anything until she's well past thirty-five; and I don't refer to her academic honours either. A little gallantry towards Pam: no more. But with regard to your own designs on her virtue . . .'

'*My* designs?'

'What else? I should be careful, if I were you. That girl is the apple of papa's eye; she's meticulously shielded; she could slip out tonight only because Saxemund and his wife are away for two or three days.'

'Now look here—!'

'Curse it, haven't you heard or read anything about them? They live in a big house full of gramophone-gadgets;

Saxemund loves gadgets and curiosities, as witness those gloves. But he'll cut up rough if he learns you've been tampering with his daughter's affections.'

The voice which had been trying to address Butler now, so to speak, stood on tiptoe and bellowed in his ear.

'My lord!' it said. 'Oi! My lord!'

Hugh recoiled. Even Butler was taken off balance.

Having before him only a distorted and guessed-at mental picture of Lord Saxemund, Hugh had a brief but wild impression that this shout was a summons; that Lord Saxemund himself, in some sinister Jekyll-and-Hyde shape, might take form against the stage door.

But he saw only the bald-headed stage-door keeper, plucking at Butler's arm, together with Johnson and a call-boy with plastered-down hair.

'My lord!' the stage-door keeper said hoarsely. 'You're to go up at once, if you please, Madame Feyoum says.'

And, though Butler himself had momentarily forgotten he was supposed to be the Most Honourable the Marquess of Dunwich, he slipped into the acting-role as easily as he would have put on another hat.

'Ah, yes,' he murmured, with a sort of broad languor. 'Please forgive my momentary inattention.' Unobtrusively a banknote changed hands. 'Er—Madame Feyoum's dressing-room is . . . ?'

'Upstairs, my lord. Johnny'll show you.' The bald-headed man nodded towards the call-boy; then looked at Hugh. 'And this gentleman?'

Again, in irritating fashion, Butler surveyed Hugh as though the latter were about the same age as the call-boy.

'My young friend here. Yes, to be sure. He is with me.'

With the call-boy's clamorous voice cleaving a way through a sullen mob, with Butler's miniatures gleaming in a long line as he sauntered, they ascended a narrow staircase on the left and went along a corridor. They could exchange only whispered remarks like boxers in a very light sparring match. But Hugh was determined to clear up one part of the matter.

124

('Listen! Did you get any information from Pam?')

('No. You mightn't believe it, but she's far too clever. I thought it best to pretend I believed she's as feather-headed as *she* pretends. Still, you might get some information.')

('I?')

('Fallen hard for you, old boy. Never carries on like that; knows what she wants, though. Enjoy yourself, but I repeat: look out for Pop. Your Helen, on the other hand . . .')

('What about Helen?')

('The fact is, *I* find her attractive.')

('You do, eh?')

('Definitely. Not thirty-five, true. But can't be far off it. More experienced, I suspect, than *you* ever suspect. You don't mind if I explore the matter, I hope?')

('Wait a minute! I'm engaged to Helen—!')

('Are you? Didn't seem so to me, the last time you two met. Got to be a sportsman, you know.')

('Now look here—!')

('Sh-h-h! Mustn't raise your voice, old chap.')

Butler quietened Hugh as the call-boy, from mere force of habit, banged a fusillade of knocks on the dressing-room door.

There was a stir inside, a whisper or two, and a rustle. The door was opened by a lady who could only be Madame Feyoum herself, giving them radiant welcome.

She was indeed a fine figure of a woman. Johnson had been correct in describing her as 'Frenchy, all curves': some of the latter were all too obvious; and clearly French, though the tawny colour of her skin suggested she had been born nearer to French Morocco than Paris, with perhaps a dash of Moorish blood. Though she had removed the stage make-up from a boldly handsome face, with wide nostrils and a broad, curling mouth, her street make-up was nearly as vivid. It accentuated glossy black hair, and vivid if rather protruding brown-black eyes. For her stage-costume she had substituted a heavy crimson-and-gold dressing-gown, under which she appeared to wear nothing at all except stockings and high-heeled shoes.

125

For an instant she gave them both a look of frank, bold appraisal, tapping a visiting-card against fine teeth. She was pleased, and showed it. Then she became very correct.

'*Monseigneur le marquis?*' she asked Butler. She made an effortless curtsey. '*Je suis bien flattée, monseigneur.*'

'*Mais pas du tout, chère madame!*' murmured Butler. He swept off his hat. Just as formally he lifted her extended hand to his lips.

Madame Feyoum accepted this tribute gravely. Then, smiling, she extended her hand to Hugh. Hugh, feeling the worst damned fool in the world, went through the same performance.

Suddenly Madame Feyoum noticed the presence of the call-boy, who was staring with all his eyes.

'John-ee!' Her contralto voice rang with heavy mock-sternness. 'You are a bad boy. Go! *Va-t-en!* Scoot!'

The call-boy, making a hideous face, hunched his head in his shoulders and stumped away.

Yet despite all her good-humour and vitality, despite the fact that she exuded sex as much as she exuded Chanel-Number-Something perfume, Hugh's first thought was that some shadow lay underneath it. Look out, look out! His next thought was for her excitable husband, who must have looked very small beside her.

Poor little devil, he thought. *Abu, or Omar, is the only person nobody seems to be thinking about.*

Madame Feyoum glanced quickly behind her. With a soft motion she closed the door so that all three stood outside. Softly but in an impassioned tone she addressed Butler.

'I am annoy,' she declared. 'Much! Very! Ah, bah! Why you twice send thees card,' she held it up, 'of some silly lord which do not exist anyway, when I much rather meet de great Patrick Butler? Eh? Eh?'

For once Butler was taken completely aback.

'And why,' demanded Madame Feyoum, 'you send your chauffeur, who is an ugly face as well-known as you are because you send him everywhere, to ask in de foyer 'ow I am doing? You theek they do not tell me?'

Butler grinned at her.

'Dear madame,' he said, 'you are an artist. Had you failed tonight, you would have been kicking the furniture to pieces and would have seen nobody afterwards. Since you so magnificently succeeded . . .'

Madame Feyoum's teeth flashed in a curling smile. Her brownish-black eyes gleamed and brightened with every flow of vitality.

'I knock dem, eh?' she beamed. 'Yes! By damn, I do!' Her manner changed. 'I like you,' she said, with more in her tone than the words convey. 'And I like you,' she said in the same voice, whirling on Hugh. 'Which is you, please?'

'My name is Prentice, Madame Feyoum. Hugh Prentice.'

Madame Feyoum's brilliant eyes narrowed between the mascara of their lashes.

'Pren-tees?' she repeated, in so much the same intonation as her husband that Hugh felt a retrospective shiver. Again the shadow came and went on her face. 'Pren-tees, you say? *Alors, c'est—*'

She stopped, lifting her full shoulders in a shrug.

'No matter!' she added. 'You are you.' She looked at Butler. 'You are you. Why do we stand 'ere? No, no, no! Come in!'

And she whisked open the door of the dressing-room.

There was no sign of a dresser. The room, in the wildest disorder, might have been her own room at a hotel if it were not for the absence of windows. The only light shone brightly round a powder-dusted dressing-table, on which the most conspicuous objects were now a big open jar of cold cream and a discoloured face-towel. Well to the left stood a big bowl of red and white carnations.

Hugh took three steps into the room after Butler, moved round to stand beside him, and stopped short.

Not far from the dressing-table sat his uncle, Mr. Charles Grandison Prentice.

Hugh's mouth opened and shut without a word. Madame Feyoum, nodding towards the flowers in the bowl and about

127

to speak, saw the look on Butler's face and on Hugh's. She said nothing.

Uncle Charles, in his usual beautifully tailored dinner-jacket, a white carnation in his button-hole and the customary large cigar in his fingers, sat as placidly as he might sit at Lady Somebody's house. He was middle-sized, bulky without being fat. His lower jowls, too heavy, thrust his under-lip almost up over his upper-lip beneath a curt grey moustache. His thin, brittle grey hair nevertheless covered his scalp.

His face, as usual, bore no expression at all.

In the midst of dead silence he arose. He put on his overcoat, taking hat in one hand and stick in the other. He wore no gloves.

'I'm afraid, Madame Feyoum,' he said in his throaty expressionless voice, 'it's getting late and I must be off. Good-night. You won't forget, I hope?'

Madame Feyoum moistened her painted lips.

'No!' she said. '*Jamais!*'

'Ah, I imagined as much,' said Uncle Charles, putting the cigar in his mouth. 'Again, good night.'

At last Hugh found his voice.

'Uncle Charles!' he exclaimed. 'They said you were at the theatre, but I didn't believe it. Is your cold better? It must be!'

Uncle Charles paused, taking the cigar out of his mouth, and regarded him with a straight, level gaze.

'You have the advantage of me, sir,' he retorted politely but coldly. 'I have never seen you before, nor do I wish to see you again.'

Bowing to Madame Feyoum, nodding very slightly and rather contemptuously at Butler, he strolled out of the dressing-room. The door closed softly after him.

Hugh, half-stunned, stared at the door. Butler went white and straight with rage. Madame Feyoum, sitting down with her back to the dressing-table, crossed her knees and looked at the floor so that her black, glossy, short-cut hair tumbled into her eyes.

128

But now Hugh understood. They were all disowning him. First Monica and Jim, now Uncle Charles. He had only ... no; he didn't have Helen, now. But that was his own fault.

The dressing-room, unlike most dressing-rooms in winter, was overpoweringly hot. Out of a great void he heard Butler's voice.

'Chin up, me lad,' the Irishman said with a sort of deadly agreeability. 'Before another day, I promise you, that damned old fraud will very much regret giving the cut-direct to his own nephew.'

'Here, no! Take it easy!'

'You're fond of the old boy, then?' Butler asked dryly.

'No. We've never got on altogether well. That's only natural, so far as he is concerned. Monica loves the social life and I loathe it. Uncle Charles is a snob. His knowledge of the law isn't what it ought to be. But he's no fraud, whatever else he is; and in his own way he's been very decent.'

Butler turned round with polished courtesy.

'And what is *your* opinion, Madame Feyoum?'

'Me?' She jerked her head up and back, so that the dark hair flew with it. 'I 'ave no opeen-ion, as you call it. 'Ow should I know?'

'For instance, why was this virtuous old gentleman here tonight?'

'It was about a letter. It was nothing. Ah, bah. If it was something important,' snapped Madame Feyoum, opening her eyes very wide, 'do you t'ink I would let you come in 'ere?'

'Touch,' said Butler, with soft pleasure. 'A real touch, a palpable hit. Madame, it is a joy to talk with you.'

And he took up her hand and again pressed his lips to it.

'You are not nice!' cried Madame Feyoum, suddenly becoming all too feminine. Tears sprang into her eyes. 'I tell you the truth. First I have see you at the Court Bailey, where you defend a Mees Gropp which is suppose to poison her boy-friend; and I admire you. Okay! I see you tonight; I like you. The audience; I knock 'em! Yes! They cheer; they applaud. I am touch and I weep. But at the beginning they do not think I will succeed. And so,' she nodded towards the great bowl of red and white carnations, 'there is nobody who has thought to send me flowers, except you.'

She lowered her head and looked at the floor.

Butler, clearly ashamed of himself because this gesture had been only a part of a plan, also looked away. But it did not stop him for long.

'Do you understand why we're really here?'

The woman nodded.

'To find the murderer of your husband?'

Again she nodded without looking up.

'Poor Abu,' she said after a pause.

'Was his name really Abu? Or Omar? Or what?'

'It was really Abu. But we call him Omar too. It make no difference. That depend on what country we are in, and which seem better.'

Suddenly she flung back her head and looked up defiantly. Tears smeared the mascara, which overran on her cheeks.

'This was a marriage of convenience, you understand? I am his ventriloquist. For most shows like dese there is a ventriloquist to break it up. He thinks a womans as a ventriloquist will be fonny; and so it is, when I do it. But thees marriage? Well! In some countries where we travel, about people in show business, they 'ave de peculiar ideas. You see?'

'Yes, Madame Feyoum, I see.'

Madame Feyoum tossed her head.

'Ah, bah!' she said, trying to glare the tears out of her eyes. *'Trop de politesse, voyons!'* She lifted her chin. 'You can call me Cécile.' She looked at Hugh. 'You can call me Cécile too.'

Both Hugh and Butler acknowledged the compliment.

'I do not love Abu, no!' said Cécile. 'But I am fond of him. And I do not 'urt his pride. When he make de great *frisson* in public, and bang de table in a restaurant and tick out the waiter to show what a big man he is even if he is little, I only say, "Yes, dear." Oo! That man get into fights even when he know he will get beat bad. You see?'

130

Hugh nodded. The dead Persian seemed to walk and talk and gesticulate in the hot dressing-room.

'But he will not let me do the magic. No, never! And, oh, how that man love to make gamblings and get something for nothing!'

Perhaps the woman herself did not realize it. But the atmosphere had changed.

'Yes. Now we come to it!' said Butler. 'The police have been here, I take it? When were they here?'

Cécile threw up her hands.

'Grand Dieu, when are they not here? They first come near seven o'clock. They tell me Abu is dead; they have find his passport in his pocket, wit' other things that prove who he is.'

'Yes?'

'Well! I say that is very sad, but I must 'urry and 'urry to get the show on. Because I can do it all myself. I! Me! There is one Inspector Macduff, like Shakespeare, who question me. He is so Scotch I only just understand him. He say, can't I cancel thees show?'

'And you couldn't?'

'No, no, no, no!' retorted Cécile, sitting up straight and rapidly smacking her hands together at each syllable. 'If there is get round the rumour your show is closed, even for one night, then you are in trouble.'

'Yes? Go on!'

'So these police all sit out in the 'ouse and watch my show. When there is the interval, at eight forty-five, I am try to rest. By damn, back they come and question me again. No, thees is too much!'

'And what did you tell them?'

'What I tell you! Only I tell you more, if I can.'

'For instance, you said your husband was fond of gambling. Cards? Horses?'

A look of heavy cynicism flashed across the woman's tawny face, and was gone.

'Cards? Horses? No. Never. That horrifies heem! He say, "No, no, that is gambling. I buy stocks; I buy shares;" I say,

"Orright; you get advice from a bank or a good firm of brokers." Abu say, "Banks? Bah! They say buy the gilt-edge, with a very little profit. No! I get fifty, one hundred, two hundred per cent." I say, "Then what is the difference between that and gambling? And anyways you will be cheated."'

She paused to draw breath, after speaking quickly and heavily. Butler did not move or speak. He only studied her.

'Well!' said Cécile, shrugging. 'A little time after, he strut home like theese,' she illustrated, 'and say he has been advised about a very big secret investment. He say he is advised by the most respectable firm of solicitors in London.'

'Solicitors?' Butler repeated sharply.

'Yes.'

'What solicitors? What firm?'

'I don' know—at that time! When it is a question of money, Abu will tell you nothing! He does not tell me the name even when . . . when . . .'

'Yes? Go on!'

'Two night ago,' Cécile swallowed, 'he walks into this theatre the colour of I-don'-know-what. His hands shake so much I must do the show for him, like tonight. Abu says he has been persuaded, since two-three months, to put six thousand pounds into a company called Angli-Ameri-Iraqui Oil. He has just found out there is no such company; and he has been swindled. But *I* don' hear the name of the solicitors until the police tell me tonight. They are Pren-tees, Pren-tees, and Von.'

The dressing-room was so quiet that you could hear the faint clank and thump of a steam-radiator.

Hugh Prentice felt another touch of nausea. But he intervened quietly and with authority.

'Butler! Do you mind if I take charge of this for a minute?'

'No; go ahead.'

Cécile turned towards Hugh. He felt a breath of fierce femininity; her eyes, though mascara-smudged, were compelling and disturbing as they searched his face.

132

'You know, I hope,' Hugh smiled, 'that our firm never give advice to clients on such matters?'

'Yes!' said Cécile. 'I know it now!'

'Would you explain that, please?'

Cécile made a grimace with her mouth. Her gaze shifted away; then moved back.

'Because,' she said as though defying him, 'that is one of the reasons how Abu learn he has been swindled. He discover first that somebody, who is not a member of thees firm, pretend to be a member of thees firm and guzzle him. Someone has imp . . . imp . . .'

Hope, a faint edge of hope, sprang up and glowed in Hugh's heart. Had his luck turned at last?

'Impersonated, Cécile?' he asked. 'Someone impersonated a member of the firm?'

'I speak very well English, thank you! I do not know whether it is a member. But someone who is connected wit' thees firm. Yes!'

(*Let me handle this properly! Let me lead her on gently, gently!*)

Hugh leaned forward.

'Cécile,' he said, 'do you know that the police think I killed Abu? Either I, or another person who's on the run: Jim Vaughan?'

'Von? Oh! But already, at nine o'clock, they have catch thees man with the German name.'

'They caught Jim Vaughan? Where?'

' 'Ow do I know, for sure?' cried Cécile. 'They talk so fast, when they all talk, I am mix-up. But I think they say: in your sister's flat.'

'And they arrested him?'

'No, no! They question him. He prove something to do with a brief-case which I do not understand. But he prove it is not his brief-case, or other things. And they say okay. He is what the films call in de clear.'

'Then that leaves only myself. Cécile, do you believe I killed your husband?'

'Bah!' snorted Cécile, with her eyes still fixed on his face.

'I know you do not. I know men. As soon as I see you 'ere, I am sure.'

'You see, I'm actually a member of the firm. I can easily prove I never sold any fake oil-shares. Why on earth should *I* have killed him?'

What *was* the expression in that woman's eyes and mouth and even distended nostrils? Commiseration? Sympathy? She breathed slowly. Her hands were clasped together in the lap of her scarlet-and-gold silk dressing-gown. She spoke suddenly.

'You really wish me to tell you?'

'Of course.'

'Well! The police think Abu has rush into your office, to get the firm to help him find the person who swindle him.'

'Yes! That's quite possible! It would explain a great deal.'

'*Bon!* He has written a letter to your uncle, yes. But *you* don' know anything of all thees. When Abu rush in and begin to rave about oil companies and being swindled by somebody, he mix it all up. Abu's English is not good. Maybe you think he mean you. You tell him he is foolish in the head. Abu go crazy and start a fight, which he always do with tall people like you . . .'

'And I picked up a Moorish dagger and stabbed him? Is that it?'

'Yes.'

Motive. Motive at last. Grotesque and absurd though it sounded . . .

Out of the corner of his eye Hugh glanced at Butler, Butler, cloak over his arm, stood facing the mirror with his eyes closed, listening.

'Cécile,' Hugh said quietly, 'I'm not doubting your story. But how did the police come to talk so much? And tell you, as a witness, what they thought?'

'Oh, don' you *still* understand?'

'I'm afraid not.'

'All the time the police is here,' she answered simply, 'your uncle is here, too.'

'My Uncle Charles?'

134

'Yes! As soon as they have found poor Abu's body, they 'phone him and ask what the 'ell. He is here at the theatre sooner as they are.'

'Yes? Don't stop!'

'When he hear about all this, and what I say, he becomes all soothy and calm. Even Inspector Macduff, who think only the Scotch is all right, think he is all right. How can they respect that old . . . staa! 'Ow they can respect him, I don't know! But they do.'

'Steady, Cécile! What did he actually tell the police?'

The woman writhed in a mighty shrug.

'He say,' she replied, 'that what the police think is probably true.'

'So!' whispered Patrick Butler, without opening his eyes.

'He say,' continued Cécile, still not removing her eyes from Hugh, 'that you are (how it is?) flight-ee. Unsta-ble. Fly off the handle boom! If you lose your 'ead, you might pick up a knife when Abu run at you and want to fight. But he say it is all right and no much harm done.'

'Oh? How?'

'Because, he say, at worst thees is man-slaughter. And, if Patrick Butler shall defend you, they could get you off on a plea of self-defence.'

Butler, eyes tightly closed, remained facing the mirror.

'I could, you know,' he remarked in a sardonic tone. 'And very well Grandison Prentice knows I could. What about it, old boy? Want to give yourself up?'

'No!' said Hugh, in a voice that seemed to make the room rattle.

A savage gleam of pleasure kindled Cécile's eyes. She half started up from the padded bench, the dressing-gown falling off her shoulders; but hastily she readjusted the gown and sat down again.

'Then you don't want to give yourself up?' Butler said insistently.

'No! Don't you see I'm free? Jim has been cleared; that's the only thing that worried me; and I'm absolved from any pledge to give myself up and confess. But that's not every-thing. Just to protect themselves from trouble or scandal, Uncle Charles and Monica and even Jim have banded to-gether to make me the goat; they think it doesn't matter so long as I don't actually hang or go to prison. Well,' shouted Hugh, 'they can all go to hell on a butter-slide. Even if it takes a miracle, I'm still going to dodge the police until I can prove I didn't kill anybody!'

'Ah,' murmured Butler, with soft delight.

Hugh controlled himself.

'But there's just one . . .' he began, and hesitated.

'Yes? What is it?'

'It's this conversation the police think I had with Abu. He never once mentioned fake oil-shares. He wasn't angry; only frightened. I don't think I missed anything. The trouble is that I'm very nearly, if not quite, as bad with French as Abu was with English. The whole latter part of our talk was in French.'

The effect of this was as unexpected as Hugh's own out-burst.

Butler's eyes flashed open. His left hand, carrying the cloak, swept out in so mighty a gesture that the big bowl of red and white carnations flew wide. The bowl struck the wall and smashed; water splashed and flowers tumbled askew.

Cécile, uttering a cry, hurried over to retrieve them. Butler turned round from the mirror, his mouth open and working. But he did not speak loudly.

'Let me be quite clear about this,' said learned counsel. 'You are sure it was in French?'

'Didn't I tell you? Twice? I'll swear I couldn't have failed to mention—'

Butler's gesture stopped him, Butler's gaze, spellbound yet restless, seemed to be anywhere except in the room.

'Then I was not wrong!' he declared, snapping his fingers. 'Indeed, I am never wrong. Prentice! All our difficulties may be resolved if I hear the answer to just one question. It is this. When Abu said—'

He stopped.

Running and clattering footsteps, like hammers in so quiet a theatre, pounded along the corridor outside. With no warning series of knocks, the door was thrown open. They saw the alarmed face and plastered-down hair of Johnny, the call-boy.

'Madam Foom!' he gulped. 'The cops are back again. Dozens of 'em! And that there Inspector Duff as mad as blazes!'

Abruptly Cécile straightened up, clasping water-soaked carnations to the breast of her dressing-gown. From acute misery her expression changed to dusky wrath.

'John-ee!' she said, and seemed to hiss it. 'What does Harry tell them?'

'Harry says you're here. With the Marquess of Dunwich and a friend of his.' Continuing to gulp, Johnny looked quickly at Butler. 'But Inspector Duff,' he continued with a very fair imitation, 'the Inspector he says, "Marquess o' Dunwich ma fute!" he says. "That's Butler and Prentice! Spread out!" he says. "Cover the theatre front and back. They'll no' ge' away this time!"'

Hugh and Butler exchanged glances.

'This admittedly,' Butler confessed, 'is bad. However, I think we can find a . . .'

Cécile threw back her shoulders imperiously.

'Bad, you say? Pah, I say!' she cried. 'Ah, *ces sales flics!*' And she regarded Hugh with overpowering maternal affection. 'They shall not take you, *mon pauvre!* No! I will make you disappear.'

'Disappear?'

Cécile had already whirled back to the call-boy.

'John-ee!' she crooned in a voice of honeyed sweetness. 'You will be nice to me and 'elp me?'

'You bet I will, ma'am!'

'The front of the house is dark, yes?'

'Sure it is, ma'am! There's nobody here 'sept Harry and me.'

'Good! Good! First you run along and turn out every light

backstage. Then you come back—I take theese gentlemen down by the iron stair—and I tell you what to do. Run!'

The door closed in a slam and gulp. Footsteps clattered away.

Cécile was now drawn up with almost regal grandeur.

'Ladies and gentlemen,' said Butler, rubbing his hands together in solemn glee, 'here we go again.'

Cécile stamped her foot, holding the carnations closer.

'You shall not joke, you!' she said. 'Afterwards, maybe yes.' She looked at Hugh. 'You say perhaps it take a miracle to get you away? Good! Come wit' me. And I will show you a miracle!'

Chapter 13

'Sн-н-н!' softly hissed Cécile, about three and a half minutes later.

'But where are we?' Butler's equally soft whisper floated back.

'Sh-h-h!'

Except that they were in total darkness, and probably somewhere very close to the stage itself, Hugh could tell nothing. There was no mistaking that vast dust-and-canvas odour; that sense of being in a kind of well amid scenery, where voices would strike up hollowly as in a cavern.

Hugh and Butler knew only that Cécile had led them, on tiptoe, down a spiral iron staircase. There, by the rustling noise, Hugh guessed she was tying the waistbelt of her dressing-gown very tightly, and knotting it. In the ghost of a voice she had told Butler to hold the dressing-gown cord at the back, and for Hugh to be guided by the two buttons at the back of Butler's tail-coat, while she guided them forward.

In this order, like a slightly erratic snake, the procession moved.

'Iss all right?'

'Dear madame, iss splendid. The temptation to administer a pinch, however, iss almost . . .'

'Mees-tair Butler!'

'Cécile?'

'Thees is not the occasion or the place that you should pinch me,' Cécile hissed sternly. 'Later, per'aps,' she added loftily, like a judge admonishing counsel that his introduction of evidence was ill-timed.

'For the love of God,' whispered Hugh to Butler, 'will you try to behave yourself?'

'My dear fellow, you misjudge me.' Butler spoke with real sincerity. 'I've already devised two plans for your escape if

Cécile fails. But this African-jungle business, with us paddling down the river while the cannibal drums throb on either bank, is getting on my nerves.'

'Yes, and it's getting on mine!' Hugh whispered back. 'Do you realize it was only by a split-second we missed Duff's charge up the backstage stairs? And they're all over the theatre now.'

This could not be denied.

The voices, the hurrying footsteps, the furtive movements both backstage and out in the stalls, were only those of men moving with quick assurance. But, in a ghostly and deserted theatre at nearly midnight, each voice seemed magnified to a cry and each footfall to an overtaking run.

Distantly, somewhere, the narrow white beams of electric torches prodded and probed. Hugh's fear was that the beam of a torch might wheel across and pick them out squarely. On occasion they could hear the bellowing voice of Inspector Duff, enumerating each entrance or way out to be covered.

This was the point at which Cécile said, 'Sh-h-h!' and Butler asked where they were.

'Sh-h!'

'My sweet charmer, it's no good repeating "Sh-h-h!" with these head-hunters all round us. What is this fine scheme of yours? *My* plan—'

'Sh-h-h!' hissed Cécile, as the little procession stopped. *'Ces sales flics!'* she breathed with venom, adding that they were *espèce* de something. 'With my 'usband, my first 'usband, I am truly in love. Oh, how I am in love! He is always in trouble with the *flics*; and I get heem away until they shoot heem. *Flic*, which is slang for policeman: how you say that in English?'

'It depends,' whispered Butler, 'on which kind you mean. Plain clothes C.I.D. men, for instance, are currently known as bogeys, busies, dicks, and scotches. The Flying-Squad people are called sweenies, from Sweeny Todd. Police-women rejoice in the title of zombies. The ordinary copper—'

'Bogeys!' breathed Cécile, with hatred. 'That is what I like. They is bogeys.'

'All the same, where *are* we?'

'Wait! I stretch out my hands in front of me, and make sure. Ah! Is right!'

'What is?'

'I am in front of the electrician's board of switches. It control most of the lights.'

'And where does that put us?'

'In the wings, just off de stage. From where you are now, if you should take a lot of paces sideways to the left, you will be bang on the stage facing out towards the audience.'

Even Patrick Butler, by the sound of his whisper, was growing rattled.

'Dear madame, this is all very interesting. But how . . . ?'

'Sh-s!' hissed Cécile, breaking up the group. 'I show you!' They heard her groping as well as breathing, and she seized Hugh's left hand with her right.

'I am your French mommy,' she said, kissing him hard on the cheek. 'The rest of your family, they don' give a hoot about you. That old *cochon* wit' the cigar, already he plan more tricks against you. But *I* care.'

To Hugh as well as to Cécile the word 'bogey' now seemed to be spelled without a letter 'e'. Endlessly they were tramping, calling, flashing their lights. There was no way out of the trap.

'Come!' insisted Cécile. 'Don' you trust me?'

'Yes,' said Hugh. 'Sorry. Where are we going?'

'I lead you, as quiet, as quiet, straight out to the middle of the stage. I come back 'ere. Then I strike a match, very quick, so I can see the right switches. And I turn on the footlights and the battens.'

Darkness moved and whirled before Hugh's staggered eyes.

'That's fine,' he said, not without bitterness. 'But couldn't you give me a good spotlight so the bogeys could see me better? And I can always sing "Annie Laurie" for Inspector Duff's benefit.'

141

Cécile was growing frenzied. 'Do you trust me, or don'
you?'

'Yes! All right! Lead on!'

'And what about *me*?' dramatically whispered Butler.

'Sh-h-h! You stay there. I come back to you.'

Whereupon a voice, which to Hugh's nerves seemed
only about twenty feet behind them, sang out of the darkness.

'*Inspector!*' said the voice.

'*Aye?*' bellowed back Inspector Duff, from some distance
incalculable.

'*We can't do this without any ruddy lights, sir! Isn't there
a central switchboard in most of these theatres?*'

'*Aye, ma lad! I mind there is!*'

'*But which side is it? Right or left?*'

'*I dinna ken! Find it!*'

'*Yessir!*'

Fortunately, the enthusiastic one had no torch. Hurrying
footsteps, magnified to thunder on a bare floor, raced three
paces and ended with a smack against a pile of canvas flats
stacked against the wall.

'Fear not!' softly called Butler, who was very much himself again at the prospect of action. 'I shall take pleasure in
knocking the blighter cold if he gets near this switchboard.
Lead him, Cécile!'

Cécile led him, both of them on tiptoe.

By a soft draught blowing about his ears, by a greater
sense of emptiness round about him, Hugh guessed they
were crossing the stage.

Briefly, at the very back of the stalls, the white eye of a
torch opened to brush across half a dozen rows of cushioned
red seats. But it seemed like walking on cobwebs over
nothingness. Cécile's lips were close against Hugh's ear.

'In the middle of the stage,' she breathed, 'there's a brick
wall.'

'What?'

'A brick wall. It is eight feet high; it is two feet thick.
Members of the audience, which is not confederates, they

142

build it wit' the narrow side towards the audience. They build it while I do illusions on each side.'

'Yes?'

'Sh-h-h! Here is the wall. Feel it.'

Already Hugh's feet had encountered an oblong of what felt like fairly thick carpet. Moving on it, his outstretched hands touched the small brick wall, narrow side towards the audience, whose plaster between the brick remained fairly fresh.

'You see?' almost silently demanded Cécile. 'First, before they build it, I show them thees carpet. People from the audience look all over it. They see it had no cut or opening in it, which is true on my honour! They spread it out on the stage, to show I cannot go down by any trap-door under it. Yes? Then they build the brick wall across the carpet. Yes?'

'Yes! But what . . . ?'

'Lee-seen! At one side of the brick wall, in the middle, they put up a folding screen with three sides. At the other side of the brick wall, also in the middle, they put up another folding screen. You see?'

'I see, yes! But—'

'Sh-h-h! I get inside one folding screen, on de right. While I go in about twenty people from the audience stand all round the wall so I can't get out. The drums roll. Boum! They take away the screen from the other side. Boum! I have walked straight through the brick wall! Afterwards they can examine it again. Iss all right.'

Memories stirred at the back of Hugh's brain.

Somebody, he remembered, had told him of having seen this illusion done. It was particularly maddening; the wall really was a brick wall, the spectators surrounded it, the carpet was solid and permitted no escape.

'Ha, ha, ha,' Cécile carolled softly. 'Thees Inspector Macduff, *he* has seen it!'

'Yes, but—'

'Almost he has gone off his onion. He rave. He rush up on de stage. It is still a brick wall with no trick.'

Even as Hugh was whispering questions and protests,

143

Cécile put his hands on a very light wooden screen, lacquer-painted, its sides hinged to form three walls of an oblong. It was on the right-hand side of the stage.

Cécile pushed him inside it, very softly drawing the two sides of the oblong against the wall except an inch or so on his left—towards the black, non-existent audience—so that Cécile could hiss through that tiny opening.

'Now crouch down and stay there!' she whispered. 'Don' move, don' speak, don't do anything no matter what you hear or what you think is going to happen. *Entendu?*'

'Cécile!'

'Yes?'

'How am I supposed to escape the bogeys just by walking through a brick wall? Even if I do?'

'Because there is one way out they have not thought of, and I knew they would not. Ha, ha, ha!'

'Cécile!'

But Cécile had gone.

He knew it only by the faintest whisper of her silk dressing-gown, the very spectre of a footstep. But he knew it all the same.

At the same moment there smote out an echoing voice from the back of the theatre.

'*Inspector Duff!*'

'*Aye?*'

'*There's somebody moving on that stage!*'

Though the aperture between the wall and one side of the screen was only an inch wide, Hugh saw the reflected dazzle of torches spring up. Over the top of the screen he had a glimpse of a flat, gilded centaur-figure against one wall of the theatre.

'*Gently, noo!*' called Inspector Duff. '*Close in, aye! But don't run! Stop! Whaur's yon lad wha' looked tae the lights?*'

'*He's here, Inspector!*' The voice jumped up from still another direction.

'*WHAUR?*'

'*Backstage, on the floor. He's knocked cold, with a bruise under his left ear!*'

144

Even Inspector Duff had no time to reply. The whole stage was illuminated with soft yet brilliant light.

Through the aperture Hugh could see an edge of foot-lights glowing through glass coloured orange-yellow. In his insecure hideaway light poured down on him even from above; a thin line of battens, rather high up, made the inside of the screen as bright as its blue carpet.

He heard two voices, obviously raised for the benefit of Inspector Duff and his men. Two persons, clearly Cécile Feyoum and Patrick Butler, strolled out on the stage.

'Very well!' loudly said Cécile, as though in anger, 'If you insist, my Patrick, then I will show you how I have walked through the brick wall.'

'Alas, my own Cécile,' Butler cried tenderly, 'but curiosity killed the cat and has nearly killed me. I must know the secret of the brick wall.'

'And if I show you,' crooned Cécile, 'you will be nice to me?'

' "Nice", my dear, is a weak and ill-chosen word. I kneel before you!—But why, may I inquire, can we not be alone even here? There appear to be many drunken and incompetent stage-hands roystering even at midnight.'

'Stage-hands, is it?' bellowed the distant voice of Inspector Duff.

Men were charging in from all directions. Sweat started out on Hugh's body.

He had a narrow view of Butler and Cécile passing the aperture, silhouetted against orange-yellow footlights. Cécile, in fact, had paused with her hand round the edge of the screen where Hugh was hidden. He saw her fingers and her red-varnished nails.

Hugh had literally obeyed her instructions to crouch down. He was crouching like a runner, left knee forward and right knee down, his fingers touching the carpet at the back of the screen. But there was nowhere to run except straight at the brick wall in front of him.

'Stage-hands, eh?' Inspector Duff's voice was much closer. Somebody, unquestionably the Inspector himself, was

145

climbing over the rail which separated the stalls from the orchestra pit. Somebody landed with a crash inside the orchestra pit, upsetting a music-stand. A chair was dragged on the floor. There were fierce scrabblings as someone attempted to drag himself up on the stage.

'By Jove, Cécile! One of your stage-hands is well and truly intoxicated! Here, my man: let me give you a hand up.'

(*Don't make him too mad!* Hugh was praying. *For the love of Mike don't send him off his rocker completely.*)

For other running thuds indicated that the constabulary were arriving from both sides of the stage, as well as from the back of it. All escape had been cut off.

There was a heavier thump, evidently as Inspector Duff sprawled on the stage and then got up. Hugh could not see him. But he could hear the Inspector breathe.

'By Jove, Cécile! This is no stage-hand! I rather imagine...'

'Ye ken fine who I am, Mr. Bu'ler, and why I'm here! Whaur's Hugh Prentice?'

'Ah, yes.' Despite all his efforts, Butler's arrogance shot up to its full height, though his tone remained quiet. 'I seem to remember, Inspector, that I was once or twice obliged to cross-examine you in the witness-box at the Old Bailey. The results for you, I also recall, were not happy.'

'*Whaur's Prentice?*'

'Wherever he is, Inspector, I presume you don't think he's anywhere near Madame Feyoum or myself?'

'No, I'll gie ye that!' the other assented grimly. 'But whaur's he hidin' noo?'

'Even if I knew, my dear sir, I should be unlikely to tell you.'

Inspector Duff's tone changed. It became quiet, and, to Hugh, horribly sinister.

'I'll gie ye a wee bit warnin', Mr. Bu'ler. Dinna gang tae far. Or I'll tak' ye in charge as quick as I'd tak' anybody else.'

'Indeed. You interest me. What is my offence?'

'Obstructin' an officer of the law in the courrse o' his duty, that's what!'

146

'I see. By the way, Inspector, what is the charge against Mr. Prentice?'

'He's wanted for questionin' in the murr-der of . . .'

'Come, come, sir!' Out rolled the courtroom manner. 'Let us have no more of these evasions, please. What is the charge against him? Do you propose to arrest him for murder?'

'Not yet, maybe! Not yet! But—'

'What, no charge?' inquired the wondering Butler. 'Yet you have the effrontery to threaten *me*?'

'No sae fast, ma mannie, no sae fast!' Inspector Duff's sinister voice told him quietly. 'There's the sma' ma'er of a police officer, one o' ma men, knocked out wi' a blow under the ear, not ten paces frae whaur ye were standin'!'

'It would be of some legal curiosity,' mused Butler, 'to learn how you could prove where I was standing. Or, indeed, how I hit anyone. Do you care to examine my hands? You will find no mark on them.'

'When ye hi' a mon under the ear? Aye, maybe not!'

'I would further remind you,' said Butler, 'that you are out of your district. You are in the Metropolitan area only by permission of Mr. Robert Lee, the Assistant Commissioner of the C.I.D. Curiously enough,' Butler added sharply, as though a new thought had struck him, 'Mr. Lee is a friend of mine. He is a barrister, like myself. He is a man of culture with a sense of humour. But the fact remains, my good Inspector: in the Metropolitan Police area you have no authority to arrest anybody at all.'

'I hae not, eh?' yelled Inspector Duff, his voice reverberating back.

'None whatever!' yelled Butler, amid more echoes.

'We'll see aboot that, ma mannie!—Sergeant Baines?'

'Sir?' snapped a young, new, alert voice.

'Ye're one o' the inefeecient, incompetent Metropolitans, are ye no'?'

'Inef—' Sergeant Baines stopped. 'Yes, sir,' he said flatly.

'Then I'm orderin' ye! Arrest yon mannie on a charge of assaultin' a police-officer in the courrse o' . . .'

'Inspector! Wait!'

'Eh?'

'Don't do it, sir!' urged Sergeant Baines. 'We can't make the charge stick; you ought to know we can't. And that's Pat Butler. What he'll do to you in the magistrates' court . . .'

'I dinna care *wha*' he'll do! He walked oot here, him and the leddy, tae—' Inspector Duff stopped. 'Aye!' he said, more evil-sounding than ever. 'Why did ye come oot here?'

'This brick wall!' As Butler spoke, Hugh saw his arm reach out and slap the wall. 'Hadn't you any ears, Inspector? Madame Feyoum promised first to show me the trick again, and then to show me how it was done.'

'I hae no concern wi—' Again Inspector Duff stopped dead. There was a strange, new, reluctant note in his voice. '*Wha*' trick, did ye say?' he demanded.

'Walking through a brick wall.'

'H'm,' said Inspector Duff, breathing hard.

'But now,' Butler said dejectedly, 'I'll never in my life learn how the thing was done. You've upset her too much.'

Throughout all this, in fact, Cécile had been weeping and sobbing with such effect as to make any man's judgment whirl.

'Eh, noo! Er—madam!' said Inspector Duff.

'No!' cried Cécile, gulping it out powerfully between sobs. 'You are a nasty man and I do not like you. Never, never I show you how it was done!'

And, to Hugh's horror, in her overpowering false emotion she dragged the screen two inches wider open.

'Madam!' the Inspector said with much dignity. 'I wudna upset a leddy. But the skellum Prentice canna escape. It'll no' tak' but a meenut. Before I lose ma mind, suppause ye show us a' how it was done?'

'*Nevair!*' screamed Cécile, with such a gesture that Hugh had to steady the screen or it would have toppled over.

'Madam, I'm no' askin' ye this time. I'm *orderin'* ye!'

Cécile's sobs stopped on a last high, dramatic note. She stepped over so that her body, dark in outline despite its scarlet-and-gold robe, blotted out the aperture.

148

'Very well. I will do thees,' she cried. 'But because Mees-tair Butler ask me and not you. I will go inside thees screen, and close it. I will cry, "Are you ready?" Then I walk through the wall, and open the other screen. Afterwards I take away both screens; and I show you how I do it. But you promise me: you shall not touch the screens until I tell you?'

Hugh could almost hear, if not see, Inspector Duff grit his teeth.

'Aye, I'll gie ye fair play. The rest o' ye! Surround the screen and the cairpet! And I'll bet ye saxpence she canna du it this time!'

Cécile, panting, swept inside the screen and closed it. She gave Hugh only one savage, gleeful look before she knelt down and gave the carpet a sharp, brief rap in the middle at the base of the wall.

And Hugh saw the whole trick in a flash.

The carpet, as she had said, really was unbroken and uncut. Yet, as in most first-class illusions, what seemed to make the trick impossible was what in fact made it easy.

For there was a trap-door under the stage, just beneath the wall. The carpet sagged down, under the middle of the wall, as two invisible wings of the trap-door fell at Cécile's rapping. There would be plenty of room for the illusionist to squirm through underneath, to the shelter of the screen on the other side, and smoothing out the carpet as she went. The trap-door would then invisibly close.

But Cécile, moving with blinding swiftness, did more.

'I give you the word,' she shouted, 'in just three seconds. I cry, "Are you ready?" Is it understood?'

'Yes!' a chorus of voices cried back.

Under cover of this Cécile had whipped out a paper-covered safety-razor blade from the pocket of her dressing-gown. The paper vanished; it was back into her pocket. With the sharp blade, just under the covering two-foot thickness of the wall, she ripped a straight line down and across the carpet.

149

'Feet first!' She did not speak; it was only a mouthing. 'Down!'

Before he knew what he was doing, still half-staggered by the simplicity of the illusion, Hugh had acted.

He lay down and writhed forward. His legs, his body, slipped with a jerk and scrape through the long, expanding cut. It caught his face as he fell.

He had heard that stage cellars are deep, and braced himself for a long drop. Instead he was caught, and sent sprawling backwards with a jerk up his thighs, by a thick supported mattress less than eight feet below the stage.

'Are you ready!' he heard Cécile cry.

The flame of a pocket-lighter sprang up. It disclosed the face of Johnny, the call-boy, standing ready on the mattress. Instantly, with a lithe expert twist but with somewhat regrettable lack of modesty, Cécile dropped down through the cut beside Hugh.

'John-ee!' she hissed. 'You are a bad boy again, but never mind. Queek! I hold you up!'

Catching him under the arms, she held him up. Carrying the lighter in one hand he jerked the edges of the carpet together in a smooth join. Then, handing the lighter down to Hugh, who had stood up, Johnny raised and closed the wings of the trap-door. Softly he shot a heavy bolt, completing a smooth floor.

Cécile, from the mattress on the trestle-table, ran lightly down a flight of wooden steps to the stone floor. The cellar was in fact very high, a bitter and musty cold. There was no illumination except the flame of Johnny's lighter, as he and Hugh stumbled down to join Cécile.

Cécile's eyes were wide open and glistening with delight.

'You see?' she demanded. 'The cut in the carpet is along under the wall. They cannot even see it, or know it is there, unless they knock the whole wall down. And they will not do that. They will theenk . . .'

What they thought was almost immediately made plain.

By some curious effect of acoustics, footsteps and voices rang down hollowly but with an unusual clarity.

'Inspector!' called somebody they could not identify. 'Isn't she taking a long time to walk through that wall?'

'Aye, that she is! Pu' awa' the screen on yer ain side!'

The screen was not only pulled; it was yanked. They heard the wooden frame bang and rattle as it fell.

'Inspector, she didn't walk through the wall! She's not on this side!'

'I see, I see! Pu' awa' the ither, currse ye!'

Bang went the second screen, falling and flying wide.

'Goddelmighty,' someone else shouted, 'the woman's disappeared.'

Cécile threw back her shoulders in lusty, unconquerable mirth.

'Ha, ha, ha,' she carolled. 'Ha, ha, ha.'

'Sh-h-h!' it was now Hugh's turn to hiss, as he clamped a hand over her mouth. 'If we can hear them, can't they hear us?'

'Not so well, no.' Cécile quietened down nevertheless.

'And shouldn't you have walked through the bricks after all? You'll have Inspector Duff ready for a strait-jacket!'

'That is why I do it,' Cécile said sharply. 'I do not like heem. But never mind. After I have take you out to the street, I go back. I do de very dramatic appearing act when I fly down from the ceiling and land on de Inspector's shoulders.'

'Oh, God!'

'You do not like thees?'

'Yes, yes; it's admirable! But how can I get out of here, even if I'm in the cellar? They've got all the entrances taped.'

'Haah!' said the pleased Cécile. 'That is what they imagine, because I have hear him call out a list. But no, no, no! There is a stage door. Inside the stage door they see stairs to de cellar. *Bon!* They theenk that is only way out . . .'

'And isn't it?'

'Ah, bah! Wit' a beeg show like thees, 'ow you imagine they get all the heavy props in and out? On the same side as the stage door, only a hundred feet away from it, there is double-doors and a ramp to the street. But people do not theenk of anything but de stage door. John-ee! Light the *briquet* so I do not stumble. Come!'

Hugh's nightmare journey through those cellars, where the face of a mummy rose suddenly, stared out at him, and a skeleton vibrated inside a vanishing cabinet, was at least a short one.

Johnny's lighter had gone out again. A more intense cold, with a draught round their ankles, gave him some indication of where they were. Softly Cécile drew the bolts, top and bottom, on double-doors. She peered out briefly.

'You see?' she asked. 'There is nobody outside. I can' help you any more. But you turn to the left, away from the stage door, and run. Yes?'

Agitation, emotion, weariness, all the events of that wild night, rose up in Hugh's throat and choked him.

'Cécile,' he said, 'I don't know how to thank you. I can't.'

'Ah, bah! I am your French mommy. That is enough, yes?'

Hugh acted instinctively; he seized her and kissed her hard. Cécile returned the kiss in a way which nobody could have called maternal; but presently she patted his cheek and pushed him away.

'Now you go,' she insisted. 'I do not mind what you do, but it is *brr*-cold and I have practically no clothes on. But you thank me again, yes, maybe?'

And she was gone, the doors closing quietly.

Hugh turned, racing on tiptoe up the stone ramp towards the foggy street—and stopped as though he had bumped into Cécile's brick wall.

In the middle of the ramp, staring at him with grey eyes so wide open in amazement that Hugh could see them by a smeared-out street-lamp, stood Pam de Saxe.

How she had got there, or by what other miracle she had been conjured into the wrong place, Hugh did not know and did not stop to think.

'Pam!' he whispered, racing up to take her hand. 'Pam, that didn't mean anything! It was only—'

'Sh-h!' hissed Pam, as everybody else had been doing. 'I hev a taxi, with the motah running, just up he-ah. Don't go

152

to the stage doah. Theah is a detective theah who ... Run!'

Softly they ran. The taxi was there at the curb, its door open. Pam dived inside (rather unsteadily, Hugh thought), and Hugh followed her after one glance at the stage door down on his right.

It was too far away in the fog, but against bright lights he had an impression of a man in a bowler hat craning around to look.

'Hoy!' shouted the impression of a bowler-hat. 'Who's there? Who's in that car? Stop!'

The cab-door slammed. The driver, evidently well-bribed, ground into gear and shot away blindly into the fog. Whether he heard the police whistles behind him, Hugh couldn't tell.

Pam, with Hugh's overcoat and hat across her lap, was sitting bolt upright with tears in her eyes.

'Well, re-olly!' she said. 'How many squick-hic women do you want? And must *oll* of them have no clothes on?'

Round her, not unpleasantly, hovered in angelic cloud a strong aroma of brandy. Suddenly he remembered that long list of wines she had ordered at the Buckingham Hotel, ending with Armagnac brandy and instructions to bring the bottle.

'Pam, are you tight?'

'Oh, how ohful!' breathed Pam, reeling slightly back with her hand pressed to her breast. 'How *mean* to think I should get myself squick *tight*!'

Then her mood changed. She rose up, moved over, sat down in Hugh's lap, and nestled her head against his shoulder.

'Nevah mind, dahling!' she murmured. 'I know those women can't help it. *I* can't.'

Curiously enough, Hugh did not mind her presence there. On the contrary, he found it much more than pleasurable when he put his arms round her.

'Pam, listen! Where are we going?'

'Only home, dahling. To my house. Theah's nobody theah, not even servants. You see ... you see ...'

'Pam!'

Pam had done much that night; but so had the brandy. She nestled trustingly against him. Her eyelids closed. And, with a sigh like the rustle of an angel's wing, she passed out cold in Hugh's arms—as the taxi clanged and plunged towards the house of Lord Saxemund, alias Father Bill.

Chapter 14

HUGH PRENTICE opened his eyes.

In the first second his thoughts scattered and ran wildly into blind corners, as they always do when we wake up in unfamiliar surroundings.

He was in a large and luxurious, if somewhat heavily and loweringly furnished, bedroom he had never seen before. He was in bed, alone. An experimental move told him he wore someone else's pyjamas; though much too short in arms and legs, and far too narrow across the shoulders, they were so capacious round the waist that it had been necessary to tie the cord in a tight knot.

Automatically, as when he was in his own flat at home, his right hand flopped out towards the bedside table for his wrist-watch.

There was a bedside-table there, right enough. But his arm struck a low projection with a line of push-buttons. Somewhere vaguely in the direction of the ceiling, out of sight, there was a whir and whush. Music, allegedly soft, smote out in full blast. It was joined by a heavy baritone voice:

> *Duh-rink to me o-h-nly with thine ey-eyes,*
> *And I will pled-dge with mine!*
> *Or leave a kiss . . .*

Galvanized, Hugh sat up.

He stabbed at all the buttons, finding the right one at last. With another whir and dying whush, the voice was strangled. Hugh remembered everything.

He was in somebody's bedroom at the house of Lord Saxemund in Park Lane. His wrist-watch lay on the table where he had left it. Though the heavy curtains were not completely drawn together on the windows, little could be told about the time because heavy fog darkened the panes and seeped in through one half-opened window.

Hugh looked at his wrist-watch. Incredulous, he then held it to his ear; but it was still ticking. In utter exhaustion after last night's weird happenings, he had slept the clock nearly round. It was half-past one in the afternoon.

'Pam!' he said aloud. 'Helen! Butler!'

He swung his legs out of bed. Then he sat to reconsider, and fit into place what had happened after his hasty departure from the Oxford Theatre.

Most of us, at least in youth, have had the experience of conveying home someone's drunken daughter. It is not a pleasant experience. You face at least one irate parent, and usually two. Your reception is either freezingly cold, or outdoes any shouting melodrama ever played at the late Adelphi Theatre. Whatever their views, papa and mama are united on one point: you have plied an innocent girl with strong waters for the most sinister purpose, to take advantage of her.

And, since we are being frank and telling the truth, it must be confessed that in many cases they are perfectly correct.

On the other hand, there are also many times when the innocent girl needs no encouragement whatever.

Quite to the contrary, despite the tears or prayers or curses of her escort, she sloshes it down until she reaches a state when nobody would think of taking advantage of her, or could derive any of the necessary co-operation if he did.

Such, it appeared, had been the state of Pam de Saxe when the taxi, in fog and cold, stopped before Lord Saxemund's home. It was one of those houses which grimly have resisted the flow of modern atrocities into Park Lane. Yellowish, thick and narrow-looking though obviously large, with a heavy three-sided window-projection on the right, it was reached by a long flight of stone steps up to the front door.

Not a light showed anywhere. Hugh breathed more freely.

Lightly carrying Pam in her mink coat, as well as his own overcoat, hat, and her handbag, he slipped open the door of the cab and stepped down. A very friendly taxi-driver, breathing awe, slid out of his seat on the other side and hurried round to lend aid.

'Got 'er key, governor?'

'No. But it's bound to be in her handbag. Mind opening the bag and having a look?'

'Not a bit. Ah! Got it!' the taxi-driver said hoarsely. 'Only key in the bag, bar car-keys. You carry 'er up the steps, sir. I'll open the door.'

'Right. Thanks.'

'Cor!' muttered the driver, shaking his head as they mounted. 'They do carry on, don't they?'

'What do you mean, they do carry on?' Hugh snarled at him.

And here it is necessary, in the interests of truth, to destroy another illusion of fiction.

When a girl in a story becomes blind to the world and passes out, the man escorting her is always pictured as being revolted and a little disgusted. It is never clear why this should be so, unless the man is so priggish an ass that he himself has never been too tight to navigate a staircase unassisted.

It was certainly not so with Hugh, who didn't mind at all. On the contrary, as he carried Pam tightly, he felt even an added tenderness.

Helen, it flashed through his mind, was much too clear-headed and sensible ever to let herself get whiffled under such circumstances. The thought was illogical; it filled him with horror; but there it was. Despite the thousand questions he wanted to ask Pam, about Helen and herself and what had happened after he and Butler left the Buckingham Hotel, even this seemed unimportant. The taxi-driver's question infuriated him.

'What do you mean, they do carry on?' he snarled. 'What's the matter with it, anyway!'

' 'Ere! Governor! No offence!'

Recoiling, the driver hastily put the key into the lock, turned it, and opened the door. Dropping the key into the bag, he closed the bag and handed it back to Hugh.

157

'That all?'

'Yes. I can manage now, thanks. Er—I'm sorry I spoke as I did. You see . . .'

'Gorn!' grinned the driver. 'I said no offence.'

Hugh fished in his pocket and handed over a banknote. 'Will that cover the fare?'

'Yes, *sir!* Thanking *you*, sir. Good night; good luck.'

Hugh kicked the heavy door shut behind himself. Silence, darkness, warmth. No more.

That immense three-sided projection, at the front, could mean only a room near the front door. Hugh blundered along the right-hand wall, found a door ajar, and pushed it open with his foot.

Faint foggy light from the street, through undrawn curtains, disclosed a six-sided room with an easy-chair near the door. Hugh carefully deposited Pam in the easy chair. He groped back to the door for a light. Finding what his fingers told him were four switches, he pressed down the topmost one—and leaped backwards as though the beam of a policeman's lantern had rested full on him.

It was Hugh's first experience with the gramophone-gadgets secreted in every room in this infernal house.

From the region of the ceiling there was a whish and a whoosh. The loud strains of the 'Merry Widow Waltz' smote his ears. Before he could shut off the diabolical contraption, from a switch hidden by the telephone on the desk, he had listened to 'Always', 'Falling in Love Again', and so spirited a rendition of 'Boys of the Old Brigade', that the combined bands of the Brigade of Guards seemed fiendishly hidden behind panelled walls.

The switch clicked loudly on a smashing cymbal-clang. The music choked and went dead. Hugh, panting, leaned against the desk. Then he hastened to draw all the heavy curtains.

True, it was the sort of music Hugh himself liked. Sitting by his radio at home late at night, with the radio turned down while he read Boswell or a noble detective novel, he would have enjoyed it. He did not enjoy it when it seemed

158

likely to rouse the curiosity of every policeman from here to the Marble Arch.

Or perhaps, he reflected, the music was not really loud. It sounded so only to his over-twitching nerves. He tried to picture the weird mentality (Lord Saxemund's, no doubt) which had set it here for the delectation of himself or his friends. He couldn't even picture Father Bill's face.

'Well!' he said aloud.

Then he set about carrying Pam upstairs.

This time, carrying her clumsily with a box of matches in one hand and a match ready in the other, he touched no electric apparatus. In his present state of mind, he would as soon have messed about with a switch in the death-house at Sing-Sing.

Upstairs, where it was also dark and heavily carpeted, there seemed to be about a dozen bedrooms. The sixth or seventh was plainly a woman's; and, instinct told him, it was probably Pam's.

He put her gently down on the bed. He removed her fur coat, not without difficulty, and also her shoes. Then, as she lay on her back, he drew up over her a quilted coverlet, folded at the foot of the bed.

Afterwards, striking still another match, he looked down at her.

On the bedside-table was a small lamp, with a white button in its white base. Hugh studied this.

'That thing,' he said to himself, 'is a lamp. Quite conceivably, should I press the button, I shall be greeted by a choir singing, "Lead, Kindly Light". But, when I pick it up, a white cord leads down to a baseboard-plug and nothing more. Let's risk it.'

He did. Only the lamp went on. As he tiptoed towards the half-open door at another side of the room, he could not have said what prompted him. Yet he wanted to see Pam's face without that mask of make-up.

Subtle, ghostly, heart-stirring are the watches of the night. While Hugh was dampening and squeezing out a face-cloth in the adjoining bathroom Pam's motionless figure stirred.

159

One eyelid quivered too, and slightly opened. A grey eye, misty and loving yet deeply puzzled, wandered in the direction of the adjoining room. Yet Pam again lay motionless, breathing gently and with eyes closed, when Hugh returned with the face-cloth.

So as not to wake her, he softly drew the cloth over her face. It was a little more difficult than he had imagined. Afterwards . . .

By the Lord, how attractive she was without that raddling of cosmetics! Framed in now-tumbled yellow hair, her face was delicate of feature but with a faint natural colour which needed little addition. Her eyebrows were arched. Long dark eyelashes lay on her cheeks. Her wide pink mouth called for no smearing of lipstick.

'Damn you,' Hugh addressed himself, almost aloud, 'what are you doing this for? What's the idea?'

He flung away the face-cloth. But, just as he turned to go, he could not resist lifting one of Pam's delicate hands and pressing his lips to it.

For a terrible second he thought he had awakened her. She suddenly stirred and twisted in sleep. She muttered something inaudible. A tear trickled down from one eyelid and ran across her cheek.

Alarmed, Hugh quickly switched off the bedside-lamp. He went softly out of the room. With the box of matches again in his hand, he groped his way to the head of the stairs. After he had picked up his hat and coat from the six-sided study, he must be out into the night again.

Half-way down the stairs, quite unexpectedly, he reeled and only kept himself from falling by seizing the banisters on his left.

That was an idiotic thing to do, missing his step in the dark! No: wait. Now he knew. He was over-tired: less from exertion than because he had swallowed no food since a sketchy lunch in the middle of the day.

Wait again! With servants and family away only for a few days, since the central heating still worked, there ought to be food in the larder.

160

And that prompted still another thought. Why not spend the night here?

After all, where else could he go? Those he had thought closest to him had chucked him out, denied him. Uncle Charles was preparing to turn him over to the bogeys. He might wake up some friend and get a shake-down; but, in decency, you can't involve a business-friend when you are on the run from the police.

'Why not stay here?' he asked the darkness aloud.

Knowing that loneliness which only an outcast can feel, he grew restless in turn. Blundering to the foot of the stairs, he found his way to the back of the house and to the kitchen. Here he snapped on electric switches, defying musical reply; and, of course, this time he got none.

The house, built in the middle of the last century, had a big and solid kitchen. Its original owners had solid Victorian notions: two iron bars were shot across the back door against burglars. Otherwise the kitchen had been redecorated in a surgical dazzle of white tile and white enamel.

He yanked the handle of a tall refrigerator. He was met by no lusty chorus, about the joys of eating, for the constant delectation of the cook. He found only an electric light, showing him cold chicken, cold ham, cold tongue, butter, and milk.

Other white enamel surfaces opened to disclose bread and cutlery, dishes and glasses. After ten or fifteen minutes' voracious eating, off a white-enamel table-top, a sense of soothing well-being stole into him. Now he wanted only something to drink and something to smoke. To his astonishment he remembered that he, normally a heavy smoker, had not touched the packet of cigarettes in his pocket since late afternoon.

To get some whisky necessitated a raid into a big dining-room, hung with curious tapestries and filled with strange furniture. Plainly it showed the taste of Father Bill, who had bought the gloves of the Scots Queen and stolen or borrowed the gloves of Charles the First.

But Hugh needed no reminder of leering enemies. When

F   161

he lifted the whisky-decanter from an elaborate silver holder on the sideboard, the holder tinkled out a series of Highland airs which brought Inspector Duff's image bellowing through the tapestries.

It was only a musical-box. He let it play while he poured out a very stiff whisky, added soda, and stifled 'Loch Lomond' by replacing the decanter. In the kitchen again, under a white-faced, loud-ticking clock indicating twenty minutes past one, he slowly drank the whisky while he smoked two cigarettes.

Afterwards, with weariness spinning in his brain once more, he turned off the lights, crept back up the stairs—and received another shock.

Somewhere from the direction of Pam's room, he could have sworn he saw a light flash on and quickly off again.

Hugh stood still in the upper passage. He rubbed his eyes. Presently he decided it had been an illusion, like some of his other illusions. At the back of the passage, on the left, he found what was clearly a man's room.

There were pyjamas, of a short but too capacious kind, in the chest-of-drawers. Hastily undressing and climbing into the inadequate pyjamas, Hugh sat down on the edge of the bed and made his plan as he wound his wrist-watch.

'Now it's all right,' he told himself firmly. 'I can set a mental clock in my head that'll wake me at six, before anyone can be about. And I can slip out without being noticed. I can . . .'

And that was how it happened.

That was how Hugh, starting awake after what seemed only a brief interval, set in motion another infernal singing-contraption, choked it off, seized his watch, and found himself again sitting on the edge of the bed holding a wrist-watch which still said it was half-past one in the afternoon.

He sat up straight and listened. There was no sound in the house.

Despite his panic, he was immensely refreshed. He felt ready to face any bogey on earth. A cold breeze stirred from

162

the half-open window, despite the faint warmth of central heating.

His clothes, slung across a chair, were still there. At his feet lay a pair of felt-lined slippers which, though they were not the right size, he could at least wear. Across the bedroom a door stood open to a sybaritic bathroom.

'Now it's all right!' he declared to himself, aloud again. 'I've got to hurry like the devil, but it's still all right! Pam probably isn't even awake yet. I can nip out of here very quickly. But I'm not going without a bath and a shave.'

He fitted on the slippers and strode into the bathroom.

The bathroom, rather regrettably, was of black marble and green tile. Facing him, in a long and broad recess, was the outer black-marble side of the tub. From here to the ceiling the tub was cut off by a wall of glass with a glass door, having a silvered handle, at the right-hand side.

Hugh saw the idea, though he did not altogether approve. High in the right-hand wall of the recess was the mouth of a shower-bath. Lower at the top of the tub, on the left, were a series of complicated taps.

'H'm,' said Hugh.

He kicked off the slippers and climbed out of the pyjamas. He opened the glass door, stepped inside the glass wall which cut off the recess, and closed the door. There, standing in the black marble tub itself, he warily considered the taps.

More than one guest in a strange house, he had discovered, has tried to turn on the bath and instead has got the stinging drive of a cold shower across the back of his neck. Besides, he must remember Lord Saxemund's passion for putting gadgets in the wrong places.

A quick shower would be best, he decided. Wherever were the taps for turning it on, they were presumably where they ought not to be.

Just over the middle of the tub, in the green-tile wall, his eye caught two small and inconspicuous black buttons. Triumphantly he pressed the left-hand button.

There was a whirr. There was a whush. Then, joyously bursting out in this enclosed space:

> *Oh, Mademoiselle from Armentieres, parlez-vous!*
> *Mademoiselle from Armentieres, parlez-vous!*

This time taken completely off balance, Hugh slipped and almost sat down hard in the tub.

He looked round wildly for the source of the demoniac voice with its full accompaniment, but couldn't see it. The joyous voice, after singing that Mademoiselle from Armentieres had been paid no attentions in forty years (an improbable statement, considering the rest of her recorded history), was warbling 'hindy-dinky-parlez-vous' when in hopeless desperation Hugh jabbed at the right-hand button.

The voice, sounding like a boxer punched repeatedly in the stomach against a ring-post, gasped away into silence.

And Hugh, in sheer elation, rushed at the taps and turned on everything he could see.

A rush of mingled hot-and-cold water from the shower, at exactly the right temperature, smote his shoulder-blades and poured down on him.

This was magnificent. This was superb. Except for his recent experiences, it would have made him want to sing as he increased the water pressure.

Long and carefully he studied an oval cake of soap, lying invitingly in a recess in the green wall. But he must have soap, no matter what sardonic ditty it sang at him.

And there was nothing wrong with the soap, when he snatched it up. Finally, with another lucky stab, he found the cold shower and gritted his teeth under it. Turning off everything by the simple process of turning off everything, he stepped outside the glass wall and closed the door. He was a new man again.

Hastily he dried himself, put on the slippers, and knotted on the pyjama-trousers. The wash-basin and medicine-cabinet, in the same wall as the door, provided luxurious shaving-tackle. He slipped a new blade into the safety-razor. He worked up a fine lather on his face. He was just beginning to draw the blade down the side of his jaw, when he stopped with something of a chill up his back.

Somebody had just opened the outer door of the bedroom.

At first, imagining it might be Pam, he reached down for his pyjama-jacket. But he let the jacket fall. The footsteps which marched into the room—short, hard, stumpy—were clearly those of a man.

There was a silence as the footsteps stopped. Hugh, the razor poised in the air, could only stand motionless facing the shaving-mirror.

Then the footsteps crossed the room.

In the open doorway of the bathroom appeared a short stout man with a red face, who was smoking a cigarette.

He stared at Hugh, his small bulbous eyes growing wider. He took the cigarette out of his mouth. Astonishment momentarily deprived him of his aspirates.

'And 'oo the 'ell,' he asked, 'are *you*?'

Hugh poised himself, making plans as quickly as he could. Turning his head sideways, he surveyed the lathered right side of his face. From the line of the side-hair he drew a long swathe with the razor; then another. He contemplated them. Then he turned round.

'Lord Saxemund, I presume?' he asked.

Chapter 15

Hugh asked this, as well as he could, in what he imagined to be the tone of the late Henry M. Stanley addressing Dr. Livingstone in the wilds of the Congo.

That, the height of *insouciance* in recorded history, struck the right note. For, as well Hugh knew, his position wasn't funny. He was in bad trouble again. Though this man might be short and fat and red-faced, wearing a suit of too-thick brown country tweeds like an india-rubber man, and with a gold watch-chain across his corporation, he was still the formidable and wire-pulling Father Bill.

What Hugh must do (or so he decided) was to imitate his hero, Patrick Butler. He must think, speak, and act as Butler would have done. It may not have been a wise choice, but he made it. The short stout man dropped his cigarette and jumped on it.

'Yes!' he said in a hoarse whisky-voice. 'I'm Saxemund. And I'm asking you,' he added, getting back his aspirates with a jerk, 'just who you are?'

For a moment, as Lord Saxemund surveyed the bathroom, it was not necessary to answer. His fat face went even more red. He did not speak; he raved.

'Sleeping in my bed!' he said. 'Wearing my pyjamas! Using my special shaving-soap! Who's been . . . ? Who's been . . . ?'

Hugh continued to shave.

'You would be more impressive, my good sir,' he said coldly, 'if you did not sound so much like one of the Three Bears.'

The fat man's eyes bulged out of his head.

Then he spoke in a low, hoarse, dangerous voice.

'You'll find out, young man, just which one of the three bears I am. For the last time, who are you?'

Whereupon Hugh lost *his* temper, and with a loud bang.

A few civil words, a faked explanation (which did not involve bringing home Lord Saxemund's daughter as drunk as an owl), and all might yet have been well.

It was the shaving that did it. To a man who is shaving, nothing is more distracting or more infuriating than to have questions fired at him while the razor navigates upside down at the angle of the jaw. It fusses him; it puts him off his stroke; it makes him want to yell.

'I'm a friend of Pat Butler,' Hugh snapped, dipping the razor. 'And he's out to have a show-down with you. You know that, I hope?'

'Butler? *That* wind-bag?'

'Wind-bag, is he? Did you ever know him to make a threat he didn't carry out to the exact letter?'

'Butler! You're scatty! Why, the reason I came back this morning—!'

'But it scares you, doesn't it? So keep your own head shut, Father Bill, before you begin threatening other people.'

There was a brief, hard-breathing pause.

'Who's Father Bill?' asked Lord Saxemund in an even lower voice. 'Who said anything about Father Bill?'

'*I* said it,' answered Hugh, lifting his head and looking him in the eyes. 'Now what do you propose to do about it?'

'You'll find that out too, young fellow, as soon as I get to a 'phone.'

'*Daddy!*' interposed a sharp, reproachful voice in the background.

It was Pam, of course. She stood a few feet back from the door of the bathroom, her chin tilted up.

It would be hard to say what Lord Saxemund was, except that for a second or two he had ceased to be either the irate householder or the sinister string-puller. The gold watch worked part way out of his waistcoat pocket from his breathing. Elder novelists would have made some reference to his ewe-lamb, the pride of his eye.

'Pammie,' he breathed—as revolting a word, Hugh thought, as he had ever heard.

Certainly there was something very different about Pam this morning.

Since she wore mules and not shoes with four-inch heels, she was not even tall. Though her thick fair hair had been carefully brushed, her face bore almost no cosmetics: a faint touch of powder and lipstick, but nothing else except a faintly defiant flush that made her lovely. Hugh could not analyse anything more, until he realized she was wrapped round closely in a thin sheer silk dressing-gown of white figured with blue dragons; nor, as could clearly be seen, was she encumbered with anything else.

'Daddy!' she repeated.

Lord Saxemund only breathed.

'Thet is the man I love,' said Pam. She coloured, and glanced away. 'Not that he cares a farthing for me, as yet; but thet is the man I love.'

Lord Saxemund looked at his daughter, looked at Hugh, and then went crazy.

This is the trouble with having a ewe-lamb. It produces emotional scenes which ordinary mortals cannot credit.

'You was—you were out with him last night, weren't you? Oh, God, that this should happen to me!' screamed Lord Saxemund. 'Your mother and I go away only for a few nights, and I have to come back on business, and ... You was out with him last night, wasn't you?'

'Yes,' Pam said coolly.

Lord Saxemund bounced towards her.

'You reek of brandy!' he snarled. 'No, m'gell, never mind all yer scented soaps and yer fancy mouth-washes. You reek o' brandy!' He glanced back and forth between Pam and Hugh, suddenly noting their costumes. His tone became tragic, almost pleading. 'He plied you with it, didn't he? He made yer drink it? Down yer poor throat he forced glass after glass, the dirty villain? And then he—he—'

'Daddy! This is re-olly the most ...'

Lord Saxemund whirled back to Hugh.

'I'll kill yer,' he declared, almost calmly. 'Ruin my daughter, would yer? Don't care twopence about her, but you'd bring tragedy and disgrace on me own grey 'airs and 'er mother's!'

'And who says I don't care for her?' thundered Hugh, losing his own head.

'I'll—'

'Daddy!' Pam cried sharply, and straightened up. 'Kindleh stop this ohful nonsense at once. Let *me* heah what he said! Didn't he say . . . ?'

'I will strangle you,' said a completely insane Lord Saxemund, 'with my own hands. With my own hands,' he explained, lifting them, 'I will strangle you.'

Hugh, past all control, flung down the razor into the water of the wash-basin.

'Now I'm warning you!' he said. 'Keep off, you tubby little egomaniac! Just keep off!'

'Aoh?' echoed Lord Saxemund, lifting his upper lip in a heavy stage-sneer. 'So 'e wants me ter keep orf, does 'e? And why does 'e want me ter keep orf?'

'Because I don't want to hurt you, and there's no place or room to let you fall soft! But, so help me—!'

'I'll kill yer,' screamed the virtuous father, and leaped at him.

Yes, it was unfortunate.

Yet in fairness it must be emphasized that, as Lord Saxemund sailed through the air, it was his feet and his legs—not his head—which struck the glass wall extending from tub to ceiling.

The thin glass burst and flew to fragments. Lord Saxemund, landing in the tub sideways with his back to them, received not a scratch. Yet, having landed in a seated position, he must have been stunned half-senseless by that powerful jar from the base of the spine to the back of the neck so vulnerable to the hangman. One of his short legs, as he flew, jabbed hard against the left-hand button of two above the tub.

And his arrival was joyously greeted.

Two German officers crossed the Rhine, Parlez-vous!
Two German officers crossed the Rhine, Parlez-vous!
Two German officers crossed the Rhine, to—

Hugh, wearing slippers and caring nothing for smashed glass, opened the unbroken door of the cabinet. With murderous and loving care he reached across his dazed host, and unerringly twisted the tap of the cold shower.

A heavy stream of bright, icy water-needles flew slantwise and downwards across the side of Lord Saxemund's cheek. It spurted upwards, it spurted downwards; it sluiced his face and ran slowly down over his tweed suit.

'That'll cool you off, you old so-and-so,' said Hugh. 'I don't give a hoot whether you're Father Bill or Father Christmas. But, the next time you want to bully one of your mob, try it on somebody who can be impressed by it.'

And he closed the glass door with a bang.

Pam, her thin white robe flying, rushed into the bathroom and stopped appalled.

'Oh, dear,' she murmured.

Even at that wild time it occurred to him that it might somewhat annoy Pam if he pitched her old man through plate glass and turned the cold shower on him. He was amazed at what happened.

Throwing her arms round his neck, she kissed him on the lips and pressed herself against him. Hugh was conscious throughout his whole body of that sensation, no doubt chemical, which is produced by very few women in our lives.

Then she pushed him away.

'Hugh,' she said with rapid practicality, 'go out into the bedroom and wait. It will take only five minutes to smooth him down. It never takes more. And you'll want that time to get dressed. But don't go away; I've made other plans to clear up the rest of your trouble. Hurry, please.'

Was it only illusion? Or did Pam speak in a soft, quick voice entirely free from those grotesqueries or affectations of plum-in-the-mouth speech?

He couldn't be sure. But he hurried out. The door was closed and locked behind him.

Still the gramophone's voice lustily sang even more adventures of the lady from Armentieres; just as well, because Lord Saxemund had begun to rave. The shower was turned off. Hugh, who had finished shaving, wiped off the remaining lather on one of Lord Saxemund's shirts from the chest of drawers. He had just finished dressing, putting his tie in satisfactory order, when the bathroom door opened and closed again.

No; he had been mistaken.

'Dahling,' she said, again with her plum-in-the-mouth speech, 'you do have a passion for throwing people through plate glass. But don't do it to me, please. I don't mind if you knock me about. But not glass; it cuts.'

'Pam, I'm sorry about that. All the same, I owed him something for setting one of his mob on me last night . . .'

'Oh, that?' Pam dismissed it with a wave of her hand. 'Reolly and truly, Daddy didn't know anything about thet, or I should have given him a piece of my mind. People do things in his name; and he simpleh nevah knows. But this,' she nodded towards the bathroom, 'may take a *bit* longah than I imagined. Meanwhile, please go down to the kitchen and eat youah breakfast. It's ohl prepah'ed; I was coming to tell you.'

'Breakfast? Who prepared it?'

'*I* prepah'ed it,' answered Pam, opening her grey eyes wide. 'And I can clean this house bettah and quickah than ouah maids put togethah. Onleh they won't let me.'

Then her tone changed.

'But, dahling, dahling,' she pleaded, '*please* don't leave that kitchen until I come and fetch you. Will you promise me that?'

'I'll promise you anything you like, Pam.'

Again Pam's eyes grew intensely tender. But she was interrupted by noises from the bathroom, suggesting that Lord Saxemund was now smashing everything except the warbling loud speaker. She hurried back.

171

Hugh tramped gloomily downstairs, wondering what was going on in his mind and heart.

In the kitchen, under metal dish-covers and on a hotplate, he found a breakfast so superbly done that he still couldn't believe Pam had cooked it. Few women (or men either for that matter) know how to prepare that most supreme of all combinations: scrambled eggs, bacon, and toast. Here was someone who did know.

He found both coffee and tea. Gulping down the tea in large and satisfying quantities, Hugh lit a cigarette and then jumped to an edge of uneasiness again as his eye fell on the loud-ticking clock.

It was ten minutes past two.

The hunt for him would still be up, harder than ever. Fog, pressing so darkly against the windows that he had been compelled to turn on lights, brought back every image of yesterday.

Why had Pam made him promise to wait in the kitchen? He must get to a 'phone; he must reach Patrick Butler, if the enraged Inspector Duff had not jailed Butler as he more than half threatened.

Hugh crushed out his cigarette. He paced the kitchen. The only telephone he had seen in the house had been in the six-sided room, to the right of the front door, which Lord Saxemund presumably called a study. So far as he could see, it wouldn't matter if he left the kitchen for a minute or two.

The passage through the house was almost dark as it had been the previous night, except for a big leaded pane in the front door. Even this was a little dimmed with white mist. Hugh groped forward. He had nearly reached the door of the six-sided room, this time on his left, when he stopped dead. Up against the oblong glass panel of the front door suddenly reared the silhouette of a head.

There was probably nothing in this. Perhaps Hugh's nerves were not at their best after so many twists and spins of adventure.

Or it may have been, as a hand of that silhouette seemed to grope out for a doorbell, that subconsciously he recognized something familiar in that caller outside the door. He did not, could not, reason why. He knew only that it was vitally important, or seemed so, for him to keep that visitor away from those in the house.

Hugh strode forward. As he passed the door of the six-sided room, he thought he heard Pam's voice speaking softly inside the room—and, too, the voice of another woman who couldn't be there.

Before a bell could be rung he had opened the front door.

The man on the doorstep was hatless; instead of an over-coat he wore only a raincoat with the collar turned up. As he stood below the doorstep he was a foot or more below. The newcomer raised his eyes. When Hugh saw that close-cut black hair, that narrow skull, the dark impassioned eyes, he remembered even as the young man spoke.

'My name is Lake.' The young man shook his head; as though impatient at the huskiness of his voice, he cleared his throat. 'Gerald Lake. I am a solicitor. Lord Saxemund would not know my name, perhaps. But, if it is possible at all, and —and on the off-chance that he might be here, I should like to see him on most urgent business.'

The fog-murk, if possible, was worse than it had been the day before. Hugh could not even see across to Hyde Park on the other side of the street.

But the idealistic, no-nonsense eyes stared up. Too well he remembered the solicitor with offices above Mr. Cotterby's antique-shop, just before that savage fight in the street. Gerald Lake, who had uttered a warning Butler would not heed.

'I . . .' Hugh was beginning in a low voice.

There was no recognition in Lake's own eyes. There could scarcely be, with Hugh standing in the dark doorway. If Lake saw anything at all, he saw only Hugh's clothes. They were the short dark coat and striped trousers of a correct professional man; but also the clothes of an ultra correct manservant.

'Will you come in, sir?' Hugh said in a very low voice.

He still did not know why the devil he was doing this.

173

But he stood back still farther into shadow, holding open the door. Lake nodded and stepped inside. Hugh very quietly closed the door.

'I do not know whether Lord Saxemund is at home.' It seemed not at all strange to be speaking in hardly above a whisper. 'But I will inquire.'

'Thank you,' said Lake. He cleared his throat again.

Hugh, his back turned, walked down to the second door on his left. He hadn't a notion where the door led; it might even be a coat-cupboard. But it led into a dim kind of back drawing-room.

'Wait here, please,' said Hugh, and nodded towards a chair.

He didn't dare turn on any lights or touch any switches; it might produce a wild burst of music which would make him jump out of his skin. But, as Lake nodded and lifted his eyes again, it seemed to him that Lake's eyes held an edge of madness.

Frightened without knowing why, Hugh went out and closed the door.

Whatever else he did, he must find that telephone in the front study. He blundered across the passage, and found the door standing just ajar.

He had completely forgotten he had heard voices speaking in there only a few minutes ago. About to throw the door wide open, he stopped when it was open only a dozen inches or so.

One of the voices was Pam's. Pam, fully dressed in a grey frock, sat with her back to him in a hard, straight chair facing the desk in the window embrasure. The other girl sat in the chair behind the desk, facing Pam. Both were only blurs in the gloom.

'. . . so I phoned and asked to come here,' the second girl was saying in a brittle, rather high voice, 'just what you think you're doing?'

As she said this, she reached out and turned on a flattish lamp with a green shade. Its light sprang across the desk, several feet above the desk, and nowhere else. Pam's silhouette, as she sat rigidly facing the desk with the light outlining the edges of her fair hair, alone could be seen. Very clear was the partly flushed, partly pale face of the girl behind the desk.

'And,' she almost snapped, in a higher voice, 'just what *are* you doing?'

It was Hugh's *fiancée*, or perhaps his ex-*fiancée*, Helen.

Chapter 16

HELEN, clearly, was in one of her sharply sensible moods. Her mouth expressed nothing. Her brown eyes, of a darker colour than the hair, expressed an anger which she clearly showed she could control. She wore her fur coat, and a coloured scarf was bound round her hair against the sombre line of the closed curtains.

'Just between ourselves,' she added, in that clear bound-to-be-fair way, 'I know you're not one-tenth as stupid as you like to pretend.'

Pam said nothing.

'And, also between ourselves,' continued Helen, her voice rising as though she would mentally slap or shake Pam out of immobility, 'I admit you got me out of a horribly embarrassing and—almost indecent position at the hotel last night. Would Hugh or Pat Butler help me out? No! They went racing off to the Oxford Theatre. And not five minutes later the police arrived. The *scandal* there could have been!'

Pam spoke at last.

'Yes. There could have been,' she said without inflection. 'By the way, do you know there's a police-car standing outside this house?'

Clearly Helen hadn't known. She started to get up, her head jerking round towards the windows. But she sat down again. Anger grew more and more bright in her face.

'No,' Helen retorted, 'and I still don't know it. The fog's thick. Maybe I missed it. But I still think . . . what trick are you playing *now*?'

'No trick,' said the motionless and detached Pam. 'Go out and speak to the men in the car, if you don't believe me.'

Helen slapped both her hands flat on the blotter. Fear blossomed up as well as wrath.

'Is that true?'

'Yes.'

'Then they've come to arrest—?'

Pam did not answer. Helen struck the blotter again.

'Tell me, you . . . you overbearing rich-man's daughter!'

'How very silly you are,' said Pam, after a pause. Still, un-cannily, she did not stir or raise her voice. 'But I'll tell you, if you like, what you really came here to ask.'

'And what's that, please?'

'The answer is no,' said Pam. 'I didn't tell Hugh.'

'Tell him what?' cried Helen.

'What you said to the police, to that Scots Inspector, when they got to the hotel after Hugh and Pat had gone.'

Now Pam did raise her voice a little, but not much: it was as though, by an effort more violent than any could guess, she kept that same detachment.

'You said,' she continued, 'you'd been lured into this, and didn't know a thing about it. You said you didn't even know Hugh was wanted by the police; you said he'd given you a false wedding-ring. When you'd discovered something awful was going on, you said,'—here Pam swallowed hard—'you dragged off his wedding-ring and his engagement-ring. They could find the rings outside in the corridor, you said. Which they did. Finally, to prove your good faith, you told the police Hugh had gone to the Oxford Theatre. Then you wept some crocodile tears and left the hotel.'

Throughout all this, Helen's face had remained expression-less.

Her colour might be high, her look a little less soft. But she looked back steadily at Pam, her hands clenched on the blotter.

'You panicked,' said Pam. 'I don't blame you. You really are kind-hearted and good-natured . . .'

'Thank you.'

'Don't drive me too far,' said Pam.

For a second, in just those five words, there was so appal-ling a cold stab that Helen recoiled. Then Pam was quiet again.

'And, when you first heard Hugh's story at Pat's house, you were deeply touched because others wouldn't support

177

him. You thought you could support him, easily. Then, when we got to the hotel . . .'

'Where you,' interposed Helen, with a quick return-stab of a smile, 'made such an exhibition of yourself at the reception-desk?'

'I did, didn't I?'

'Yes.'

'Yes,' agreed Pam, with a kind of hypnotized nod. 'But that wasn't difficult, you see. I've had to play silly all my life, because my father and my mother preferred me to be like that, and wouldn't let me be anything else. So it wasn't difficult, when—'

'When you lost your head over poor old Hugh?' inquired Helen, again smiling and again hitting her hard. 'And behaved entirely like a child? And yet didn't accomplish very much after all? You didn't, did you?'

'No.'

'And you never will, dear. Don't you understand that, now?'

'Yes,' said Pam, and lowered her head. 'But I haven't answered the question you really came here to ask.'

'Question? What question?'

'I didn't tell him you disowned him and gave him away, just as the others did,' said Pam. 'I was tight, sloshing down drinks and trying to think of lies to mislead the police. But I wasn't as tight as that. I haven't told him; I'll never tell him. I want him to think, in all that crowd of bloody snobs round him, there was at least one who'd stand by him to the death. Even if it happened to be you. And yet you . . . you were almost the worst of the lot.'

All the colour drained out of Helen's face. Her eyes seemed to become enormous.

'And shall I tell you,' asked Pam, 'why you found you couldn't stand by him?'

'Really,' said Helen in an unnaturally high voice, 'it's hardly necessary to go into matters that—'

Pam's head whipped up.

'Because you don't love him,' she said with fierce intensity. 'You never have.'

178

'I can only repeat,' cried Helen, with a shrill laugh, 'there are certain matters I don't care to dis—'

'Oh, come off it,' said Pam, exactly as her father would have said the words. 'Do you think *I* didn't know that? As soon as I heard the awful, unnecessary fuss you kicked up with him in the corridor?'

'What fuss? What corridor?'

'In the hotel corridor between the Bridal Suite and the Royal Suite. Oh, don't pretend you don't remember! He was with me in the sitting-room of the Bridal Suite, while I ordered dinner. He remembered you, and ran out into the corridor. He met you there; I heard it. And smile all you like. It may not have been as much of a victory as you think.'

Helen, so furiously angry yet so unnaturally calm, was in fact smiling with a kind of bare and primitive cruelty.

'You pitched into him,' Pam went on remorselessly, 'about me. *Me!* But that wasn't the real reason, and you know it wasn't. You weren't jealous of me; you were far too contemptuous.'

'Perhaps, dear, I still am.'

'Smile! Go on! Because you won't think it's funny for much longer. You tried your tricks once too often—and he saw through you.'

Dead silence.

The smile did vanish. There seemed to exist, in this overheated little room with all emotion packed into that little circle of light at the desk, only these two girls and nothing else in the world.

'Shall *I* tell you what had happened?' asked Pam. 'You'd been talking to Pat Butler in your suite, hadn't you?'

'And if I had?'

'Up to that time,' said Pam, 'you'd thought this adventure was frightfully good sport. All larks, wasn't it? But Pat knew. He loves danger; but he knew just how dangerous and risky it was. You weren't angry at all; you were scared. So you ran out to find Hugh. And to make a scene with him, as you always do: not because you were angry; only because you were scared.'

179

Pam gave her no chance to argue or even reply.

'Don't deny it!' she cried. 'You've always been a little contemptuous of Hugh, haven't you, for being so patient? But you didn't get away with it that time. He saw through you. He told you a few truths; and how true they were! You made a worse scene; you threw the rings away. Not because you loved him, and he'd hurt you; it was because he'd hurt your vanity by telling you the truth. Now tell *me* the truth. You don't really love him, do you?'

The subject of this conversation stricken and tongue-tied, still held the door half open without being able to move.

Hugh wanted to move; long before this, he had wanted to run. And, quite literally, he couldn't.

There are some situations that go far beyond the merely embarrassing. There are times when you can't think what a gentleman does do, or doesn't do, in the matter of eavesdropping, because feelings have flown beyond control.

Pam couldn't see him; her back was turned. Helen couldn't see him; the soft light of the desk-lamp put a glow between her eyes and the door. Hugh, in a humiliation beyond anything he had believed could happen to him, remained where he was.

He had got to the worst, he thought. Beyond Pam's cry, 'You don't really love him, do you?' he believed it couldn't be more awkward.

But he was wrong. The worst had not yet come.

With dazed eyes, as he tried to study Helen's features, he knew Helen must always hold the advantage over Pam when Pam left her heart and soul wide open with a question like that.

'Love him?' Helen repeated. She seemed to consider. One gloved hand moved across the desk-blotter and touched her handbag. 'Well! I think I've told you twice before, dear, that there are matters I don't care to discuss.'

'All right! Then do you *respect* Hugh?'

There was a pause.

The question, in all honesty, had taken Helen completely aback. She looked at Pam. Her lips were half-parted. Then

180

she laughed: more loudly and shrilly than usual, because she was upset, but quite sincerely.

'Well!' she answered with real amusement. 'Respect old Hugh? I really don't know. I'm afraid I hadn't thought about that part of it.'

And Pam screamed at her.

'You fool,' Pam said. 'You empty-headed, insensitive damned *fool*!'

Helen leaped to her feet.

'I've had quite enough of this, thank you,' she said with dignity. 'If you don't mind, I shall just . . .'

Pam also jumped up.

'Oh, no, you won't!' she retorted, advancing a step towards the desk. 'You'll stay where you are. Or I'll slap your silly face off, as I nearly had to do last night. Don't you remember?'

'I—'

'Don't you remember?' Pam insisted. 'When you were lying in the bedroom at the Royal Suite, sobbing and sobbing because your vanity'd been hurt? And the police burst in on both of us? And I had to run across and knock some sense into you, so you could even talk to the police?'

'You're being rather vulgar, aren't you?'

'Of course I'm vulgar. I'll be more vulgar still. If our original scheme had worked when we went to the hotel; if the police hadn't found us; if I'd let you occupy the Bridal Suite with Hugh Prentice (which I didn't intend you should, thanks!)—well! Would you have gone through with it?'

'I don't think I . . . gone through with what?'

'All right! Then I'll use words of one syllable. Would you—'

'Stop! Oh, really! Stop!'

'Well, would you?'

'I don't know,' Helen answered quietly. 'I simply don't know.'

'You wouldn't have,' Pam said just as quietly.

'And that makes you a little contemptuous too, doesn't it?' asked Helen in the same even tone. 'You people with

181

money!' she added, with sudden and passionate envy. 'It doesn't matter to *you. You* can do anything you like.'

Pam began to laugh.

'Have I said anything so very funny?' inquired Helen.

'No. I'm sorry. It's simply, "You can do anything you like." Applied to *me.*'

And Pam, with all the life and fight drained out of her, turned back and sat down again.

'Well, can't you?' demanded Helen. 'Clothes! Furs! Cars! Jewels! Anything and everything you want; anything most of us would give our souls for!' Her voice was going up with each syllable. 'You're saying, or trying to say, I'm—well! that I should have been too cautious to—well! to have an affair with Hugh . . .'

'Oh, no!' said Pam. 'I didn't mean that at all. I meant you were falling hard for Patrick Butler.'

There was another pause.

Then Helen snatched up her handbag from the desk.

'That's not true.' She spoke evenly. 'But, since we're being so frank now, I can tell you it might very well *be* true.'

'Yes. I thought it might.'

'When I first met Pat a long time ago, and heard him in the courtroom,' Helen went on in her clear, ringing voice, 'I wasn't much impressed. But I didn't know him then. Until he kidnapped us all into that car last night, and he talked to me while he took us home, I didn't understand how—how hypnotic he can be. I was attracted even when I fought him; perhaps I fought him *because* I was attracted. He *does* things! He doesn't let anything stand in his way! Hugh's a dear; but Hugh's not like that.'

Once more Pam's head jerked up straight; every muscle in her body seemed to grow tense.

'No!' she said. 'He's not spectacular enough, is he?'

'Spectacular?'

'He doesn't boast about the things he can do. He just grits his teeth and does them.'

'When I came here,' said Helen, now flushed and lovely in the joy of pouring out confession, 'I didn't want to quarrel with you. I never do; with anybody. But you would have it. You wanted to know whether I was in love with Hugh. Very well: the answer is yes. That takes the wind out of your sails, I think?'

It did. Pam started to speak, but looked at the floor instead.

'To be exact,' said Helen, her fingers trembling as she tried to open the catch of her handbag, 'I'm quite as much in love with him as I need to be. If I want to laugh at him, I'll laugh as much and as hard as I please. If I want to keep him guessing, by moods or scenes or anything, I'll do it.'

Here Helen paused, more flushed and lovely than ever.

'I think you honestly don't understand that,' she said, between wonder and contempt. 'You'd hand your whole life over to a man, and on a plate. Wouldn't you?'

Pam nodded without looking up.

'Yes,' she whispered. 'My life. Everything else. On a plate.' And she put her hands over her eyes.

'Then you are the fool,' Helen stated calmly, 'and I can't see how you haven't learned it. Unless you keep a husband where he ought to be, you'll never be free. Oh, I shall weaken! Often! That's my nature. But, in the main, I'll do it.'

Whereupon, drawing a deep breath, Helen for some reason launched out on a matter which upset her worse each time.

'Well, *Lady* Pamela!' she said. You may be the daughter of the Earl of Saxemund. Your father's money may buy you the mink coat you were wearing last night. It may buy you cruises in the Mediterranean. It may buy you most things you're greedy for. But it can't buy this.'

Scrabbling and scrabbling in her handbag, Helen at last found what she had been seeking. She held it up. Pam's gaze instinctively followed, to a tiny circlet which flashed and glittered in the light.

It was the diamond engagement-ring Hugh had given her, the ring which first she and then he had flung away in the hotel corridor.

'If *you* remember,' she cried, 'that police-inspector gave it back to me. I'd intended not to wear it for a while, to punish Hugh a little. But, since it's you who deserve having your face slapped (oh, metaphorically, of course!), I'm going to punish you, young lady, and punish you just as hard as I know how. So I shall put the ring back on my finger. I shall—'

Helen stopped abruptly, her eyes flashing up.

Hugh, with a kind of soundless violence, had pushed the door wide open.

'Hello, Helen,' he said.

His most passionate wish was to shield Pam, to spare Pam any knowledge that he had heard anything. He saw her shoulders grow rigid.

'Sorry, Pam,' he added, in the same casual tone. 'But I stayed so long in that infernal kitchen I couldn't wait any longer to 'phone Pat Butler. I've just come up here to 'phone, if you don't mind.'

And yet all the time, with intensity, his gaze was locked against Helen's across the length of the room. He was daring her to put the ring on her finger.

Helen, quick-witted as ever, saw he was. She stood motionless, the glittering circlet in her right hand poised just above the third finger of the left. The edge of her smile appeared: that mouth, which, for all her soft-looking appearance, showed she could endure not one word of opposition from any man on earth.

Carelessly, slowly, defiantly, she began to lower the ring towards her finger.

Hugh also smiled a little, and the set of his shoulders altered. Helen saw that, too.

If she did as she intended, he had quietly resolved to rip it off her finger if he broke her wrist too. On the desk, at one side, lay a heavy stone paperweight. This would do to smash the ring to flinders; to pound and crush its diamonds, if that were possible; but, at least, to batter the trinket shapeless and destroy even the last breath of its symbolism.

As once before in that room, Helen's face went white.

Her tongue crept out and moistened her lips. Still she stared back at him. Then she lowered her eyes.

She glanced down at the open handbag. As though she were not doing it at all, as though neither ring nor handbag existed, she dropped the ring into the bag and closed its catch with so light a snap it was barely audible.

In another instant she had become the humorous, carefree, laughing girl Hugh thought he had always known.

'Pam and I,' she said with a light laugh, 'have been having a talk about the troubles you and Pat Butler made for us last night. We're seriously annoyed with you both, I can tell you!' Another laugh mitigated this; then Helen grew serious. 'I do hope you get out of your own troubles, Hugh. Now I must be off; and I only hope the police-car outside doesn't catch me.'

She nodded at Hugh. She touched Pam affectionately on the shoulder. A few seconds later she was gone. The door of the six-sided room closed; a pause; then the quiet, decisive closing of the front door.

Pam still sat facing away from him. Hugh went slowly to the middle of the room, trying to clear his throat and finding it difficult.

'Pam,' he said huskily, after a little time.

She had been dabbing furtively at her eyes. Now, with an effort, she sprang up from the chair and faced him with a desperate brightness and gaiety.

'Hullo!' she said brightly. 'You've—you've had your breakfast?'

'Yes, thanks. It was admirable. I . . .'

'And you don't need to ring Pat Butler!' she assured him in a rush. 'I've done that. And he's arranged to . . . to . . . What was I saying? Oh! Daddy! Well, he was in an awful rage. I've got him smoothed down, and more than that. *He's* promised to . . . to . . .'

Pam faltered and stopped.

Hugh hadn't a poker face. He had often wished he had one, but he hadn't. He was looking straight into Pam's eyes; and she could not have mistaken what she saw there.

'Last night,' he said, 'you were only pretending to be knocked out by all that brandy, so you wouldn't have to answer questions about what happened at the hotel. And that was because—'

Oh, God!

He could have bitten his tongue out to recall those words. He had blurted out, by implication, that he knew everything. He saw the reflection of it in Pam's eyes and mouth. Even now, with some quick lie, it might have been possible to cover it up. But his own dogged honesty kept him butting away.

'Yes!' he said. 'Yes, I heard it! But I'm sick to death of lies. I want people to say what they mean, and mean what they say. Pam my dear, what I'm trying to tell you . . .'

'You heard what *I* said? Everything?'

'Yes! But what does it matter?'

Now, to his horror and astonishment, Pam was retreating from him. He was confused. He couldn't understand how it had come about, but he loved her and he wanted to tell her so.

But she was retreating as though in half a panic. She stumbled against the back of the chair in which she had been sitting. She almost fell. She retreated round the desk, where Helen had been before. There was a swivel-chair in the niche. Seeming almost to crumple up, Pam sat down in it, swung it away from him and faced the curtains.

'Go away,' she whispered.

'*Pam!*'

'Please go away,' she said in a low, shaky voice.

Well, that was that.

Hugh turned round. In an idle, dazed kind of way he observed that someone's overcoat and bowler hat had been left lying across an easy-chair to the right of the door. Hullo! They were his own overcoat and hat. He had left them there last night when . . .

Feeling in his right hip-pocket, he found the bulge of a pair of gloves. They were squashed nearly flat; the right glove would have dried bloodstains on it; but they remained usable as gloves.

186

He put on the overcoat and the hat. Drawing out and shaking the gloves, he fitted them on his hands. He opened the door, leaving it carefully half-way open. He walked to the front door, opened it, went out into the mist, and closed it behind him.

In the six-sided room there was a sudden stir and a heart-cry from Pam.

'Hugh! Where are you going?'

He did not hear it, because he had closed the door. He went down the stone steps to the pavement, and peered round him.

The car was drawn up discreetly a little way down to the left. The mist was heavy, but he would have recognized it even without the glowing yellow letter, *police*, like the illuminated sign at the top of a free taxi.

Hugh walked straight up to the car and addressed the driver.

'I presume,' he said, 'you're looking for me?'

The two men in the front seat, one of whom was trying to read a newspaper by the glow of the dashboard instruments, looked a little startled. But there was another man in the car: a thick-set, heavy-featured figure who leaned forward from the back seat.

'Aye!' grunted a familiar voice. 'And that we are, tu!'

In an abstracted kind of way Hugh realized he had never before seen Inspector Duff's face. He saw it now.

'Well, gentlemen,' said Hugh, 'the fun's over and the game's finished. I'm giving myself up, if you don't mind. Move over, Inspector.'

Chapter 17

MOVING comparatively fast in the lamp-starred murk, the police-car circled the island at Marble Arch, moved east along Oxford Street, crossed Oxford Circus, and had nearly reached the intersection at Tottenham Court Road.

And still nobody had spoken a word.

Hugh, his arms folded, sat plunged in such gloomy and near-suicidal thoughts that silence wrapped him only in balm. Being taken up by the police, as a contrast to the behaviour of Pam, now seemed to him a matter so trifling as to be not even worth consideration.

At first, it occurred to him vaguely, this was an odd route if they were taking him to Scotland Yard. Ah, but they weren't! They would be taking him to the City, of course: to the lair of Inspector Duff.

And, if this happened to be some kind of 'silent treatment', Hugh gloated and tightened his teeth. He loved it.

But Inspector Duff did not appear to be happy. Once or twice his rather Cromwellian face, with a bowler hat pulled down nearly to his ears, turned sideways for a quick, sharp glance at his captive. Once (the single exception to the dead silence should be noted) Inspector Duff leaned forward and, to the empty air, malevolently said, 'Hoots!'

However, since this seemed to be merely an outlet for his feelings, neither of the two uniformed men in the front seat commented or turned round.

But Inspector Duff could not contain himself. The car crossed Tottenham Court Road, into New Oxford Street, making for High Holborn and the City. Inspector Duff turned to Hugh.

'Hoots!' he said again. 'I'm wonderin', Mr. Prentice, what ye'd be thinkin' about.'

'You are, eh?'

'Aye. I am.'

'You really want to know what I'm thinking about?'

'Aye.'

Hugh tightened his folded arms. He glared ahead and uttered one word.

'Women,' he said.

This roused the sudden interest, even approval, of the uniformed men. But Inspector Duff was scandalized.

'Weemen?' he exclaimed. Then, with reflection, he swallowed in silent fury. 'Ah! Ye'd be thinkin, nae doobt, o' yon godless hussy at the Oxford Theatre? Wha' dropped down on ma neck out o' nowhere, after she'd deesappeared under ma ain eyes? And her wearin' nae mair breeks than a babe unborn? And d'ye ken what was done by certain incompetent ne'er-do-weels, callin' 'emselves Metropolitan Police, when she landit on ma neck?'

'No.'

'They laughed,' said Inspector Duff, as though describing some darker abomination of the Black Mass. 'They *laughed*.'

Hugh twitched his head round.

'Inspector,' he snarled, 'are you a married man?'

'Aye.'

'Then do you understand your own wife? Do you understand any damn' woman you ever met?'

The uniformed policeman sitting offside front, with a gleam on his flat cap, suddenly turned round and extended his hand to Hugh. Hugh shook it. The man turned back and folded *his* arms.

Inspector Duff's face assumed a look more than definitely sinister.

'Meestair Prentice! This is no time tae be thinkin' aboot the sins o' the flesh!'

'And who's thinking about the sins of the flesh? Only you, apparently. Your mind—'

'Meester Prentice!' choked Inspector Duff, hammering his fist on the back of the dividing seat. 'My patience is a thing o' the past. Ye'd best be quiet and pray. Ye've much, much to answer for.'

189

Hugh, with the image of Pam even more vivid before him, was in no mood to be badgered by any mere police officer.

'Now what, exactly, have I to answer for?' he asked. 'Before you tell me, remember I'm a lawyer too. What have I to answer for?'

'Ye hae constantly avoided and obstructed officers of the law who were tryin' tae question ye—'

'Any person, with no previous criminal record and no current charge laid against him, is entitled by law to avoid questioning by police authorities as long as he can. This principle was laid down in the case of Rex v. Walker, 1811, and upheld by Lord Chief Justice Ellenborough. Anything else?'

'At a certain antique-shop in the deestrict of Seven Dials . . .'

'At a certain antique-shop in Seven Dials,' Hugh interposed smoothly, 'two hoodlums, each armed with a deadly weapon, knocked each other out in a fight. No doubt you have a witness to this, in the person of the shop's proprietor, a Mr. Cotterby?—Yes; I see you have. Anything else?'

Inspector Duff looked back at him.

'Eh, ma Goad!' the Inspector said almost quietly. 'Ye're near as bad as Patrick Bu'ler himsel'!'

'Of whom, I believe, you have the very lowest opinion?'

Even in angry preoccupation Hugh was surprised that Inspector Duff hesitated, scratched his chin, and seemed to be pondering. At length he delivered judgment.

'Mr. Bu'ler,' he stated, weighing his words, 'is no' a God-fearin' man. His mo'ives, in escortin' hame last night yon sinful French hussy wha' wore nae breeks, wouldna stand scrutiny and are open tae the deepest suspeeceon. Forbye! It may be that sometimes (not always, mind, but *sometimes*) Mr. Bu'ler is a mon o' judgment and even guid sense.'

'*What?*'

'Aye.'

Hugh had to look at him twice. He could not have been more amazed if Inspector Duff had rolled down the window,

190

stuck his head out, and uttered a loud wolf-whistle at some young lady passing by.

'But, hang it, Inspector, you've been saying . . . !'

Smoothly the car drew up at a left-hand kerb and stopped.

Instead of uttering any phantom whistle, Inspector Duff opened the offside door, stepped outside, looked sternly at Hugh, and pointed to the pavement.

'Oot,' he said briefly.

The culprit, who had been paying no attention to where they were going, peered out and then stared round.

They were in Lincoln's Inn Fields. Not only in Lincoln's Inn Fields, but just outside the steps leading up to the door of number 13, on whose top floor were the offices of Prentice, Prentice, & Vaughan. That was where Hugh felt, with unexpected dread, that the whole affair might be entering a new and deadly turn.

'Inspector, what's the game?'

'*Oot!*' the other repeated sternly.

'But what is all this? Why are you bringing me here?'

'Look, sir,' the driver of the car interposed rather apologetically. 'This may not be as bad as you think. You see—'

'I'll hae silence,' roared Inspector Duff, who was now in his own domain and swelled like a figure in an allegory. 'I'll hae silence as deep and dark as the blessit braes of Inverary at midnight. *Oot.*'

Hugh, lifting his shoulders, stepped out. Inspector Duff's flight of fancy might almost have described Lincoln's Inn Fields. There was thicker fog than yesterday; in addition, it seemed to be growing dark.

Inspector Duff led the way up the front steps. The echoing foyer, the lift-cage without any lift visible, the tile-floored stairs down which Hugh had clattered yesterday afternoon, were still dimly lighted and deserted.

Now Hugh trudged upstairs, with Inspector Duff behind him, until they reached the top floor. In the left-hand wall were the closed double-doors leading to the offices of Prentice, Prentice, & Vaughan.

'In,' said Inspector Duff, pointing.

'Now look here!' said Hugh. 'You haven't cautioned me. I take it there's still no charge and I'm not under arrest?'

'Ye may take it so.'

'Then what in blazes . . . ?'

'*In*,' the other repeated sternly, and pointed again.

Hugh opened the right-hand door, instinctively removing his hat as he stepped inside—and then jerked back as though he had been struck in the face.

He had expected the offices to be as dark, as empty, even as eerie as they had been yesterday afternoon. And yet, like a transformation-scene, all the lights were on and at least many of the rooms seemed occupied. It might have been a normal, quiet, busy working-day.

The broad central corridor, with its conservative frayed carpet, was well if murkily illumined because of fog-wisps. As he looked down its length, he could see that a light burned under the closed door of his own office. Side by side with it, the door of Jim's office was partly open; there was a light in there, too.

A faint but steady ticking of typewriters issued from behind a door down on the left. Nearer at hand, from the cubby-hole beyond the ladies' and the gents', teacups rattled against the side of a small gas-range.

It was true that the biggest and most impressive office, his Uncle Charles's, half-way down on the right and overlooking the Fields, appeared empty. Then Hugh glanced at the waiting-room, immediately to your left as you entered.

In that bleak little place sat Cécile Feyoum; and beside her, smoking a cigarette with a languid man-of-the-world air, was the call-boy named Johnny. Hugh swung round towards Inspector Duff, who pushed him into the corridor, followed him, and closed the doors.

Tick, tick, tick-tick went the murmur of the typewriters. From the cubby-hole where tea was prepared issued a loud pop and then a hiss as somebody lit the gas-range the wrong way, and then had to turn it off for a second. The sweet voice of Miss Ogden, Jim's secretary, cursed softly.

192

Hugh spoke in an instinctive whisper.

'There are three of 'em still missing,' he said, 'but the rest seem to have had a simultaneous recovery from 'flu like a lot of dead people.'

'Aye,' agreed Inspector Duff, and pointed ahead. 'Doon!' he said.

'What the hell do you mean, doon? What's—?'

'Go doon ta your ain office; open the door; and walk in.'

'And what happens then?'

'That, ma lad, ye'll discover for yersel'.'

'Do you go with me?'

'Oh, I dinna think so,' replied Inspector Duff with massive carelessness. Without a further word he marched into the waiting-room.

Cécile uttered her ha-ha burst of mirth, winked at Hugh, and then became overnaturally solemn under the eye of Inspector Duff. Dressed in a leopard-skin coat over a scarlet frock, her dark hair framed in an Oriental sunburst of a hat, she was perhaps a little conspicuous for London. Johnny eyed the Inspector and then blew a smoke-ring.

Hugh walked slowly down the corridor, trying to shake away illusions.

At the same moment the door of his office opened and closed briskly. Down the corridor marched Miss Prunella Watts, his own secretary, with a bundle of paper files over her arm.

Miss Watts, though not perhaps the handsomest of girls, had always been pleasant, always sympathetic; and sometimes referred to her own deep sensibilities. Now her mouth dropped open. She clutched the paper files as though about to scream.

'Mr. Hugh!' she said at length, in little above a whisper.

'Forgive me, Miss Watts, but is there anything strange about me? You *have* seen me before, I take it?'

Miss Watts, as they say, couldn't cope. She gave a nervous little ha-ha, like Cécile in diminutive, and bolted into the secretaries' room as though she had seen a ghost.

Hugh, striding towards his own door, saw the partly open

door of Jim Vaughan's office. He hesitated there, and opened the door wide.

Jim, seated behind his own desk, was addressing someone hidden by the opening of the door. On the right of Jim's desk, in a chair fully in Hugh's sight, sat his sister, Monica.

'. . . and so, according to what Monica tells me—' Jim was saying to the invisible person. Jim glanced sideways.

Jim was always irreproachably dressed when Monica was there to oversee the matter. Seen in profile, the dark-haired Monica seemed to have a brow and nose like a knife-edge; seen full-face, she was merely a good-looking, not ill-natured girl in her late twenties, but with a gloss of clothes about her and a mouth as prim as it had been when, as a child, she gave make-believe parties and compelled her friends to adopt names out of Debrett or Burke's peerage.

Jim's sandy eyebrows went up over the bright blue eyes. He had started to his feet with instinctive friendliness.

'Good God!' he exclaimed warmly. 'Hugh, old son! What on earth . . . ?'

He was moving round the desk when Monica looked at him, and he stopped.

'Jim, please remember yourself. If you have any clients, your secretary can send in their names.'

Hugh looked at Monica for a moment, and then closed the door.

He took a step sideways, opened the door to his own office, went inside, and closed it with a soft snap. He hung up hat and overcoat, thrusting the gloves into one pocket.

A roaring fire again burned in the fireplace beyond the black leather sofa. At Hugh's desk, his bulky back turned to the door and his thin, brittle, grey-white hair like spun glass in the glow of the desk-lamp, sat Mr. Charles Grandison Prentice.

Uncle Charles was going through a small pile of documents. Every drawer in Hugh's desk stood wide open; so did every drawer in the greenish-metal filing-cabinet between the two windows on the right.

Every paper file preserved by Hugh, every letter he had

kept, every paper he held sacrosanct, had been dragged out. Some had been torn up and thrown in the waste-paper basket. Most, it is true, were stacked high in neat piles on desk or filing-cabinet or sofa. But there can be business-letters of a human personal value; these were in the waste-paper basket, like the armful of detective novels from the lowest drawer of the filing-cabinet, and these had been discarded in the waste-paper basket with the same disdain. Uncle Charles did not turn round. His voice, when not addressing clients, was always faintly superior or faintly unpleasant.

'I was not aware, Miss Watts, that I had rung for you.'

'No,' snapped Hugh. 'And nobody rang for me, either. But I'm here.'

It never seemed possible to surprise Uncle Charles, in the sense of upsetting or disconcerting him. He swung slowly round in his swivel-chair. His heavy jowl had again pushed its lower lip well above the upper. His eyelids drooped.

But his expression showed only a sort of weary patience.

'You again?' he asked.

'At least, I see, you recognize me this time.'

Uncles Charles ignored this. He was utterly calm.

'You seem—ah—again to have escaped the police. But, if you hope to find sanctuary here, I fear you are mistaken.' Uncle Charles's hand slid out towards the 'phone.

'Thinking of ringing the police?'

'Of course. What else?'

'Only that it's not necessary. Inspector Duff is in the waiting-room now. There's a police-car outside the building. You've only to shout.'

'Oh, then you have been brought here under arrest?'

'No,' Hugh answered clearly. 'Something I can't explain tells me that I shall never be under arrest. Meanwhile, haven't you rather a cheek to pry into my papers and take everything out of my desk?'

'I hardly think so. Since you are no longer a member of this firm; since automatically you will be struck off the register—'

Uncle Charles's bulky figure conveyed the effect of a shrug

without going so far as actually to indulge in the gesture of one. Even while he touched the white gardenia in his button-hole, his heavy-lidded eyes made an unexpected, weary effort.

'For many years, Hugh,' he said, 'I have tried to understand you. And I can't. I can only conclude you are too much like your late father.'

Crack went a coal on the gushing fire. Flame flared up. Hugh took a step forward.

Uncle Charles held up a cool hand.

'Please understand,' he said, 'that I make no remark against your father. He was my elder brother. He was a barrister; and, many have held, a brilliant one.'

Here Uncle Charles could not quite keep the sneer out of his voice. Another coal cracked in the fire.

'*But,*' pursued Uncle Charles, 'he had almost as little sense of his social obligations as yourself. He drank heavily; can you deny it? He was addicted to loose women; can you deny that? He lost his clients. It required my utmost efforts to keep the matter from becoming a public scandal.'

'Now listen to me, said Hugh, in a thick unsteady voice. 'You were going on to say my father had no respect for money?'

'None whatever. Can you deny that?'

'This business,' Hugh swept his hand round, 'was two hundred years old; it was dying. He set *you* up in it. He financed you. He propped up your weak knees when you were young and needed it.'

'And when,' inquired Uncle Charles, his upper lip sticking up still further, 'have I ever denied that? Or failed in my obligations to his children?'

A serene, fishy expression of virtue held Uncle Charles indomitable.

'No, no, no, Hugh. It really will not do.'

'What won't do? If I wrung your bloody neck, as you deserve—!'

'And if you did, what would it gain you? Come; this is stupid. You are a romantic, like your father. You are quixotic,

196

like your father. He would not see the world as it really is.'

'If you're saying—!'

'I speak the truth,' Uncle Charles said gently. 'And it is often painful. But what did it gain him? You, I believe, always admired your father. Had you possessed more self-confidence as a boy, you would have disobeyed my orders and become a barrister as he was. But others, I regret, did not share your view of him. Your mother left him. He died, quite unmourned, at the early age of fifty-two. Ask your own sister, even now, what she thinks of him. I shall not prompt her, Hugh. Simply ask her.'

Hugh could not meet his eyes. He turned away. He saw a waste-paper basket piled high with bright-jacketed novels; it seemed to be all he saw.

'Do you deny this, Hugh?'

'He was the best man I ever knew!'

Uncle Charles sighed.

'I have no doubt you think so. That is the pity. You will not treat or see the world as it is. You have chosen to go your own way ...'

'I've no complaints to make, thank you!'

'With an arrest for murder imminent? Come,' sneered Uncle Charles, 'don't talk foolishness!' He controlled himself. 'Let me make myself clear. You have chosen to make your friends on the grounds of whether you liked them, rather than the more intelligent grounds of whether they could be useful to you. You have refused invitations; you have avoided polite society. Indeed, I have even heard you laugh at those customs, nowadays called "social contacts"—'

'I only said, as I say again—!'

'Kindly do not interrupt me, my dear boy. What is the result of all this? You have disgraced the firm worse than ever your father disgraced his own profession.'

'I've been a fool, if you want to call it that.'

Up went Uncle Charles's eyebrows, though the heavy lids scarcely moved.

'A fool?' he repeated. 'Well! That is perhaps one term.

197

But what is the result? You have chosen to flout every convention and everyone (including myself) who might have given you assistance. A little influence here, a little pressure there; and much might have been done for you in a path you must walk alone. There is not a soul on earth who will help you.'

'*Now isn't there, by God!*' said a new voice.

The door opened and closed softly.

And Patrick Butler, carrying a brief-case and girded for war, towered up against the doorway.

He did not speak these words loudly, you understand. He spoke with deadly quiet and affability; as when he had cornered a witness and was about to administer the stroke of less than mercy. Evidently he had been there for some time. He wore no hat or overcoat; his fashionable dark-blue suit, with grey tie and white collar, had a kind of grim gloss in the old office.

'You must forgive me, my dear fellow,' he continued, slapping Hugh affectionately across the shoulders, 'if I didn't 'phone you this morning. But I have been about your business all day. And with satisfactory results, I think.'

Uncle Charles's expression did not change, except that it grew a little more superior. His jowls seemed to grow thicker as he eyed his visitor up and down.

'Now what are you doing here, sir?' he asked. 'I was not aware I had invited you to my office. Be good enough to leave at once.'

Butler took a step forward. His voice changed.

'The back of me hand to ye, ye sanctimonious old divvle!' he snarled vulgarly. 'I'm here to settle the score.'

Chapter 18

In leisurely fashion Charles Grandison Prentice drew out a leather cigar-case. From this he took a cigar. Piercing it with a silver instrument at the end of his watch-chain, he then calmly put back both piercer and case.

'If you refuse to go, Mr. Butler,' he went on, raising his eyes again, 'it will be necessary to summon the porter and have you put into the street. Let us see.'

Butler was again all smiles and urbanity.

'Indeed,' he agreed, 'let us see.'

Uncle Charles reached out and pressed the buzzer on Hugh's desk.

Butler, still more urbane, tossed his brief-case into a chair and strolled towards the desk.

'Now, *I*,' he remarked, 'carry evidence with which I propose to send you to prison. Will you listen to it here, among ourselves, or will you listen to it in the presence of a police-officer?'

Raising his eyebrows in cool contempt, Uncle Charles again pressed the buzzer and struck a match for his cigar.

Butler nodded. Turning back, he went to the door and threw it wide open.

'*Detective-Inspector Duff!*' he bellowed down the corridor.

Hugh, in whirling despair and with no notion of what could be happening, saw the whole length of that familiar corridor with its doors on either side. The grim face and bowler hat of Inspector Duff appeared from round the side of the waiting-room door, far down on what was now Hugh's right.

'*Aye?*' he yelled back.

'*Will you come here, please?*'

Uncle Charles, in the act of putting the match to his cigar, blew it out.

'One moment!' he said sharply.

Butler bowed and turned back to the corridor.

'*The old bastard,*' he shouted down its length, '*prefers to have you wait for a time. Right?*'

Inspector Duff nodded and withdrew his head.

The ticking of typewriters abruptly ceased. Miss Ogden, distantly emerging from the cubby-hole with a tray of tea-cups, skidded so badly that the cups slopped over badly and she had difficulty in holding the tray. Back she dived into the cubby-hole.

Uncle Charles's stomach was moving in and out like a frog's.

'These words are actionable, sir,' he snapped.

'I was quite aware of it,' suavely agreed Butler, without closing the door. 'When I have finished with you, my man, we shall see whether you care to take action.'

He faced Uncles Charles, his head up and back. Automatically his left hand went up to hold the lapel of a black silk gown, just as though he were in a courtroom.

'You are acquainted, I think, with a Madame Cécile Feyoum?'

'I have met her, as you know,' snapped Uncle Charles.

'You have met her. Very well.'

In the paralysis which held that whole suite of offices, it had taken Miss Prunella Watts, Hugh's secretary, this much time to steady her legs and answer the summons of the twice-pressed buzzer. As she appeared in the doorway now, Butler greeted her with a smile of compelling charm.

'Ah, now, me dear,' he said, and chucked her under the chin, ''tis envious I am of any man with so pretty a secretary as yourself. Would you be doing me the great favour, now, of asking Madame Feyoum (she's in the waiting-room, me dear) to join us here?'

He chucked her under the chin again.

Miss Watts went scarlet. She has since told her friends that this was from indignation and outrage. Anyway, she tossed her head and said she would.

'That's me girl!' beamed Butler, closing the door. He turned back to Uncle Charles.

200

'And now, sir,' he continued. 'Last night your nephew and I interviewed Madame Cécile in her dressing-room after you had gone. She doesn't much like you, as her behaviour showed. That's true, is it not?'

Uncle Charles, having struck another match and got his cigar lighted, spoke with soft malice.

'I am no authority, Mr. Butler, on the likes or dislikes of French prostitutes. Perhaps you are?'

Butler smiled.

'You flatter me,' he said. 'However, call her a prostitute again and I shall have even less mercy than I had intended.' His voice changed. 'She is an honest and straightforward woman. She does not enjoy telling lies. Her statement to us, in the main, was quite true. But she did (under compulsion!) tell us one untruth.'

Butler swung towards Hugh.

'My dear Hugh!' he said, with a kind of friendly ferocity. 'She was answering your questions when she told the untruth. Her eyes shifted as she said it; her eyes shifted, and she spoke next as though defying you. Didn't you notice it?'

'Yes!' Hugh exclaimed. 'I noticed it, right enough. But I couldn't see what application it could have. It was when she said—'

'One moment,' Butler interposed softly.

There was a quiet tapping at the door. Miss Watts opened it to admit Cécile, after which Miss Watts closed the door hastily.

At the beginning, it was plain, Cécile had been badly frightened despite her brave show of leopard-skin coat and scarlet frock and Oriental hat. But now, seeing Butler and Hugh together, she took heart. And there was more.

Butler, like a good tactician, merely waited. It was Charles Grandison Prentice, removing the cigar from his mouth, who made an error.

'Let me warn you, my good woman,' he said in his throaty, superior voice, 'you are in the presence of a solicitor. You had better be careful.'

Cécile stopped. Her coat moved in and out at the breast

with her hard breathing; her dusky face lit up, like her intense black-brown eyes, with a physical sweat and glow of wrath; and her dark-painted lips were drawn back from her teeth.

'By damn!' she whispered.

'Quite so,' smiled Butler. 'And you know, don't you, that no harm can come to you while young Prentice and I are here?'

'By damn, I do!'

'Then you have only to sit down,' said Butler, indicating a leather chair facing Uncle Charles, 'and answer me a few questions as you did (hem!) somewhat later last night.'

Hugh, also smiling, led her to the chair. After sitting down, arranging her skirt and coat while Hugh sat down on the arm of the chair, she gripped his hand in both of hers. Her eyes searched his face.

'I am your French mommy, yes?' she demanded, with passionate anxiety. 'I am all right?'

'You're very much all right, Cécile. Just pay attention to Mr. Butler.'

'Cécile,' said Butler, with a scornful gesture towards Uncle Charles, 'did you ever see that man before?'

'But I have already tell you!'

'No!' Butler's voice chopped like a cleaver. 'This must be done exactly in accordance with the rules of evidence.—Did you ever see that man before?'

'*Mais oui!* Yes! Once!'

'When and where?'

'At the Oxford Theatre. Last night!'

'Was this before or after the arrival of the police there to question you?'

'But I have tell you both,' she glanced between Butler and Hugh, 'the same thing last night! It was before the police get there.'

'How long before, please?'

'I don' know! Not exactly, that is. He—'

'Try to give a rough estimate. Five minutes? Ten? Fifteen? What?'

'Fifteen minutes, I theenk. About that.'

'Fifteen minutes. I see. What did he say to you?'

Cécile was catching fire from Butler's manner. The barrister's every gesture, every inflection, so conjured up the courtroom atmosphere that the woman thrilled to it, responded to it, enjoyed herself as hugely as the smiling Butler himself. Her brown-black eyes were gleaming as she leaned forward in excitement. She flung back the answers as quickly as he snapped out the questions.

'He has say,' she replied, 'his name is Mees-tair Charles Pren-tees, of Pren-tees, Prentees, and Von. He say he is oh, so distress!' she acted it out, shuddering on the words, 'to hear from the police on the 'phone that my poor 'usband, Abu, has been stab with a Moorish dagger in his nephew's office.'

'One moment, please. A Moorish dagger, I think you said?'

'I . . .'

'Please speak up, madame. Don't be afraid. Did he describe this dagger?'

'No! He only say a good client of theirs, who live at Casablanca in French Morocco, has sent it as a present to thees firm.'

'And what did you say to all this?'

'I say, "Oh, God!" That is what I feel, to hear poor Abu is dead.'

Butler studied her. Her head was up, her mouth trembling a little, but her eyes as steady as ever.

'With your permission, madame, we shall revert to another aspect of the matter. Had your husband told you anything of his dealings with Prentice, Prentice, and Vaughan?'

'Yes!'

'What had he told you?'

'Abu say he has met a member of thees firm, a beeg partner—'

'A big partner, perhaps a senior partner?' Butler interposed swiftly. 'You are quite sure of that?'

'Yes! That is what Abu say!'

'Continue, if you please.'

203

'Well! Abu say thees member of the firm has persuade him to invest six thousand pounds in a beeg, secret investment called Angli-Ameri-Iraqui Oil. Abu has given him a cheque, and he has receive the shares.'

'Have you these alleged shares now?'

'Yes. They is in my handbag!'

'We shall produce them presently, as exhibit number one. In the meantime, will you tell us what happened to your husband then?'

'Abu has discovered (I don' know how!) there is no such company as Angli-Ameri-Iraqui Oil. He find out thees man has swindle him!'

'I see. Now did you tell all this last night to Mr. Charles Grandison Prentice?' Butler pointed inexorably. 'That man there?'

'Yes!'

'Indeed? And what did he say?'

'Him?' Cécile's voice rose on a high, almost hysterical note. 'He has become all smarmy and goozy wit' me. The maddened woman acted this too, with much shoulder-lifting and drooping of eyelids. 'He take my hand and say no, no, no. He say I must not tell thees to the police. No, no, no! He say I must tell the police that the person who swindle Abu is not a member of the firm at all. He say I must tell them the swindler is a impostor which has only im-per-sonate somebody in thees firm.'

'And that is what you did tell the police?'

'Yes!' Cécile made a helpless gesture. 'This is why I act so fonny with you and my French son afterwards. I can' help it.'

'Then what you told the police was a lie?'

'*Grand Dieu*, what am I to do?' cried Cécile. Tears menaced the mascara of her eyelashes. 'I 'ave no way out!' She stabbed her finger towards Uncle Charles. 'That man has threatened me...'

'Ah?' The syllable struck across like an arrow. 'He threatened you, then?'

'Yes!'

204

'Will you please tell his lor—hem! will you tell us how he threatened you?'

Cécile let her hands fall flat in her lap. But her head was raised proudly.

'Me, I am French,' she announced. 'But I was born in Morocco. About my first husband I tell you and you,' she touched Hugh's knee, 'last night. He is a burglar they call *Le Renard*, the Fox. I love him. Pah! You men cannot understand how much I love him! Often I help him escape. Until they shoot him at Nice, and for a long time I think it is not good to live at all.

'But that man,' she pointed at Uncle Charles, 'say he know all about me, from the client who live in Morocco. He say Interpol, which is the international police, they are still looking for me to put me in prison for I help my husband. He say, unless I tell the police 'ere what he wish, then he will tell Interpol and they will put me in prison even now.'

Butler, head back, left hand on the left lapel of his coat, contemplated her gently.

'And if I were to tell you, madame, that Interpol has no charge whatever against you?'

The woman opened her mouth, but did not speak.

'I do tell you that, Madame Feyoum, with all my heart. There is an English office of Interpol, just off the Information Room at New Scotland Yard. An hour there this morning, by courtesy of Mr. Lee; and I learned what I tell you now.'

Cécile's face and mouth began to work. Butler gave her no time. Out went his hand again.

'But that man threatened you?' he asked.

'Yes!'

'Was there any other witness to this threat?'

(Quietly, over and over, he was hammering the word 'threat'.)

'Yes. It is a call-boy which is named John-nee. He is outside the door; I do not think the fat sneerer know he is there; but he hear it.'

'Would you be willing, madame, to swear to all this in the witness-box?'

'If you ask it, yes.'

'Are you familiar, madame, with the full meaning of the English term generally known as blackmail?'

Cécile hesitated. 'It mean you ask money from somebody, yes? If the money is not paid, then you tip the beans and say something bad about him?'

'No!' said Butler with sharp clearness. 'That is the general belief. But blackmail has a wider application.'

'*Pardon?*'

'Should any person use illegal threats to force any other person into making a prejudicial statement, especially a false statement,' and Butler folded his arms, 'he is even guiltier than though he has asked for money. Blackmail is a felony, madame; it entails a long term of penal servitude. I will see that your sneerer serves every year he deserves.'

Whereupon Butler, bowing slightly, stepped back and swept out his arm.

'That is all,' he said politely. 'Mr. Charles Prentice may cross-examine.'

Uncles Charles would not cross-examine.

It was another of those knockout blows, shattering and paralysing, for which 'that damned Irishman' was famous.

Long ago Uncle Charles had ceased to be superior. With a shaky hand he had put down his cigar on the edge of an ash-tray. Even his beautifully cut morning-coat, with gardenia, seemed to sag as though it covered a laundry-bag. His swivel-chair creaked as he tried and tried to stand up. But he couldn't stand up.

'Butler!' he said. His throaty voice sought several levels. 'You're joking!' he cried. 'You don't *mean* this? You wouldn't really do it?'

'Ho!' said Butler with uninhibited joy. 'Wouldn't I?'

Hugh sprang up from the arm of Cécile's chair.

'Here, stop a bit!' he protested. 'I never meant . . . I never wanted . . .'

Butler stalked over and gripped Hugh by both shoulders.

'My dear fellow,' he said quietly, 'I promised you that damned old fraud would regret having said he didn't know you and didn't want to know you. I promised you that, I think?'

'Yes; but—!'

'You see the game, don't you?' Butler asked gently. 'He's disliked you since you were a boy. You wouldn't conform; you wouldn't fit into his mean little pattern. To give him his due, he wouldn't have let you hang for murder; he'd have arranged a matter of manslaughter or even self-defence. But that was the farthest he'd go. He didn't mind a murder here, if you committed it; in his mind you're flighty, unstable, quite unworthy of him. But a swindle, in a firm like this? That *would* bring the whole firm down to ruin. He knew he couldn't hope to fasten a swindle on you; but he could do it with the murder. Or thought he could. Listen! When Abu first walked in here, by your own testimony, didn't Abu ask to see *the* Mr. Prentice?'

Hugh put his hands to his head.

'Yes! Yes, come to think of it, he did!'

'And now what could that have meant, if ye please, except the senior partner?'

'I—'

'By Cécile's testimony last night,' Butler nodded at the half-paralysed woman, 'Abu wrote a letter to him several days ago. Ah, bedad! And didn't he know all about it?'

For the first time Hugh Prentice understood that Patrick Butler's friendship could be as overpowering as his enmity.

'Don't worry, me bhoy!' Butler continued, slapping him on the shoulder. 'He'll get everything that's coming to him.'

'But I don't want that!'

'Don't want . . . Can ye deny ye hate his guts?'

'No!' Hugh yelled back. 'I don't deny I hate his guts. But I don't want to see him in jail. If he swindled Abu,' Hugh swallowed, 'well—maybe he needed the money, or thought he did. Couldn't we make some kind of compromise? If you've got to the end of your fireworks . . .'

Butler took a step or two away from him. Butler threw back his head and laughed.

207

'*End* of the fireworks, is it?' he asked. 'Man, man, you haven't even seen the beginning of 'em yet. Pray observe.'

He stalked over to Hugh's desk, where he jabbed and jabbed at the buzzer-button for Hugh's secretary. Deplorable though it is to state, Miss Prunella Watts must have been listening outside the door; it opened with too much celerity for anything else.

Instantly Butler had become all smiles and charm.

'Ah, me dear!' he welcomed her. ''Tis the sight for sore eyes ye are! And is it possible, now, that Lord Saxemund is here?'

'Ye-y-yes, Mr. Butler. He's in the waiting-room now.'

'Then would ye have the extreme kindness, acushla, to go and fetch him here?'

'Y-yes, Mr. Butler!'

The door closed with a scurry.

Lord Saxemund?

Hugh Prentice's soul, silently uttering a deep groan at the prospect of an encounter between the Earl of Saxemund and Patrick Butler in the latter's most devilish mood, also figuratively beat his head against the wall.

Nor was the downward plunge of his spirits lessened by the mood of a wide-eyed Cécile, who kept plucking at his sleeve.

('That man,' whispered Cécile, fiercely nodding at Butler, ''e iss awful. By damn, I tell you! I think my first husband is bad, but *him*? When he has gone home wit' me last night, 'ow long do you think he has keep me up this morning?)

'Sh-h-h!'

('I know; but, by damn! 'Ow long—!')

'For heaven's sake, hush!'

What hair-raising confidences Cécile might have imparted, if Miss Watts had not again hurriedly opened the door, Hugh never knew and never wanted to know.

Lord Saxemund, appearing shorter and tubbier than ever by reason of a pearl-grey overcoat with black lapels, stumped in with an air of belligerency. A soft grey hat increased the

208

effect by being pulled down over one eye. He was again smoking a cigarette.

At his side was Pam.

Pam tried hard to convey the effect that she was not there at all. Her grey eyes, softer and even more beautiful without the slightest make-up on her face, wandered casually round: anywhere except at Hugh. She exhibited the deepest interest in a bookcase. The fireplace seemed to fascinate her. But she did flash a glance at Hugh, and immediately looked away. Hugh, nearly turned to stone, could only stand by Cécile's chair and look at her.

Lord Saxemund stumped forward towards Butler, who stood with his fists on his hips.

Yet nothing, nothing in this whole affair, would ever go as Hugh Prentice expected it to go.

'Well!' growled Lord Saxemund, taking the cigarette out of his mouth. 'Came all the way up from the country this morning, I did, just because you 'phoned. It's to be peace between us, then?'

And, somewhat grudgingly, he extended his hand.

'Peace,' Butler said heartily, and gripped the hand. 'And goodwill and co-operation. If I can do you any favour, I am henceforward at your service.'

'Well!' grunted Lord Saxemund, eyeing one of Butler's waistcoat buttons so as not to look up at his face. 'Don't mind admitting, between ourselves, I'd rather have you on my side than against me. Fees,' and he waved the cigarette impatiently, 'we'll talk about later. You'll not find me tight-fisted. Meantime, as I said on the 'phone, any little favour I can do you . . .'

Here, in his effort not to look straight at Butler, Lord Saxemund's gaze moved to the right. And he saw Hugh.

His button-mouth went wide open. He looked, and looked again.

'Daddy!' Pam cried warningly—but all in vain.

Lord Saxemund was not merely an angry man. He had gone beyond all reason human or divine.

He flung the cigarette on the carpet and stamped on it.

Dragging the neat grey hat off his head, he held it high in the air and then fired it on the floor.

'There's the man,' he screamed, ''oo led my daughter astray. Fed 'er brandy, 'e did, when the pore lamb's never once been allowed anything stronger than lemonade.' Another enormity smote him. 'Slung me,' he shrieked, 'through the glass wall of me own tub. Turned the cold shower on me, too. Oh, God 'elp me!'

'Pam!' cried Hugh, who was nearly as upset as her father.

Pam gave him one look of love; then hastily averted her eyes.

'*Pam!*'

'I'll kill 'im!' yelled Lord Saxemund. And once more he charged.

Hugh, in spite of his state of mind, had no intention of allowing any further occurrences of the sort which had disgraced this morning. As the enraged little peer swung a right fist which a blind man could have dodged, Hugh seized him firmly under both arms and swung him high in the air.

Lord Saxemund's fists and feet flailed the air. His curses blasted the whole suite of offices. Stalking over to another leather chair near the door, Hugh deposited him in it with what he believed to be a more or less gentle thump.

'Come, come!' said Patrick Butler, clucking his tongue as at some mild intrusion. 'My dear fellow, there is an inquiry in progress. This is scarcely the time . . .'

'Oh, be hanged to swindles and who was swindled and who's the head of the firm!' shouted Hugh. ;This is really serious. Pam, come with me.'

And, seizing a not-too-reluctant Pam by the wrist, he flung the door wide open and dragged her out into the corridor.

Chapter 19

In the long and sedate history of Prentice, Prentice, & Vaughan (est. 1749 by Jos. Prentice, Esq.), there had perhaps never been such a scene.

It was not that the staff joined in. From the offices on either side of the long corridor there was only a kind of pressure, a keyboard muffle which indicated that people were peering round doors and then rushing to whisper in corners.

Miss Watts, it is true, was running down the corridor as though for her life. Miss Ogden, essaying another sortie from the cubbyhole with a second tray of teacups, hastily dived back in again. But the uproar came from Hugh's office, where he had left the door wide open and where everybody appeared to be talking at once.

'By damn,' cried the awed voice of Cécile Feyoum, 'but I do not know which of dem is de worst!'

Lord Saxemund, sitting back in the leather chair and crying out, 'Kill! Kill!' like a Zulu war-chief, was choked off only when Butler jabbed his left hand across the man's neck. Whereupon Butler pointed the forefinger of his right hand within a quarter-inch of Lord Saxemund's nose.

'Now listen to me!' roared Butler. 'If you say one more word, so help me, I won't defend Joe the Peterman. Understand?'

Lord Saxemund, though growing purple in the face, still kicked out with both legs.

'If Joe does a stretch, what happens? I'll tell you!' said Butler, 'Big Louie won't have one single man who can screw a pete (hem! I mean, open a safe) worth two whistles and a groan in Tartarus. Finally, all this talk about gallons of brandy and the ruin of your daughter.'

Lord Saxemund ceased to kick.

'Your daughter,' pursued Butler, 'can put down more

brandy, champagne, and assorted drinks than you ever could yourself. She always can; she always will. And what's wrong with Hugh Prentice? He's of better family than any goat you could buy out of the peerage; he works like blazes; he's the only man who ever had the nerve to pitch you through your bathtub-wall without caring who you were. He loves your daughter, and she loves him. If I know anything of his character, his intentions are strictly honourable . . .'

'*Hey?*' demanded Lord Saxemund, his first coherent word.

To add to the wild confusion, the door of Jim Vaughan's office was hurled open. In the aperture appeared the faces of Jim and Monica Prentice.

'Hugh!' Jim called in a heavy stage-whisper. 'What in merry blazes—?'

'Sh-h-h!' hissed Hugh.

Still dragging Pam, he could see no sanctuary except the close double-doors, now on his left, leading to his uncle's office. This, at least, would be empty.

He opened one door, hurried Pam inside, and closed the door with decision.

It was a large office, far less austere than the others. Also it was warm, lighted now only by an immense fire in the big marble fireplace. The light of the flames wavered and glowed in softness over heavy furniture.

Just across from the doors, occupying the middle space of the wall, hung a full-length oil-painting of Jos. Prentice, Esq. (1714–1772). Jos. Prentice wore a powdered wig, a full-skirted brocaded coat, and a repulsive smirk. But just underneath the portrait there was an eighteenth-century sofa. Seating Pam on the sofa as though she were going to have her own portrait painted, he stood over her.

'All right!' he said. 'Now what was the game?'

'Well, reolly!' murmured Pam, tossing her head. 'Of ohl the disgraceful pehfoahmances I have ev-ah witnessed, I do think . . . !'

'Oh, Pam! Drop it!'

'D-rop what?'

'That ridiculous accent. Where on earth did you learn it?'

Silence, while the firelight moved yellow on walls and ceiling.

'I'm s-sorry,' said Pam in her normal voice. 'But that's what they teach you. It's very hard to get rid of it, sometimes. Daddy and Mummy love it; they think it reflects credit on them, and won't let me speak in any other way.' Then her tone changed. 'Why,' she asked passionately, 'did you walk straight out of the house and give yourself up to the police? It was because you thought nothing mattered any longer, wasn't it?'

'Yes.'

'Yes! You thought nothing mattered, because you'd seen through that dreadful woman Helen, and you didn't care about anybody but her . . .'

'WHAT?' shouted the completely staggered Hugh.

'Well, wasn't it?'

'No, no, no!' Hugh dropped on his knees in front of her, and seized Pam's knees. 'Are all women completely insane?'

'W-wasn't it? I know I have no right to ask,' said Pam, lowering her eyes and picking at the brocade surface of the sofa, 'but that's what you did.'

'No, no, no! I was trying to tell you I love you . . .'

'WHAT?' cried Pam in her turn.

'Yes! I was trying to say that. But you backed away as though I had leprosy. You told me twice to go away. Naturally I thought you couldn't bear the sight of me, so . . .'

'O, dear,' cried the distracted Pam, 'are all men completely insane?' Tears glimmered in her eyes. 'Come up here,' she gulped, patting the sofa. 'Sit beside me. Put your arms round me: I mean, if you want to. Tell me what dreadful nonsense all this is.'

'What do you mean, nonsense?' demanded Hugh, jumping up and sitting down beside her. 'That's what you did, wasn't it?'

'Well—that was because you humiliated me.'

'*I?* Humiliated *you?*'

'You heard everything I said. Oh, don't you understand?'

'No, I don't. In all this,' exclaimed Hugh, with a powerful

oratorical gesture, 'there may be some cryptic meaning which escapes my too-earthy mind. At the same time . . .'

'Listen!' begged Pam, with her face against his shoulder. 'Please listen!' She was silent for a moment. 'Ever since I met you, I've made the most shocking advances to you. Because I meant to; because I wanted to.'

'I still don't see—!'

'But I didn't really mind. Because I was wearing a mask.'

'A mask?'

'Yes! My accent! Those weird clothes the people Mummy and Daddy so approve of say are just too-too and *the* thing! The clown's paint of make-up! The affected, silly behaviour Daddy's always insisted on! Don't you see? It was like being at a fancy-dress ball, where nobody can recognize you. You can do as you like, and play the idiot and not care a whoop, because you're wearing a mask. *Now* do you understand?'

'Yes. I think I do.'

'But today, when I had that horrible talk with your Helen . . . !'

'Go on!'

'I was myself,' said Pam, and shuddered. 'I hadn't any mask. I hated myself. Every little hatred, every spitefulness I must have been hiding for years, came pouring out. And then, I discovered, you'd heard it all. I couldn't endure that. That's all.'

There was a pause.

So much humility of soul, in a person whose kindness and good heart and fighting-spirit had never shone so vividly as when she fought the tough Helen to a standstill for someone else's sake, was too much. It brought a lump into Hugh's throat. For a few seconds, in the firelit room, he couldn't see.

Then he put his hands on either side of Pam's cheeks, and raised her head.

'Pam, my dear,' he said gently.

'Yes?'

'It never occurred to you, I suppose, that this same terrible interview showed you as the most lovable woman God ever made?'

'Don't hurt me!' said Pam, and writhed away. 'Please, Hugh, don't hurt me. You needn't do that.'

'Hurt you? My God, do you think I'd do anything in the world to hurt you? I love you too much. And it was at the interview I understood how much I cared about you.'

'You—you mean that?'

'Pam, will you marry me?'

'I . . .'

'Yes,' Hugh muttered, with despondency descending on him like all the world's gloom, 'I know. It's difficult.'

'Difficult? How is it difficult?'

'For you, I mean. There's got to be no nonsense about using your old man's money. You'll have to live on what I earn and nothing else. Would you be willing to do that, my dear? Could you?'

'I'd have you know,' cried Pam, genuinely annoyed for the first time, 'I can keep house as well as any woman in London! My mother taught me when Daddy hadn't twopence to his name. I tried to tell you that. Only Daddy won't let me; he says it's not dignified.'

'Yes, and that's another thing. I've got to fight your father, Pam. I may have to sling him through half a dozen windows. I want you as you are, not as that bloody old fool has tried to make you. Could you stand that?'

'Darling, please, please choose the biggest window at Selfridge's. I'll back you up!'

'But if you don't marry me . . .'

'Won't? Oh, you know I will! How can you be so silly?'

'What I can't understand,' said Hugh, with deeper gloom strangling him, 'is how all this happiness should have come to me. I haven't had it before. I don't deserve it.' A horrible possibility occurred to him. 'It isn't a joke, is it? You really do love me?'

'Do I love you?' sobbed Pam, and stretched out her arms. 'Come here. I'll try to show you a little of how much.'

There was, as they say, an interval.

How long this lasted, while yellow firelight trembled across walls and ceiling and the powdered wig of Jos.

Prentice, Esq., it would be impossible to state. Estimates of time would have to be taken from Hugh or from Pam, whose notions always remained vague. But it was broken by the scandalized voice of a woman, saying:

'*Oh!*'

The scandalized expression, of course, did not come from Pam. It came from Miss Prunella Watts, who stood in the open doorway with the light of the corridor behind her.

'I knocked three times!' Miss Watts cried out, backing away as though from some orgy of Ishtar: which, in fact, the scene rather resembled. 'I knocked *four* times! But I couldn't make you hear.'

Both Pam and Hugh were so angry and so highly unstrung as to nerves that the latter shouted at her.

'And why should you have knocked at all?'

'Well, really, Mr. Hugh! I mean to say!'

'No! I mean . . . that is . . . what is it?'

'I'm s-s-swhick-sorry, Mr. Hugh! But Mr. Butler wants you in your office. Perfectly *dreadful* things are going on there! Please!'

Miss Watts ran. Hugh and Pam, trying to think reasonably and collect their wits, presently decided they had better follow in haste.

'Hugh!' Pam gasped, as they went down the corridor. 'You—you won't speak to Daddy now, will you? About us?'

'As soon as possible, yes.'

'But not *now*, don't you see? If there's any row, Daddy's sure to be in it.'

She was perfectly correct. In Hugh's office, and between Butler and Lord Saxemund as might have been expected, there was progressing a truly memorable schemozzle.

'Oh, you'll do it!' screamed Lord Saxemund, jumping up and down on his own hat. 'I'm employing you, ain't I? And you'll do it! 'Cos why! 'Cos yer must!'

Butler, towering and imperturbable, very slowly surveyed him up and down.

'Little man, little man,' he said, '"must" is not a word that is used to Patrick Butler.'

216

Again Lord Saxemund danced on his hat.

'He's crackers!' yelled the infuriated peer to the whole company in general. 'He's scatty! He's orf his blooming chump! I ask yer!'

'Small and intolerable vermin,' Butler intoned, 'I will take the risks for you. When have I ever done anything but take risks? Should I appear for a friend of yours, it is understood that your name is never to be mentioned or so much as hinted at. As for the moral side,' he snapped his fingers, 'that is purely academic. If possible, I prefer my clients to be guilty.'

'Then wot are yer making all the row about? Wot—'

'There is no man born,' said Butler, 'who lives or has ever lived to give me orders.'

'And 'oo's trying to give yer orders? I only—'

'Ah, that is understood? Very well. Then hand over the cancelled cheque.'

Lord Saxemund's hand went inside the breast-pocket of his suit under the pearl-grey overcoat. Then he hesitated.

'Yes, yes, yes!' said Butler. 'We quite understand you have no connection with the firm in question. It was given to me by Mr. Louis Refton, sometimes called Big Louie. The cancelled cheque, please.'

Lord Saxemund gave over the grey slip of a cheque, attached by a paper-clip to another piece of paper.

And, subtly, the whole atmosphere changed.

Cécile Feyoum, her eyes still wider, sat in the same chair. Uncle Charles was still at the desk; but he had turned his back, elbows on the desk, head in his sagging hands. Jim Vaughan and Monica Prentice had come in; up to this time Jim, lounging against the filing-cabinet, seemed to be hugely enjoying the battle between Butler and Lord Saxemund. Monica, frightened, clung to his arm.

But there was no battle now.

Lord Saxemund, a puzzled and rather uneasy expression on his red face, sat down in the chair where Hugh had deposited him. The fire crackled and popped under the hood of the fireplace, below the tilted mirror.

217

Butler, the cheque in one hand, picked up his brief-case from Lord Saxemund's chair. As Butler glanced out of the open door, it seemed to Hugh—near the door with his arm round Pam—that Butler made some kind of signal. Hugh, looking over his shoulder, saw Inspector Duff at the end of the corridor; and he thought he saw the Inspector nod.

Butler closed the door.

Carrying cheque and brief-case, he sauntered over to the hearth-rug. He stood between the fender round the fire and the leather sofa: his back to the fire and to the tilted mirror. He glanced down briefly at the dried blood stains on fender and hearth-rug. He glanced at the stacks of detective novels piled on the sofa, where he deposited his brief-case.

Then Butler faced them all. It was not only the force of his personality which dominated that room. It was something else too.

Hugh could have sworn that Butler was about to begin, 'May it please your lordship; members of the jury.' But he remembered himself suddenly, his nostrils pinched in, and didn't.

'It seems to have been forgotten,' he said, 'that in this room, almost twenty-four hours ago to the minute, a man was stabbed to death on this sofa in front of me. And no one seems able to say how or why he was killed in an apparently locked room.'

Bong! Smote the note of the clock, distantly across Lincoln's Inn Fields.

Heavy, fog-muffled, the notes quivered across as Hugh had heard them yesterday. Butler waited, watching them, until the clock had struck five.

'To be exact,' he went on, 'it is now precisely twenty-four hours since Abu of Ispahan walked in here through that door.'

If any persons had wished to speak, it was those notes of the clock which held them dumb. In a leisurely way Butler picked up several bright-jacketed detective-novels from the sofa. He dropped most of them, and casually held up one whose title they could not see.

'It is not at all irrelevant,' he said, 'that Mr. Hugh Prentice's hobby should have been the reading of these stories. We've all read them. And very often we have found the same wearisome device.

'A victim, murdered and dying, is just able to speak a few words. He would, of course, speak the name of his murderer. Instead, in some of these stories, he blurts out some weird gibberish which nobody would ever say, and which has been designed by the author merely to baffle detection. Such—it appeared!—was our own problem. The difficulty seemed to be gloves. It was raining gloves. And all because, apparently, Abu of Ispahan had gripped Hugh Prentice's wrist and with his dying breath said, "Your gloves".'

Butler paused.

And Hugh could be quiet no longer.

'But I heard him!' Hugh exclaimed. 'That's what he did say!'

'Oh, no, he didn't,' replied Butler.

There was a little thump as Butler dropped the book on the sofa. Again he addressed the whole group.

'When the problem was first presented to me,' he continued moodily, 'and explained by my young friend Prentice at Scotland Yard, it seemed straightforward and simple. As, in fact, it was: except for the one puzzling point about the gloves.

'Afterwards, and not long afterwards,' Butler scowled, 'there occurred other events which for a short time made me doubt my own judgment. By God! To doubt my own judgment was an act of unparalleled folly.' He made a slight apologetic gesture. 'It was unpardonable. It shall not happen again.

'Upon reflection, before Prentice and I had even gone to Madame Feyoum's dressing-room, I became sure I was right after all. Then, when we were speaking to the lady, the last inspiration was supplied. It dazzled. It explained everything. I learned that, during the whole latter part of Hugh Prentice's conversation with Abu, they had both been speaking French.'

Now it was Cécile who could not remain still.

'French?' she cried out.

Butler regarded her with a slight satiric smile, and bowed.

'Dear madame,' he reminded her, 'you were there. It was in your dressing-room. Most unfortunately, in my excitement, I swept a whole bowl of red and white carnations off your dressing-table.'

'But—French?' protested Cécile. 'What difference does it make what they speak?'

'I shall try to show you. As I have had good occasion to know,' remarked Butler, with his eye on a corner of the ceiling, 'you wear a very dark and vivid shade of lipstick. May I borrow your lipstick, please?'

'My lipstick? What you want with it?'

'Let me have it, if you don't mind!' said Butler, extending his hand and snapping the fingers.

It seemed to take an interminable time before Cécile, fumbling in her handbag and spilling things wide, produced the thick little gold-coloured tube. Even then Butler remained motionless, his hand extended.

Despite her magnificent carriage, Cécile almost stumbled as she went round the desk and gave him the lipstick.

'I still ask,' she insisted, 'why you want it?'

'I want it,' said Butler, 'as a kind of pencil.'

Moving sideways, he partly turned towards the long horizontal mirror above the mantelpiece. Raising his right hand high, he rapidly printed two short words. Out against the mirror, in dark red, the words appeared in block capitals.

VOS GANTS

'And the words *vos gants*, as I scarcely need tell you, Butler said sardonically, 'are elementary French for "your gloves".' He looked at Hugh. 'Pronounce it!'

'What's that?'

'I said pronounce it. Just as you ordinarily would. Pronounce it!'

'Well! The sound, roughly, would be like *voh-gan*. You wouldn't pronounce the "s", of course; there'd be a fairly sharp nasal sound on the *ghan*; and it would sound nearly like one word. That's the best I can do. *Voh-ghan!*'

'Right!' said Butler. 'Your pronunciation is a trifle erratic, but that's the general effect. Now we all know the way in which people who speak mostly French and little English, as Abu did, *will* pronounce English names in the French manner. Even when they speak good English, they still pronounce English names as the French do. Madame Feyoum ! Imagine that you speak little English! And pronounce the name I am going to write on the mirror!'

Again he swung sideways. The lipstick moved rapidly. Underneath the words 'vos gants' there appeared an English surname. Hugh stared at it; then he stared again, because he couldn't believe his eyes.

'Pronounce it!'

'But the French pronounce it just the same as the other!' cried Cécile. 'It is *voh-ghan*, both for "your gloves" and for that name you write. Me, I do not know; I have never seen the name written. But you iss fonny. For that name you make a sound like "Von". But *we* say . . .'

The name which had sprung out in the mirror was VAUGHAN.

And Butler's voice rolled across the room.

'There's your murderer,' he said, pointing. 'The spoiled favourite of this firm, Mr. James Vaughan. And Abu, with his last breath, cried out that name!'

221

Chapter 20

'However, for those who speak no French,' Butler observed dryly, 'let me say it's the merest trifle of all the evidence against him. Under favour, I should like to address a question to Miss Monica Prentice.'

Up went Butler's hand to the left-hand lapel of his coat.

'I would not distress you, Miss Prentice. But is it true, or not true, that your marriage to Mr. James Vaughan has been twice postponed? And postponed because Mr. Vaughan had been playing the horses and had no money?'

For a moment, however, Butler's voice fell as though into a void. It was a void of overstrained nerves, during which people pressed away. Even Pam and her father, who scarcely knew Jim except by name, flinched back.

Uncle Charles whipped up his head. Though his back was still to Hugh, his spun-glass hair shone. Jim Vaughan, whom Hugh had thought his best friend, pressed his stoutening body back against the filing-case. Jim's bright blue eyes wore a glazed and stupid expression; his upper lip was lifted unpleasantly. And the self-reliant Monica, instead of clinging to his arm, had stumbled away and was running towards Hugh.

Three voices spoke out at once.

One was Uncle Charles's: 'Do you consider this legal evidence, Mr. Butler?'

One was Butler's urbane: 'I do, sir.'

The third was Monica's piteous: 'Hugh! Help me! Please help me!'

It flashed through Hugh's mind, across the years, that not since she was fifteen had his sister cried out to him for help, when she was hurt and afraid. He put out his arm; Monica ran behind it, as though for protection from those bigger than herself.

'It's all right, Mon. Don't fret.'

Raised, pitiless, Butler's voice sought her out.

'Credit me, Miss Prentice: to clear away these things now is far less cruel than if you had married that ingratiating and murderous swine writhing against the filing-cabinet. *Is* it true? Was your marriage twice postponed because he had got into trouble over backing the wrong horses?'

'Yes!' snapped Hugh, trying to protect her. 'But how did you know that?'

'You told me.'

'*I* told you.'

'You are probably not aware you told me. Witnesses seldom are, when they are asked to repeat a story several times. But I imagine you had been thinking about it last night?'

It was true. Hugh remembered how, as he plunged away in blind flight from number 13 Lincoln's Inn Fields, his mind had dwelt on Monica's twice-postponed marriage, the reasons for it, and the necessity of concealing all this from Uncle Charles.

'Now I have here,' inexorably Butler caught them all again, 'a cancelled cheque. It is drawn on the lower Regent Street Branch of the Capital and Counties Bank, drawn to the favour of Mr. James Vaughan, and signed by Abu Feyoum for six thousand pounds. Madame Feyoum! Will you identify your husband's signature?'

Cécile, who had remained by the desk staring blankly sideways and up at the mirror, woke up. She glanced at the cheque, and uttered a not-often printed word in French.

'Yes!' she added. 'Yes, yes, yes! That is Abu's writing!'

'Now would you, Mr. Vaughan, care to identify your own endorsement on the back of the cheque?'

Jim screamed back at him in a high-pitched, unnatural voice.

'What the hell do you think you're doing?' He caught himself up. His old, ingratiating smile made his mouth look grotesque as it flickered here. 'Hugh, old son!' he appealed. 'I didn't do this, you know. If you've got any sense of fair play—!'

'I think, Jim, you've made a fool of me long enough.' Hugh

223

felt almost physically, literally sick. But old associations can't be broken like this. 'Still! If there's anything I can do . . .'

'I didn't do it, Hugh! I s-swear I didn't do it!'

'No?' inquired Butler, smashing that thin protest like glass. He detached the cheque from the paper-clip holding it to the other piece of paper. 'The stamp on the cancelled cheque, together with a file-copy of this letter here, show it was paid in to the account of a firm of bookmakers deplorably named Messrs. Joe Jollyboy Ltd., at their principal branch in Oxford Street.

'The accompanying letter-copy from Messrs. Jollyboy signed by Mr. Louis Refton, acknowledges receipt in full for Mr. Vaughan's debts of four thousand five hundred pounds. It begs to enclose Messrs. Jollyboy's cheque for the remainder, fifteen hundred pounds, to be used in his merry career. These, together with the false oil-shares with Mr. Vaughan's name so clumsily signed as one of the directors, are admirable evidence.'

Carefully Butler put down cheque and letter on a pile of detective novels.

'Exhibits number two and three,' he said.

Charles Grandison Prentice tried to pick up his dead cigar from the ash-tray.

But his hand trembled too much. Instead he smote the flat of his hand on the desk-blotter.

'I had imagined, Mr. Butler,' he said with something of his old superior manner, 'you were going to call *me* swindler and confidence man?'

'You?' Up went Butler's eyebrows. 'Oh, come! Your character is not high. You cannot be trusted with the contents of a child's toy bank. But you are too wary to try so clumsy a trick as this. Cheques instead of cash! Names all over the place! Mr. Vaughan disgusts me.'

'Another actionable statement, sir!'

'And again I invite you to take action,' said Butler. Then Uncle Charles jerked back from the most terrifying expression on Butler's face.

'Do you imagine, good sir, that in the Bar mess we know nothing of your history? You have never forgiven that boy's father'—his finger shot out towards Hugh—'for being a far abler man than yourself. It is to your credit that you were fond of the sister. Your *protégé*, Mr. Vaughan, seemed to have all the qualities your nephew lacked. *He* would obey your tongue-lashings. *He* would conform. *He* had the winning manners, the smoothly greased and obsequious tongue. A marriage between your niece and Mr. Vaughan seemed to you ideal. At all costs you would protect it.

'My dear sir, you knew several days ago that James Vaughan had swindled Abu Feyoum for six thousand pounds. You knew it because Abu wrote and told you—'

Uncles Charles lurched blindly to his feet.

'This must stop!' he said.

'Stop?' cried Butler. 'Stop, you say?'

'Insulting . . . insufferable . . . actionable . . .'

'The result,' said Butler, 'was sufficient to keep you at home, with a convenient attack of 'flu and the horrors. Then murder was done. You were compelled to emerge and take action. It was a joy to guard the others and let your nephew fend for himself.' Butler checked himself, and spoke quietly. 'And yet, when the test came, it was the despised nephew who fought for you and would have protected you. God alone knows why.'

Pam put her head on Hugh's shoulder. The latter, crazily embarrassed and unable to look at Monica, wished for a miracle to sink him through the floor.

But there was worse. Lord Saxemund, his red face even redder as he slumped in the chair, unexpectedly swung round and pointed at Hugh.

'He's not bad, that feller!' rasped Lord Saxemund. 'Mind, he sauced me wors'n anybody ever did! He pitched me—ah, never mind. But he's not bad.'

'Stop, you say?' thundered Butler, whom the word seemed to madden. 'Let us see. I will clear up, very briefly, one extraneous matter which all but led me astray. Then I will

H 225

show how Vaughan, and Vaughan alone, could have killed Abu Feyoum.'

Butler leaned forward and pressed the desk-buzzer.

'There was only one person,' he spoke more mildly, 'who knew Hugh Prentice had gone to me; knew we were working together; knew our mutual tastes; even knew we were at my house. That was James Vaughan. The fact was so obvious I wonder it has escaped notice. But . . .'

A frightened Miss Watts opened the door. To Hugh it seemed that another person, some person he could not identify, slipped past out of sight.

'Ah, me dear!' said Butler. 'And would there be a Mr. Gerald Lake in the waiting-room now.'

'Y-yes, Mr. Butler.'

'And would you be kind enough to send him in here, if ye plase?'

'Lake!' Lord Saxemund snorted suddenly. 'Is that—?'

'Have no fear, Father Christmas. He will say nothing incriminating.'

Gerald Lake, when he did enter, seemed unlikely to say anything incriminating. He still wore no hat. His raincoat was buttoned up to his chin. The young man, who last night had seemed so confident and even contemptuous, was now even more hesitant than when Hugh had seen him that morning.

His close-cropped dark hair and narrow face were damp from the fog. He looked ten years older even than he had seemed that morning. His hands, thrust into the pockets of his coat, opened and shut as he cleared his throat.

Butler addressed him with formal courtesy.

'Mr. Lake,' he said, 'let me be the first to apologize. When we met in Mr. Cotterby's antique-shop, I considered you insufferable though you were only being idealistic.'

'Idealistic!' whispered Lake, with intense self-contempt.

'Nevertheless, it is true. You see, I am as much a Conservative as you are . . . otherwise. When you said you hated violence, I did not believe you. When you said it was your duty to advise poor men, I thought it hypocritical. When you

begged us not to go out into the street, I thought that hypocritical too. Political feeling can affect even me. You were
being perfectly honest . . .'

'By taking Big Louie's money?' demanded Lake. His dark
eyes blazed.

'Well, you had done it in the past . . .'

'To help fellow creatures,' said Lake, 'you must have
money from those you hate. You can't help it. You think it
will do no harm to use bad money for good purpose. But
that's the worst fallacy of all.'

'Never mind that. Tell us what happened last night.'

'At about a quarter past eight,' Lake showed his teeth, 'a
man named Big Louie Repton 'phoned me at my office above
the antique-shop. He said he'd a message from a client of
theirs, a good client, who wanted a little favour done. It
wasn't much of a favour, Big Louie said, so it would be all
right.'

'Who was the client?'

'Mr. Vaughan, I think, James Vaughan. I don't know him.'

'Ah! And what was the little favour he wanted?'

'He wanted *you* to be beaten up so badly,' Lake swallowed, 'that you'd be in hospital for a month and couldn't
interest yourself in a murder case you were supposed to be
solving.'

Jim Vaughan, his mouth pulled square, took a jumping
step forward from the filing-cabinet. Butler merely looked at
him. Jim sagged back.

'I see,' said Butler. 'How was this to be done?'

'As far as I could gather, you and a Mr. Prentice and two
ladies were at your house. After a lot of delay, you all started
out in a big car for the Buckingham Hotel . . .'

'Just a moment!' Butler interrupted very sharply. 'This
Vaughan, whom you haven't had the pleasure of meeting,
knew we were at my house. How did he know where we
were going afterwards?'

'I think it was your housekeeper. Vaughan was a close
friend of Mr. Prentice, it seemed; he'd been ringing up all
evening, and you'd been telling him everything. So, when

227

he rang up just as you left the house, she didn't see any harm in telling him that.'

'No, of course not. What did our good Mr. Vaughan suggest?'

'Must I . . . must . . .'

'Gently, Mr. Lake! I shall not keep you much longer!'

'He said, from what I understood, there was only one route you could take. The best thing would be to get you into Mr. Cotterby's shop on the way.'

'How?'

'Historical relics. Anything to do with historical relics! But gloves would be best, it seemed, because for some reason you both had gloves on the brain and couldn't resist them. Big Louie said that was easy. The boss—'

'Steady!' snapped Lord Saxemund.

'*Somebody*,' Lake spoke through stiff jaws, hatred in his eyes, 'owned a collection of such gloves. Big Louie (how strange it is!) is a rich man too, with a house not far from Park Lane and a key to somebody's house in case it were needed. If he put a man in a fast car, especially since you'd drive slowly in the fog, he could get the gloves to the antique-shop before you got there. The trouble was . . .'

'Go on!'

'It might take much longer,' answered Lake, taking his hands out of his pockets, 'to get the boys there for . . . for . . .

'Smashing us up?'

'That's what I heard on the 'phone,' Lake said, ignoring the question. 'I knew at last what I'd let myself in for. I was caught. The thought of violence makes me sick. I was going to warn you, though poor old Cotterby believed I was as bad as any of them.

'But your manner isn't very conciliating, Mr. Butler. When I tried to get you up to my office and keep you there . . . well, there's no need to argue. It was you and Mr. Prentice who did the smashing up. I sat up all night, and saw my duty this morning. I went round to *somebody's* house to say I must end this. That gentleman apparently has made some bargain with you; he sent me to your chambers.'

228

Lake paused. He lifted a hand and rubbed his thin, damp, bony cheek. The hand trembled.

'To all this,' he added in a voice that sounded half insane, 'I am willing to testify in the witness-box without involving one other person. I shall say it was all my own idea. Deluded persons must pay for thinking they have ideals.'

He opened his mouth to say something else, but refrained. Nodding his cropped head, he turned round, went out of the office, and closed the door.

'That man,' exclaimed Uncle Charles, who had swung round, 'is as mad as a hatter! He's dangerous! Stop him! He—'

Now it was Uncle Charles who stopped, as he swung the swivel-chair back.

With a leisurely air Butler was opening his brief-case. From this he took out a tapering sheath, made of roughish dark blue cloth, some seven inches long. From it projected the smoky-brown ivory handle of the dagger.

'Lake's testimony,' pursued Butler in the same casual tone, 'will not be needed in a court of law. My own demonstration, of how Vaughan killed his victim, *will* be needed.'

And he drew the straight-bladed, six-inch dagger from its sheath.

Though it had no hilt, and only a thin blood-runnel down the middle, it was stained to the handle with dried blood. Butler blew off what remained of the grey powder used to take fingerprints.

Somebody cursed. With a pounce and a cry Cécile retreated from the desk, and flopped down in her chair. Uncle Charles rose up from the swivel-chair on his stumpy legs, also moving away. Butler put the empty sheath carefully on the right-hand side of Hugh's desk, where the light of the green-shaded lamp picked out its rough blue cloth.

'Now!' he said to Hugh. 'Will you be my next witness?'

'Yes! If I can.'

'Oh, you can.' Butler closed his eyes. 'You told me, I think, that when you left Abu alone here this dagger was missing from its sheath? You had last seen it in the sheath about two hours before. Someone, therefore, had stolen it during that time?'

'Yes.'

'There was nobody in any of the offices. Had there been any visitors, any person here at all except Miss Helen Dean, during that time?'

'No! Nobody! Jim asked me the same question himself!'

'A neat, quick, misdirecting question. Who, then, could have taken the dagger except James Vaughan himself?'

Hugh opened his mouth, and shut it again. There wasn't any answer.

'The neglect of the obvious in this matter,' said Butler, 'has constantly amazed me. Vaughan was in the office next door. I have no doubt your uncle had 'phoned him and told him Abu would be coming here at five.' He swung towards Uncle Charles. 'Hadn't you?'

'I refuse to answer!'

'You will,' said Butler, with a broad and terrifying smile. 'Pray be assured, sir, you will.'

'I had no participation—!'

'No; but let us return to the entrance of Abu at five o'clock. He entered rather dramatically, throwing the door almost wide open. Will you show us just how wide open?'

Monica, even Pam, jerked back as Hugh opened the door and set it a dozen or so inches from the left-hand wall as you faced the corridor.

'He then entered. Did he do anything else!'

'Well!' Hugh hesitated. 'First I thought he glanced in a very apprehensive way towards his left . . .'

'Ah, yes. We may guess he did. James Vaughan was in the office there; Abu knew it. He was shrewd enough to guess Vaughan was a dangerous man, who wouldn't hesitate to kill him with half a chance. But Abu entered—'

'And mistook me for my uncle?'

'Yes. He asked if you were *the* Mr. Prentice. You simply said your name was Prentice; and he assumed the rest. He may have been surprised to find you younger than he had

230

imagined, but what of that? Young men are often senior partners. His story about his "brother", and his brother being in danger of murder, is the most easily explained of all. All lawyers, all doctors, know it; if people have been swindled or caught some disease, they don't like to admit they have been done or have been infected; wildly they create a situation belonging to somebody else, and only afterwards admit they are talking about themelves. So he began to pour out his story . . .'

Butler, handling the knife which held everyone's eyes, paused and raised his eyebrows.

'Could Vaughan,' he asked, 'have overheard every word you two were saying?'

'Yes. Easily.'

'How so?'

'Well, look at these doors! They don't nearly touch the floor; you can see light under them from all the way down the corridor.'

'Very well. Vaughan, in his office with this dagger, knows that whole story must not be told. He must strike, and strike at once. You, as you informed me, took off Abu's overcoat. You and Abu sat down on this sofa, facing the fire, with your backs to the open door. *Did either of you, at any time, look round behind you?*'

'No. I told you that.'

'Did you glance up at the mirror?'

'No; I told you that too!'

Again, with hypnotic effect, Butler's voice rolled out.

'And so,' he said, 'you did not see Vaughan slip into the room and conceal himself flat behind the open door.'

The silence seemed to stretch out unendurably.

Not one person seemed able to take his eyes off the rust-coloured blade of the dagger, with its smoky-brown ivory handle, which Butler was turning round and round in his hands.

'You told Abu you must leave immediately, to see me, and suggested he speak to your partner. Abu cried out in protest; naturally he did; he would not like to see the man he feared.

231

He consented to wait; he thought he had come in so quietly that nobody would know he was here.

'You gave him a newspaper. You put on your hat, gloves, and overcoat, and took up your brief-case. As you went out Vaughan was behind that open door. Naturally you didn't see him; do you ever look behind an open door as you go out? You simply pulled it nearly shut, glancing back towards Abu.

'And then? Follow it carefully; measure it by the second-hand on your watch. It took only ten seconds. You went next door, to see your partner. You knocked at the door; no reply. You opened the door, and actually went inside the room to find him. He wasn't there.

'No! He was in your own office. As you left it, he moved quickly across towards a man sitting with back turned. The ingenious Mr. James Vaughan wore a pair of white cotton gloves; we shall see them in a moment. He had been trained in the Army to kill instantly, with a knife. But an ivory handle can slip in a cotton glove; he struck downwards, with a death-blow, yet it did not instantly kill.

'He struck. He slipped the gloves into his pocket as he crossed the room, went out, and joined you. Time, I repeat, about ten seconds and no more. Then he was speaking behind you—and you hadn't seen the direction he came from —and saying he'd approached from the other end of the corridor.

'That's all. That's the whole simple story. A very brief time afterwards, you looked round the edge of the door into your own office. And what did you see?

'You saw the back of Abu's head. You saw him apparently slapping at a newspaper, and muttering rather wildly to himself. You couldn't see his face; he was too small, as you noted, for his face to be reflected in this mirror. You couldn't see his chest, where the dagger had been thrust down. You assumed he was unhurt.'

Weirdly, in imagination, the whole scene took form. All he could say was that there had been something odd, something strange . . .

'Wait!' Hugh protested.

'Yes?'

'Wouldn't Abu have screamed when the dagger struck him, as he did afterwards? Wouldn't he have jumped up or done something else, as he also did?'

'No,' replied Butler, with a rounded and distinct syllable. 'You saw the very same scene played afterwards, under your own eyes, though it wasn't fatal. You saw it in the street outside Cotterby's antique-shop.'

'What the devil are you talking about?'

'You saw Cotterby throw a knife at a hoodlum. And what happened?'

Again Hugh began to speak, but stopped because he knew the answer.

'Almost any man, unexpectedly struck by steel or a bullet,' Butler went on, 'is too stunned to cry out. He doesn't know what has happened to him. Shortly he may mutter or make slight movements, as Abu did. Only a little afterwards, when he realizes, does he begin to scream and go into a frenzy. That is what Abu did too. It provided the alibi of Mr. James Vaughan and the quite unintentional sealed room.'

'Then Jim was trying for an alibi? He was trying for a sealed room?'

'No!' Butler said, again with that rounded clearness. 'What did he want with a sealed room? He wanted this to look like suicide. Didn't he try his best to persuade you it was suicide? Didn't he use every argument, every piece of eloquence, every spellbinding effort? If you correctly described his behaviour after that murder, he almost went off his head to persuade you it was suicide.

'But you weren't having any. You insisted it was murder. And so, though he really didn't want to do it . . .'

'Yes?'

'He had to put the blame for the murder on you,' said Butler.

Hugh felt that the room was moving round in a slow dance.

'But Jim lost his head and bolted; He got the police on his own track! He had the police suspicious of him . . . !'

Butler's sour expression stopped him.

'Really?' the barrister inquired. 'When you accidentally ran away with his brief-case, it gave him a heaven-sent opportunity. He simply put the blood-stained cotton gloves in your brief-case and waited. The police were bound to find them. Never once did your precious friend lose his head. His dash away from the police was very carefully calculated: not to make people suspicious of him, but to make them suspicious of you.

'Couldn't he easily explain it, once found? Yes; he did. Outwardly, didn't it look as though he were gallantly shielding you? Yes; that did. It was the one clever thing he did. He even persuaded you, over the 'phone, that you ought to give yourself up for murder. It was a good performance, but a sickening one. And his course is run.'

From the desk Butler picked up the blue sheath. Into it he pushed the stained dagger, and dropped both into his brief-case.

'I ought to explain, finally,' he said, 'my own authority in this matter. The Assistant Commissioner of the C.I.D. is a barrister and a friend of mine. The City of London Police, as you may or may not know, is governed by the Court of Common Council. Its head, despite the legend of rivalry, works very closely with the head of the C.I.D. Both agreed to let me have a try at this, always subject to the approval of Inspector Alec Duff.' He raised his voice. 'Inspector Duff!'

'Aye?' said Inspector Duff.

'In this brief-case,' Butler tapped it, 'you will also find the cotton gloves—they are the sort used for gardening—used by Vaughan. Had he bought them at any time except the end of November, he might have gone unnoticed. As it is, two sales-girls have identified him out of a number of photographs. Do you find the case good enough for a jury?'

'Aye,' said Inspector Duff.

'Then there's your prisoner.'

Jim, bracing himself, yelled some words Hugh never

understood. Then, head down, he charged at Inspector Duff. There was a brief, very ugly business before the Inspector quietly locked his arm up behind his back, said, 'Hoots, hoots!' and gently led him away. Butler's brief-case was in the Inspector's other hand.

Again a dead emptiness hung on the office. Cécile was the first to break it.

'Well!' she said, brushing tears out of her eyes, slapping her knees, and getting up. 'I have a show tonight, by damn! Thees is bad and sad. But I go now?'

'And, if I may,' Butler told her with his most gallant air, 'I shall accompany you? If you will wait until I get my hat and coat from the unspeakable Vaughan's office—?'

'Oh, by damn, yes!'

'Butler,' said Hugh, with a thick feeling in his throat, 'how I'm going to thank . . .'

'My dear fellow! It was nothing. However, Butler added, lowering his voice to a whisper, 'I have invited your friend Helen Dean out to dinner tonight. You don't (hem!) mind if I pursue the matter?'

'Great Scott, no!'

'Ah, good. My intentions there may even be serious. I consider her a magnificent girl; and I flatter myself that I am never wrong. Good-bye!'

And he and Cécile made a flourishing exit.

'As for me,' muttered Uncle Charles, chewing at the underside of his moustache, 'I—think I shall go to my office and sit down for a while.' He turned towards the door; then hesitated. 'Hugh, my boy. If I have been unjust . . .'

'There's nothing to say. Please forget the matter.'

'But your position in the firm—!'

'You'll have my resignation in due course; I'm setting up on my own. I've saved something, and I have friends.'

And he went out too.

But dark-haired Monica, white-faced and rigidly drawn up in her dark green coat, would have none of Hugh's attempt to speak to her.

'I don't want sympathy, thanks,' she said. 'And I don't

wish to be accompanied. I shall go alone, as I've always gone alone. He wasn't much good; I knew that. But he was all I had.'

She marched out, unshaken and tearless, closing the door very softly.

And so, as darkness and fog grew thicker outside the windows, there were left only three persons. Lord Saxemund, grumpily and uneasily musing (perhaps the old sinner had a conscience after all) appeared not to have heard.

Hugh glanced at Pam. Her lips framed the silent words, 'I love you', and he knew what he had to do.

'Lord Saxemund!' he said.

'Hey?'

Pam knew what he had to say, too. Instinctively she looked at the windows; they were four floors above the street, and Pam felt a momentary alarm. But she was too happy to care.

'Lord Saxemund,' said Hugh, with a wide and dangerous smile, 'I have something to say to you.'

COUNTY COUNCIL OF THE COUNTY OF STIRLING EDUCATION COMMITTEE

COUNTY LIBRARY

This book should be returned on or before the latest date entered below. If desired, an extension of the loan period may be granted. A fine of **2**d. per week or part of a week will be charged on overdue books.

DATE OF RETURN	DATE OF RETURN	DATE OF RETURN
25 OCT 1956		
14 FEB 1957		
11 APR 1957		